# MESSAGE OF THE PENDANT

THOMAS THORPE

BLACK ROSE writing™

First printing



ISBN: 978-1-61296-292-4
PUBLISHED BY BLACK ROSE WRITING
www.blackrosewriting.com

Printed in the United States of America

*Message of the Pendant* is printed in Times New Roman

For Janet and far away places

# MESSAGE OF THE PENDANT

# CHAPTER ONE

"We're all suspects until this business is sorted out."

William Darmon surveyed weary party guests seated on hastily arranged side chairs along the grand ballroom's perimeter. The tall, round-faced gentleman held up a serving knife, identical to the one Constable Matthews removed from Louisa Hurst's body six hours earlier. He raised its shiny encrusted handle to display the Darmon family coat of arms.

Once more, he admonished restless guests with a five-shilling oath.

"Who in God's name did this?"

Golden patterns of sunlight sprinkled across the pink marble floor, a sign evening fast approached. Despite the ordeal of police questions, friends and family remained assembled, waiting for leadership from their host. Instead, long pauses of silence punctuated by soft ticking of the hallway's pendulum clock were to be endured, and only questions came forth from the master of the house.

Elizabeth Darmon sat amid guests, losing patience with her husband, who apparently expected answers to fall from the sky.

"Why would a killer use our knife?"

William met the eyes of his spouse of two years, smiling thinly.

"It is an odd weapon for a carefully planned murder. A gentleman would likely bring his own instrument, and a lady opt for less violent means. A servant would surely employ a less incriminating tool. Must have been a spur-of-the-moment choice."

She watched him fidget with the knife.

"There's always the possibility it was used to cast blame on us. I thought we were all good friends. Who harbored resentment against poor Louisa?"

Elizabeth's brother-in-law, Charles Bagwell, stood up. "I agree with Lizzy. Whoever did this probably seized the knife because it was convenient."

"In such cases, one might also become regretful," Charles' wife, Emily offered. "Is there anyone who wishes to unburden his conscience?"

Elizabeth fingered her dark brown curls, watching faces turn left and right expectantly. Losing hope their collective insight could resolve the crime, the short, stocky woman of twenty-three stood up.

"William, surely none of the family is suspect. Our parents, my sisters and your aunt, Lady Carlisle, are out of the question."

"I wouldn't be so quick to rule out Lady Carlisle," Elizabeth's youngest sister, eighteen-year-old Victoria interrupted. "Her intolerance of everyone might be a motive. I can't imagine why she left Rosewell Park to move in here. And where is she now?"

"Has anyone seen her since last night?"

"What of your family, Charles?" Emily blurted. "You and Madeline were close to your sister, Louisa, are there any grudges lurking among your relations?"

Charles harrumphed. "Ask Arthur. Maybe Louisa finally had enough of her husband's drinking and gave him an unwelcome ultimatum."

"Anyone notice if they had words before he passed out last night?"

William flung his utensil down atop a nearby table.

"Let's stop finger pointing. We're confusing bickering with a motive for murder. Can we all agree to look beyond our relations for now? That leaves eighty-one guests. Who among the rest of you had frequent exchanges with the deceased?"

Crowd murmurs erupted, while some shifted uncomfortably, casting sidelong glances at fellow acquaintances.

Feeling bruised and tired, he scanned the audience. Words came harshly in his throat.

"Well, I can think of four of her associates present at the time of the murder."

"John and Estee Black of London,

"Sir Terrence Winthrop formerly of London now of Paris,

“Jack Crullage, Victoria's friend from Hunsford…"

Despite William’s pronouncement, Elizabeth’s thoughts drifted to events leading up to their party.

Carriages began arriving two days before the night of their second anniversary ball. It was one of few occasions which could make a nobleman and his lady journey thirty-five miles from cherished London addresses. A tradition of early arrival permitted guests to spend a restful night within the thirty-two-room Darmon estate known as Mayfair Hall to be at their best for the gala affair.

By eight, couples in evening dress and black ties crowded into the grand ballroom. Light from chandeliers shone brightly off red and white streamers, and a blue-suited orchestra created rhythm echoing loudly off marble columns from a second-floor balcony. Three-quarters of the participants swirled in country dances, leaving the perimeter for conversation among dowagers and the unattached.

Elizabeth gazed with satisfaction at the resplendent event she both composed and conducted. Each dance, each grouping, and each discussion were movements within her concert. Tireless attention to detail created an unforgettable evening among London’s exclusive social gatherings of 1818.

A flaw in this tapestry arose when Sir Terrence Winthrop tripped over the outstretched form of a besotted Arthur Hurst whose rotund figure created a formidable obstacle, weighing more than three hundred pounds. The toppled victim righted himself and glared at the cause of his embarrassment. Summoning a semblance of sobriety, Hurst drew his legs under and laboriously struggled to his feet. Conversations hushed, and celebration hovered on the brink of a distasteful incident. Wiping his mouth with a damp handkerchief, Louisa’s husband loudly apologized. Winthrop bowed stiffly and turned away, shaking his head disgustedly at the man’s condition.

At ten, Lady Carlisle, no longer entertained by idle conversations, sought out Elizabeth. The bejeweled dowager, dressed in flowing blue satin cloth, announced her intent to retire witth yet another hint of criticism. "I expect this to be the last of these affairs requiring my attendance."

She took William's arm and expressed congeniality seldom seen by Elizabeth.

"I'm certain your generous efforts are much appreciated by everyone. I must, however, bid you a good evening."

She nodded toward the other guests as William escorted his aunt upstairs.

An hour after midnight, the crowd began to thin.

Orchestra members packed their belongings and retreated to the servants' quarters. Emily and Elizabeth talked in one corner of the large space, while her parents and Victoria conversed in another. Arthur awoke briefly, attempting to pay attention to nearby utterances of Mr. and Mrs. Black. In the study, William and Charles debated the best shooting grounds in Kent. Among withdrawing guests, Madeline and Louisa joined the flow of patrons upstairs.

By 3:00 A.M., stillness settled over Mayfair Hall while revelers slept. The estate remained undisturbed until sunrise when household domestics began to quietly restore order.

As morning progressed, the dining room began to fill with emerging guests hunting for breakfast and cures for a night's indulgence.

Elizabeth and William sat at opposite ends of a long table set with gilt-edged plates holding fruit and bread. William's black hair tumbled in several directions over his forehead, reflecting the morning's casual demeanor.

Through half-opened eyes, he envied his wife's alertness.

"Happy anniversary, my dear. I enjoyed last night immensely. Where you find the energy to manage such undertakings is a mystery to me."

She smiled, about to respond when Sir Winthrop abruptly sat down.

"Jolly good party, indeed, Darmon. You should be congratulated for maintaining civility here in the backwoods."

The couple blinked, uncertain whether to acknowledge a

compliment or back-handed criticism.

Only slightly familiar to the Darmons, Sir Terrence Winthrop had the reputation of a gadabout, common trait of the idle rich. His well-groomed features included a graying manicured mustache, sharply defined cheekbones and soft white hands, suggesting abhorrence of manual labor. A lithe body displayed athleticism younger than age fifty, and his keen interest in the affairs of anyone who gave him word endeared him to party hostesses everywhere. Among these allies were Charles' sisters.

At exactly 11:23 A.M., a tortured scream pierced the premises from an upstairs hallway. Julia, the second-floor maid, ran to the stairway, gesturing breathlessly to the melee below. “Come quick! I think she's dead!”

William reached the landing a half-step ahead of Sir Winthrop. Together, the two raced to the rooms above and arrived at Lady Carlisle's doorway behind several others.

By the time Elizabeth came up, the two men were already bending over a motionless figure sprawled on an unmade bed. As she approached, the victim’s blue party gown came into view, heavily stained with blood.

“What's happened to Lady Carlisle?” Elizabeth gasped.

William’s contorted face turned. “It isn't my aunt. It's Louisa Hurst with a serving knife in her back!”

Madeline rushed into the room. The tall, dark-haired woman pushed by Elizabeth and elbowed up next to William. At the sight of her sister, color drained from her face and she abruptly fainted. Sir Winthrop grasped her arms and lifted her onto a nearby chair. He called for water as Charles entered, looking horrified.

The crowd of onlookers sealed off the doorway. Someone shouted for Arthur to be awakened. Elizabeth dispatched a servant to fetch Doctor Gracepool and a policeman from the town of Langdon ten miles away.

As guests milled about the bedroom, Elizabeth's eye caught a reflection near the foot of the bed. Reaching down, she discovered a small pendant the size of her thumb engraved with an emblem in the shape of a fleur-de-lis. Turning it over, she found a tiny inscription on the back.

*Colombe du Paix. Bonaparte.*

The name startled her. She quickly closed the object inside a fist and deposited it within a pocket of her morning dress. Just then, a flustered Arthur Hurst barged through the entry, stumbling toward the bed. William and Sir Winthrop stepped away while he knelt by his wife. His body shook as he reached out to gently caress her hand. William requested the onlookers assemble downstairs to wait for help to arrive. Charles, his sister and the deceased's husband stayed behind to mourn their loss.

No one called attention to the absence of Lady Carlisle.

Six years earlier, amid the ruins of a small town near the Franco-Prussian border, a young girl picked her way through the rubble with other orphans, searching for crumbs. Her tattered soot-stained, yellow smock showed an empty pocket embroidered with the letters: *Nina.* Straggles of blonde hair streaked with dirt covered most of her face while she carefully placed bare feet on muddy ground littered with hastily discarded artifacts. Bits of clothing hid half-buried bodies, but shoes were seldom left behind on picked-over remains. Every now and then, she glanced up, wary of adults, since neither beggars nor the militia would give her reward.

A thin man dressed in dark coarse clothing watched from a nearby doorway.

The determined girl continued to meander, searching passageways for food or anything of value to be used to provide a means to eat. A child's doll stuck out of sludge near the watcher's entrance. Nina let out a squeal of delight and jumped toward it.

The dark figure grabbed her arm. She screamed, flailing at the grip which pulled her into the interior of the building.

In the dim light of a deserted room, the villain picked up a cloth sack and yanked it over her head down to her knees. Clutching the thrashing body, he lifted Nina over his shoulder and tightly pressed her legs against his chest. Without a pause, he carried her out the back door into an alley.

Nina felt the man's strength confining her as he walked stridently while supporting his burden. Finally, he stopped. She fell rudely to the ground. The sack came off and a coarse rope wrapped around her hands and feet. Strong hands shoved her into the back of a wagon where a tarpaulin was briefly raised, revealing four other waifs bound shoulder to shoulder. She landed between them and quickly plunged into darkness amid soft sobbing sounds of children who met a similar fate.

The wagon jerked forward.

Hours of bumping and jostling followed. None of the captives spoke. Nina did not understand what was happening as the cart climbed ever upward.

At last, the conveyance halted.

Creaking noise of a massive gate preceded further movement before they finally stopped for good. Two men lifted prisoners from the vehicle and herded them into a wooden shed's dark, foul smelling room. The door slammed shut.

Nina could barely see in dim light filtering between wallboards. Five straw mats lay on a dirt floor. Odors of horse manure filled her nostrils. She slumped to a mat and cried with despair while other children felt around the room.

"Where are we?" another girl asked.

"I think this is the Castle du Philippe," replied a boy taller than the rest.

An adult voice from a dark corner startled them. "You're correct, young man. You have been chosen to become kitchen flies for cooks of the chateau. Come with me, I will feed you."

The youngsters followed an elderly gentleman outside across a small courtyard to a plain oak door at the rear of a large stone building. Inside, they faced a spacious kitchen and were told to sit on the floor. Each child received a bowl of cold porridge and a piece of bread. When their portions were eagerly devoured, Nina pulled on the man's cloak.

"What's a 'kitchen fly?'" she asked, summoning her courage.

He gave no reply.

Days passed, and duties of kitchen flies became clear. The captives performed fetching and cleanup tasks required by meal preparation and disposal. In time, Nina learned the castle was actually an expansive villa located atop a mountain near her town. Residents included a gentleman and his wife, three daughters, a son and their servants. Contact was not permitted between kitchen flies and the family, but daily routine permitted time with other abducted children, and she became friends with a few of the hired staff.

One day, the master's son jumped in front of her as she returned from her duties. "What's your name?"

"Nina," she answered without fear, for his smile was disarming. She wanted to appear defiant, but his fine clothes with boots and gloves of tooled leather put her at a disadvantage despite her improved appearance since days among the ruins.

"Mine's Francois du Hurst. You must come and see my horse. He's going to be the finest in Napoleon's cavalry. Soon, I shall ride into battle for the glory of France!"

His enthusiasm struck her as arrogant. "Soldiers wrecked my home and took my family. You'll be despised by your victims."

"And what does a girl know of war?" he burst with disdain.

"Only that I hate it and would rather have peace," she retorted.

"Hah! Peace is for women!" the boy sneered and ran off.

Nina's days at the Castle du Phillipe stretched into a year. The youngsters grew close, often meeting behind the kitchen for short walks.

A second year passed before news of Napoleon's retreat from Russia reached the castle. Soon, thousands of bedraggled troops could be seen below, making their way across the Rhine Valley over the Alsace Lorraine countryside.

Late one afternoon, two soldiers banged on the front door with news that Bonaparte, himself intended a brief stay at the villa. The kitchen erupted in a flurry of activity. Courses simmered on massive stoves. Nina helped carry in preparations, busily following instructions of the chef-du-maison. She helped set the main dining room, and carried refreshments to oak tables within several rooms for late evening discussions.

At 8:00 P.M., the great leader strode into the dining room with an entourage of generals. Despite their weariness and rumpled uniforms, Nina could not imagine more impressive soldiers. For an instant, she understood why Francois dreamt of the glory of war.

During dinner, the Emperor directed conversation toward his aides with little attention to family members. Nina sensed an air of desperation among the officers, but Bonaparte remained calm in his address. Once the last course was consumed, everyone retired to the study, where Nina served cafe and liqueur. Large maps were unfurled. She caught snatches of discussions referring to troop movements. "...forces must be marshaled to the west...more men must be deployed to suppress the German states...the English blockade can be broken only if the Americans prevail..."

Late that night, while Nina cleaned dishes, she overheard an outburst beyond the kitchen door. The voice of Monsieur du Hurst protested, "No, you shall not have him."

"...they're but children. It could have inconceivable consequences," Madam du Hurst added. Somewhat later, another rebuff came. "...and if Monsieur Clay should refuse?"

When the kitchen was finally clean, Nina retreated to her room. She lay on her mat staring into the darkness, wondering out loud. "What does this mean? How are the du Hurst's involved?"

After a while, she drifted to sleep.

A hand shook her arm, awakening her. It was Francois.

He spoke barely above a whisper. “Nina, wake up. Pack your things. We must leave the castle at once. We have a mission to perform.”

Three days elapsed since discovery of Louisa Hurst's murder.

The doctor removed the body for transport to Liverpool and burial in the Bagwell family plot. Charles left Emily at their manor in Surrey and took a carriage with Madeline to attend their sister's funeral. The police constable was unable to find any new evidence and, consequently, he decided to seek help from the London metropolitan police at Palace Yard. An extensive search was underway for Lady Carlisle, but she vanished without a trace.

It was dark by the time Elizabeth and William nestled in front of a large fireplace. Light from the fire danced about the study, and a strong wind howled outside, the last of winter's fury. Flames crackled, casting flickering shadows among floor-to-ceiling shelves of weathered books. They drifted in thought, lounging together on a rose-patterned settee.

William gazed intently at the fire. He shook his head with frustration. Drawing a maroon silk robe tightly about his neck, he sat up.

“I guess Lady Carlisle was either abducted by the killer or she did the job herself, and then fled.”

“Or perhaps, she was so frightened, she remains in hiding," Elizabeth offered. “But what business do you suppose Louisa had in her room? There's no account of anyone hearing a conversation between them the entire evening.”

William regarded her face in the changing light. She was not a beauty by most standards, plain features highlighted by ruddy cheeks and a rather large nose. But her eyes were so expressive.

“A key point, indeed. You always seem to deduce the most important interactions. I doubt my reticence with strangers makes me useful to investigate this crime."

Elizabeth smiled, taking his arm. "And I envy your talent for selecting a course of action and doggedly following it through to the end."

He kissed her lightly on the cheek. "Just not knowing any better..."

She reached into her pocket and pulled out the pendant. "I'd almost forgotten. What do you make of this, my insightful detective?"

He looked at the spheroid with interest. "Where did you get it?"

"I found it on the floor under your aunt's bed when we first arrived that morning," she answered, knitting her brow.

He turned it over and read the inscription.

"My God, can it be from the Emperor himself? I once read that French agents carried jewelry cases for secret exchanges during the war. Do you think it belonged to Louisa or her killer?"

Peering more closely in the sparkling firelight, he noticed a fine line below the emblem. He gave it a sharp twist, and two halves separated. A tiny, tightly rolled piece of paper fell to the rug. He quickly retrieved it and unrolled thin parchment into a three by ten-inch sheet. A message was inked in fine handwriting:

*Bonaparte*
*Castle du Philippe*
*Secretary of War, John Armstrong, has dispatched a privateer under the command of Commodore Rodgers, expected to reach Dover the tenth day of April. Fifty men with the help of Minister Fouche's agent F.D. will make their way to London, raze Parliament buildings, and set sail for home within a month. May this act serve both our countries!*
*Henry Clay*
*14th day of March 1814*

"What does this mean, 'raze Parliament buildings'?" Elizabeth gasped. "Did the Colonials attempt such a deed?"

He bit his lip. "I never heard of it. Clay is now Speaker of the

American House of Representatives. Of course, we know if such a mission was tried, it didn't succeed. I wonder what prevented it."

Elizabeth reread the note. "Who's this Minister Fouche?"

"Joseph Fouche was Napoleon's Minister for Espionage," he replied, squinting at the flames once more. "I believe he's now in Italy, but his men were everywhere during the war."

She winced. "Why would Louisa be carrying such an article?"

He tried to smile. "Perhaps she purchased it not knowing the contents, a souvenir to be worn as an ornament."

Elizabeth frowned.

"She must have seen the inscription, which would hardly promote use for adornment. And who is: 'F.D' operating as a French spy in London? These are your initials. How diverting!"

F. William Darmon was not amused.

"It may be a key to the murder. Perhaps it's the identity of an agent who double-crossed the French and alerted the authorities. Maybe Louisa Hurst was that person, using a code name, and she was recognized at the ball. Someone took the opportunity to avenge her betrayal."

He climbed to his feet and began pacing. Pausing for a moment at the dormer window, he gazed at blowing branches.

"The answer may lie at the Castle du Philippe. I know its location in the East of France. How would you like a vacation from this spring of foul weather?"

Within the space of two weeks, the Darmons left London, arrived in Paris, and proceeded by carriage into the countryside. Elizabeth's channel crossing was not without trepidation, given a tendency to seasickness, but it was now behind her.

Paris was chaotic. Ravages of war lay everywhere. Ancient monuments, reduced to chunks of marble spread among pieces of buildings cluttering avenues and walkways. Government buildings bore scars of cannon fire, other structures stood unoccupied, blackened by raging fires. Peasants, young and old, meandered in the streets, grimly beginning new lives of poverty.

They spent one night in the city. From an upstairs window of their lodging, Elizabeth spotted a stranger across an alleyway staring at her window. From then on, she could not suppress a feeling someone was following their activities.

The French countryside retained a good deal of beauty. Rolling hills and occasional farmhouses gave a sense of tranquillity Elizabeth appreciated after recent events. Villages were another matter. Many offered little accommodation for travelers. Beggars populated every corner, and noblemen could find little protection from a gendarmerie in disarray.

At last, the English couple's carriage climbed a winding road leading to the mountain castle. Their driver carefully negotiated hazardous turns over a deeply rutted path before the transport finally arrived at the villa, two hours after leaving the town below.

At the gate, a winsome boy escorted them inside the chateau. They were shown to a sitting room with breathtaking view of the valley below and the Rhine River winding its way east to the horizon. Elizabeth looked away as a matron entered the room.

*"Guten Morgen. Bitte, geben Sie mir Ihren Namen."*

"Do the German states now extend past the Rhine?" Elizabeth whispered with uncertainty.

William gave her a reassuring glance. "I have some fluency in the language."

While William stepped away to converse with the lady, Elizabeth directed her attention to lavish furnishings in the room.

After a moment, he returned.

"Apparently the family who lived here left about the time Prussians advanced into the area near the end of the war. She has no knowledge of their whereabouts. However, there's a servant here from that time. We've been given permission to interview him."

They followed closely behind the heavy-set woman as she

descended stairs and passed through a narrow hallway. Gray, porous walls displayed paintings of surrounding mountains. Near the end of the passageway, Elizabeth stopped abruptly and gaped at a portrait of a gentleman.

"Look, William! Isn't that a good rendition of a younger, thinner Arthur Hurst?"

William paused. Quickly, he said something to the matron.

He grinned at Elizabeth. "The name of the family was 'du Hurst'. If Arthur was here at the time Bonaparte visited, it could tie him to the pendant."

"Now, we're getting somewhere."

At first, the servant was painfully shy. A Frenchman, possibly twenty-five, he remembered little of the family, never having spoken directly to any of them. Servants were not permitted to initiate conversation with their masters. Nevertheless, he did recall a few interactions between residents and household staff members.

"The boy became a friends with one of the servant girls," the attendant stammered. "'Er name was Nina. She worked in the kitchen. They both up and ran off one night near the end the war. Maybe eloped, she being a servant and all."

Elizabeth showed him the pendant, but he showed no recognition.

"Too bad. I presumed it was a gift to someone at the villa from Bonaparte. We heard that he stayed here in the spring of 1814."

The young man brightened. "Bonaparte! Yes, 'e was 'ere. I saw 'im. 'E and some generals spent two weeks at the 'ouse."

William's eyes widened. "Was it when the son and Nina left the premises?"

The servant fell silent for a moment.

"*Oui*, it was. We 'ad to look after the soldiers, and Nina's absence made more work for the rest of us. They said the mother locked 'erself in 'er room for a week, crying over the loss of 'er son. Francois was 'is name. 'E was always playing war games."

"And you never found out what happened to them?" Elizabeth asked anxiously.

He rubbed his chin. "After the soldiers left, I never 'eard word. Some letters arrived after the family moved out. I remember making trips to town to forward the expresses on to Paris. I was directed to send any correspondences with the address, Colombe, to Monsieur Lebec at Ministere des Affaires Etrangeres."

William thanked the servant and paid him a small reward.

As their carriage retraced its path down the mountainside, William smiled with satisfaction. "It's not a great deal of information, but it at least gives us a direction."

"What do we really know of Arthur Hurst?" Elizabeth asked. "He's always over-indulgent and uninterested in anything besides his own amusement. When he's sober, cards are his passion. He seldom speaks of any issue of significance. Do you think he has some sort of sordid past which drives him to drink?"

William shrugged, then, turned to her. "Do you suppose that Nina and this Francois could actually be Louisa and Arthur Hurst?"

# CHAPTER TWO

"Just how are we going to extract this information on Colombe?" Elizabeth asked, trying to add a note of practicality. "As English citizens, we can't simply walk into the French Foreign Affairs Office and demand to know the identity of one of their spies."

William looked out the carriage window at the approaching Paris skyline.

"I thought we'd inquire after my nephew, Francois du Hurst, who's been missing since wartime. If this Monsieur Lebec can't help us, at least, we may find out where they keep their personnel files. It might be possible to return after hours and look further."

She raised an eyebrow. "After hours? You mean, to catch a spy, we have to behave like spies?"

The following day, they stood in front of a three-story granite building situated just west of central Paris. Six thick white columns capped with a traditional gray dome indicated one of the Ministry's more important office buildings. War had not left its mark on the aging facade, but a host of workers busily attempted to remove all references to Bonaparte.

Footsteps echoed off a shiny marble floor as they passed through a large circular lobby toward the receptionist's counter. In a perfunctory manner, a slender clerk clad in formal blue waistcoat and high wing collar, informed them the *Registrar du Ministere des Affaires Etrangeres* could be found down the west corridor in Room 37.

Inside the hallway, the pair sidestepped ladders, canvas and paint cans spread about by maintenance people refinishing office doors and nameplates. Between these obstacles, determined clerks hurried recklessly back and forth, toting stacks of papers pertaining to displaced persons. Their progress was further impeded by bewildered-looking visitors hunting for information regarding the location of loved ones, associates and debtors.

At Room 37, the English couple gratefully slipped inside to a space of comparative calm. They stood by the door for a moment, gazing around the chamber and smelling musty odors of ink and dust. Drab, cracked and peeling walls lit by two south-facing windows suggested an interior eroded by decades of service. The room held three long tables, chairs and an ancient wooden desk, giving area for assistants to conduct research. Bookshelves crammed with aged bindings stocked the perimeter beneath maps spread over remaining wall space, and numerous piles of papers covered every inch of the tabletops. At the far end of the chamber, they could see a plain brown door with a large keyhole and, in front of it, a scholarly-looking gentleman furiously writing at the pine desk.

William reached the end of his survey and announced their presence.

The gray-haired administrator did not look up, but absently waved toward two chairs near his station.

"Mercel Lebec, Registrar du Ministere des Affaires Etrangeres. Please sit down."

Elizabeth hesitated, eyeing two rickety seats, which would surely collapse if they leaned back in them. She followed William, who chose to stand while he explained their plight.

Lebec listened attentively, then opened a desk drawer, took out a wooden box and removed a large set of keys. "Excuse me. I will check the records."

He unlocked the door behind him and disappeared into an adjoining room. They stood quietly waiting, hearing faint sounds of ruffling paper. Returning empty handed, the official put away his keys. "Francois du Hurst has no record of military service."

Elizabeth feigned alarm. "Poor Francois. Did he forsake his duty? Whatever has become of the boy?"

The clerk's face transformed into a reassuring smile.

"This isn't uncommon. Near the end of the war, many served Napoleon without record. Unfortunately, I can't offer much hope for his recovery; the number of missing persons without a recent residence is enormous. The young man may have left the country. You'd have a better chance seeking his acquaintances."

William thanked the bookkeeper with an apology for taking up his valuable time. Elizabeth smiled understandingly. They shook hands with Monsieur Lebec and left the office.

In the hallway, William looked satisfied. "Now we know the location of his files. At midday, it's customary for the French to have a meal that may last up to two hours. It's likely Lebec will leave the building within the hour. There's an inconspicuous area down the hall where we can wait and see."

Precisely at noon, passageways quickly emptied. The clerk came out and disappeared opposite their direction.

To their relief, they found Room 37 unlocked and entered without notice.

William regarded the desk Monsieur Lebec had bolted. He bent down to inspect two left-hand drawers where the attendant stored the anteroom and file keys. The top drawer holding the wooden box would not budge, but the larger drawer underneath could be slid out an inch.

Elizabeth watched her husband scratch his head. "What now? Can we force the fileroom door without the key?"

William remained pensive. "If we can pry the bottom drawer out, there may be a way to get into the top one from underneath. It would be helpful if we could find a stiff lever. There's a toolbox down the hall where those workers are repairing the molding..."

His wife nodded and tiptoed out.

He looked around the room. A map pointer, one inch thick, caught his eye. Seizing it, he wedged one end into the bottom drawer and pried it backwards. It snapped with a loud crack, leaving a four-inch stub blocking the top drawer's travel. William tried to remove the stick but it would not budge. He glared at the protrusion. Not only had he failed to reach the wooden box, but now evidence of their presence would be left in the room.

Outside, having located the toolbox, Elizabeth fumbled through its implements. The sound of approaching footsteps reverberated around the corner. Anxiously looking for a hiding place, she spied a narrow door down the hall. She hurried through the passageway and squeezed inside a storage closet.

In the darkness, she stood with pounding heart while clicking noises passed and faded away. After a moment, she reached for the doorknob, but found none. Frantically, she pushed against the frame without success. A shaft of light under the door gave a dim outline of her shoes, but the space was so tight she could not even turn around. She dared not call out. With rising frustration, she pressed her back against the wall and lifted she her knees to force the panel out, but it did no good. She remained trapped inside.

William's impatience continued to grow. Once more, he looked around the room for a tool to pry the drawer open.

His eyes focused on the rickety chairs. He grabbed one and brought it behind the desk where he inserted a leg into the bottom drawer. Then, he gingerly stepped around to the front of the desk while holding the projecting seat. Braced against the writing surface, he yanked with all his might.

The drawer abruptly released and flew out of the frame.

William tumbled backward. Still grasping the chair, he landed with a loud crash against a table, sending piles of paper scattering and books thudding to the floor.

Dazed, he sat for a moment.

In the hallway, a staccato of running footfalls rose. William jumped to his feet, horrified at the mess. The door burst open.

"Arretez!" two bulky Frenchmen commanded, blocking the only exit.

They sent for a gendarme to arrest the intruder.

A policeman escorted William ignominiously through the streets to a gendarmerie five blocks away where he was shoved into an crowded jail cell. He picked himself off a grimy stone surface, glancing at the dingy surroundings.

Most of the inmates were beggars, unclean with foul odor. They milled about with threatening glances. A cluster of nearby prisoners edged closer, their hands reaching out to grab the sleeve of his waistcoat. William shook his arms and lunged forward to gain some free space. The stench of urine and sweat tore at his throat.

He managed to work his way to a bench in a far corner of the room. At one end of the seat, an unusually well-clothed individual sat facing the wall. William plopped down a few feet away, causing the gentleman to twist around. William's jaw dropped at the sight of Terrence Winthrop.

"Winthrop, what on earth are you doing here?"

Sir Winthrop regarded him with uncertainty for a moment, then he smiled through glazed eyes. "Darmon, my man. 'Ow good it is ta see a friendly face."

William grimaced at the slurred speech and sour breath.

The nobleman shrugged at William's reaction. "I really don't know why I've been locked up. There was a party last night. I'm told I made a few ill-calculated advances toward the 'ost's wife. Before I knew it, 'e 'ad me removed from the premises and deposited 'ere. But, I must say, your presence 'ere might be the more surprising. What 'ave you done to offend the ministry?"

William made a fist remembering his bad luck. "Elizabeth and I are searching for clues to the death of Louisa Bagwell. Local civil servants don't take kindly to Englishmen poking into their affairs."

"Terrible business, that. You've a lead then?" Winthrop responded.

"We've some suspicion Arthur Hurst may be involved," William said with affected nonchalance. He shot a quick look into the man's eyes. "You two are old friends, aren't you?"

"I've known 'im for many years," Winthrop retorted with a smirk. "Met in London back in '07. 'E had a successful import business, as I recall. Arthur and Louisa used to spend a month or two over 'ere every year. I believe 'is sister lived in the Eastern mountain region." He paused with a frown. "'Ave you uncovered something that connects 'im to the murder?"

William sighed, spreading his hands. "We may have a clue..."

The cell gate opened noisily, bringing a hush of expectation among the detainees. A guard called William's name.

As William pushed his way to the entrance, Sir Terrence waved. “Good luck then.”

Appearing before the magistrate, William solemnly hung his head. “I apologize for my behavior. Loss of my nephew affected my good judgement. I assure you I'm not in the habit of breaking into government offices and will make full amends.”

“This action was indeed contemptible," the magistrate pronounced. “However, you seem to be a man of good character. Therefore, the court will accept your remuneration and advises you to leave our city without delay.”

William met the judge’s eyes squarely.

“Thank you. By the way, you've another Englishman incarcerated here, Terrence Winthrop. May I also request his release for a minor misunderstanding?”

The magistrate turned to an officer of the court. After a few words, he looked back and shook his head.

“There’s no one in custody by that name. You're the first Englishman to be arrested this month.”

William emerged from the gendarmerie in darkness. He began trudging the cobbled street to their lodging, wondering about the judge’s statement. Suddenly, he remembered Elizabeth. She must have retreated when the commotion broke out. His pace quickened, hoping she escaped trouble at the Ministry.

Climbing stairs to their room, he paused, fumbling for the key. Sounds of conversation came from inside. He unlocked the door and found Elizabeth seated next to an older woman dressed in work clothes.

“William!” Elizabeth said, rising to embrace him. “Thank God they let you go. Tomorrow, I was going to seek out our consulate.”

His lips tightened.

“I guess I’m just not cut out for this espionage business. Who is this?”

Elizabeth tried to smile. “May I introduce Jossette Reme. She's a cleaning lady at the Foreign Affairs center. I locked myself inside a maintenance closet. She let me out, and we began talking. She informed me of your arrest and cautioned against my getting involved. But, come see, I believe she has a way of getting into Monsieur Lebec's personnel files."

A middle-aged face looked at William with dark hair drawn up under a red kerchief. Her features were regular, and she wore a plain cloth dress covered by a full-length apron befitting her profession.

"*Oui*, there's a back entrance to the building for workmen. You can slip inside after the clerk leaves for the day. I 'ave a spare set of keys. Tomorrow, I will leave eeze file chambre door unlocked at the end of the day."

They talked for a while over a glass of wine.

William accompanied Madam Reme back to her apartment. Upon his return, he related details of his encounter with Sir Winthrop at the gendarmerie.

Elizabeth appeared equally mystified. "Perhaps he visits under another name."

William frowned. "But, the magistrate said no Englishman had been held there for some time. I can't imagine Winthrop being mistaken for a French citizen."

Following sunset the next night, the Darmons set out to gain access to Room 37.

Entering through the Foreign Affairs Building's rear door, they found empty stillness. They quietly felt along a pitch black hallway to Room 37. Once inside, William lit a candle and led the way to the rear door. He sighed with relief his mess had been cleaned up.

Within the storage room, they faced huge stacks of boxes piled floor to ceiling around its perimeter. William took a deep breath before removing his coat and rolling up his sleeves. Under candlelight, they began rummaging through box after box.

By midnight, Elizabeth's head throbbed, trying to focus bleary eyes on yet another handful of military discharge records as they fell one by one from her hand.

"I don't know how much longer I can keep doing this. These

papers are beginning to all look alike."

William looked up wretchedly from heaps of documents, worried they were approaching a dead end.

"I just can't believe Lebec threw the Colombe correspondences away."

He gazed inside a last box now nearly empty. Among remaining leaflets at the bottom lay a bulging envelope. Curious at this new form of archive, he hastily opened the packet allowing three thin paper rolls to plop into his hand. He remembered the tiny parchment found folded within the pendant. Awkwardly, he fumbled to unroll the missives.

"Lizzy, come, look at this!"

They began translating the first roll together.

*J. Fouche*

*I have dispatched Colombe to the port of Marseilles where she will board the La Coquille, setting sail for Boston on the 13th. Once past the English blockade, our message should reach agent Aigle by 1 March. The Americans are expected to make land near Hastings. A two-three-two signal will alert Faucon Deux to their arrival off-shore. Your man is to provide safe lodging at Rosewell Park where the mistress of the manor will provide a secure location to conduct operations. May we strike for liberty!*

*Bonaparte*

"Oh my God! Aunt Catherine's estate?" William exclaimed.

"William, this is unbelievable! Lady Carlisle was involved in this French plot four years ago!"

He scowled at the note. "It must mean Uncle Lewis' shipping business fell prey to French conspirators after his death in '06. I remember Aunty had a lot to cope with during the war just to keep the line in operation. I know she thinks herself to be an independent woman, but to commit treason?"

Elizabeth shivered convulsively, suddenly more afraid than when they found Louisa's body. "It's unfathomable."

He grimmaced. "I never knew her politics, but such traitorous accommodation is still a hanging offense even if the mission was never consummated."

Elizabeth picked up the parchment once more. "From this note, at least we know Colombe was a woman, and 'F.D.' mentioned in the pendant's missive is likely to be short for agent Faucon Deux."

"Wait a minute," she sputtered. "In this letter, Bonaparte tells Fauche the landing is to be at Hastings. Doesn't our pendant message contain confirmation of a request from Bonaparte asking Clay to send troops to Dover?"

"Oh my God, you're right! Did Napoleon change his mind?"

She frowned. "Why would he tell Fouche one thing and ask Clay for a different landing spot?"

"Unless this Colombe changed the message before giving it to Clay."

"But why would she do that? Did she want the mission to fail? Maybe she was really a double agent working for our side."

"Or, it's possible someone blackmailed her to force the substitution and kept the false message as evidence of her duplicity."

A flicker of compassion passed his eyes. "If my aunt knew the pendant was at Mayfair Hall, it may be the reason she went into hiding after the perpetrator killed Louisa. I wish we had a clue to her whereabouts."

The second paper was carefully unrolled.

*J. Fouche*

*Commander, we've waited every night since 5 April to no avail. American ship did not arrive. Soon we shall be forced to withdraw. Please advise.*

*Faucon Deux*

*15 April 1814*

"I wonder if the ship ever made it to Dover? Was it lost at sea?" Elizabeth wondered.

They opened the third roll from the envelope:

*J. Fouche*

*Commander, we have learned the American ship attempted to make port at Dover! The British frigate 'Essex' waited offshore and fired on the privateer before it could escape. The ship was lost with all hands. We were unaware of a change in plan or we might have intercepted the Americans in time to prevent a Dover landing.*

*Faucon Deux*

*20 April 1814*

"Oh, those poor men!" Elizabeth lamented. "It proves Clay got a false message directing a landing at Dover."

He shook his head in disbelief. "And Fouche never knew it. Our pendant contains Clay's response confirming the intended landing at Dover, but Bonaparte never got it or he would have realized something went awry."

Elizabeth's eyes widened. "Maybe this Colombe was sent back to France with his reply, and once again she removed it and put a forgery in its place confirming the Hastings landing."

He nodded. "And Louisa kept the Dover landing confirmation hidden all these years because she was the double agent, Colombe."

She carefully replaced the rolls.

"If she did substitute a false message, someone with French ties may have recognized Louisa at our ball and killed her in revenge."

William laughed. "Hold on. You can't have solved the mystery so fast. There are still other explanations. Perhaps, someone other than Colombe got hold of the request and substituted the wrong message. He had only to copy the one in her possession and change a single word. Fouche would go after Colombe for treason, and the perpetrator would be free from suspicion."

They continued searching Lebec's vault and found one more scrap of paper in a separate file:

*J. Fouche*

*Message delivered. Response returned in same package. Mission under threat by British agents. Will try to intervene.*

*M. Aigle*

*16 March 1814*

Elizabeth scowled. "I don't understand this at all. Since it's dated before the others, I guess it only confirms some note actually reached Henry Clay."

William sighed with resignation. "So where are we? We still cannot be certain of the true identity of Colombe and have no idea when she returned to Europe. These events are clearly tied to our family through my aunt, and possibly to Louisa's death unless the pendant's discovery was purely coincidence. But without either woman, how are we to figure out the agent's identities or their motives?"

Elizabeth agreed. "Well, I doubt Monsieur Fouche will tell us."

He scratched his chin. "I guess our only hope is to interview Henry Clay."

She gasped. "You're suggesting we sail all the way to the colonies?"

"Former colonies," he corrected. "Now the war has ended, perhaps he will set aside his former French sympathies. He might cooperate if a description of Colombe or this Aigle could help solve a murder."

She swallowed hard. "So we must follow the trail to America to arrive at a resolution."

He looked hesitantly. "Can you possibly withstand an ocean voyage?"

La Coquille rocked gently side to side. Three days after setting sail from Marseilles, trade winds pushed the fifty-foot ketch close to twenty knots. A crew of six and nine passengers were relieved to be underway, but anxious at the peril of running a British blockade to enter Boston harbor.

Nina and Francois remained inside a small partitioned cabin below deck. The first night at sea, Francois spoke quietly after the other passengers settled into their bunks.

"Nina, I will now tell you our mission. Bonaparte, himself directed us to deliver a message to an American statesman. If we succeed, it could help France win the war. We've been given great responsibility, but there are dangers ahead."

He reached inside his coat and pulled out two small pendants.

"There are messages inside these pieces, one real and one false. You've been given the honor of carrying the actual message. I'll carry the sham. Your code name is Colombe du Paix, but, if this name, 'dove of peace' is ever addressed to us, I'll act as if I'm the Colombe."

He looked deep into her eyes. "You must trust no one 'til we reach our contact in Boston. If we're ever separated, go to the Inn of the Black Whale on Riverfront Street and find a man named Aigle. Identify yourself as Colombe and give him the pendant. He'll arrange for your return voyage."

Nina raised her eyebrows with surprise. "I'm honored by the trust placed in me by our great leader, but how could I perform such a liaison on my own? I don't know any words of English. I couldn't even ask for directions."

"Don't worry. Hide the pendant. We'll pretend to be brother and sister on our way to visit grandmother," Francois directed with authority beyond his years.

During the following days, La Coquille enjoyed good weather and no other vessel appeared on the endless sea. Passengers kept to themselves, clustered in tiny groups topside, waiting for the voyage to pass.

One night, Francois and Nina crept out on deck. They made their way to the bow and watched a myriad of stars stretch down to the horizon. In silence, they gazed into darkness, exhilarated by sea breezes while the vessel softly splashed through ink-black waves.

A low voice resonated behind them. “Have you got the message?”

Startled, they turned to face the dark outline of a man with a stocky frame, shorter than Francois.

“What are you talking about?” Francois answered. “Who are you?”

“Name's Jean Noire. Minister Fouche sent me to make sure you reach your destination. Is it secure?” The dark form spoke softly.

Francois relaxed a bit. He reached unconsciously into his pocket to feel the metal object. “I assure you it's safe.”

“May I see it?” the man persisted.

Francois hesitated. The man sounded legitimate and seemed to know about the mission. He wanted to show he could be trusted. Since the actual message was safe, he decided to reveal the pendant. In the darkness, Francois did not see a thin sneer forming on the man's lips as he withdrew the object.

“Here it is!” he announced with satisfaction.

In an instant, the man grabbed Francois’ wrist. With his other hand, he swung a fist into the young man’s stomach. Nina screamed, paralyzed with fear. The seaman wrestled the pendant loose and wrapped his arm around the lad's neck. The surprised youth could barely struggle as Noire dragged him toward the rail. In one swift motion, the individual lifted the young emissary over his head and heaved him into darkness.

Nina cried out at the splash.

Jean Noire turned from the rail, but sounds of voices alerted him to others climbing onto the deck. He paused menacingly, then ran off toward the stern.

Nina lunged to the side. Desperately, she called for Francois, but she could see only blackness beyond their vessel. She began to sob uncontrollably as other passengers arrived. A man put his hand on her shoulder. “What is it, girl?”

Between gasps, she managed two words. “Francois! Overboard!”

The captain brought the ship about, but no trace was found of the young man who wanted to be a hero.

***

Two weeks passed slowly. Nina anxiously kept in the company of fellow passengers, praying she would not see Jean Noire again. No one recognzed his name or the vague description she provided. Each day, she became more fearful of a terrible fate waiting in an alien country that lay ahead.

Two days from port, a posted lookout shouted. “Ship ahoy!”

Passengers followed the mate’s outstretched arm toward the stern’s starboard side. In the distance, sails of a frigate came into view.

The captain bellowed. “More speed! Raise the topsail!”

A fury of activity followed on deck.

At the captain's command, everyone scrambled to find objects which could be thrown overboard to lighten their craft. With sails bulging, the ketch moved faster, but the frigate’s image grew in size. Less than a mile away, Nina could make out a British flag.

Tiny puffs of white smoke erupted on its hull.

A whistling cannonball plunged into water twenty feet from her rail. The plume’s spray doused fearful La Coquille passengers. Nina anxiously looked back at the captain.

Another zinging sound passed overhead with a resounding fountain of water towering on the opposite side. Distant thunderclaps signaled more cannon fire from the warship.

Nina stared with strange fascination at the ominous hunter bearing down on its prey.

A distant splash appeared in front of the frigate.

Nina started with excitement. “Are we shooting at them?”

Cowering passengers straightened and charged over to her railing. They wildly gestured at a second ship off to the west. The English ship slowed and began to turn. The other Man-of-War rapidly enlarged while plumes of water sprouted around the English vessel. A passenger recognized the black and white sides of the new challenger. “It's the USS Constitution!”

Nina cheered at the sight of an American ship in pursuit.

Quickly, the two frigates receded behind them. A collective sigh of relief came from frightened voyagers, collapsing around the deck.

The next day, land hove into view and not long afterwards, grateful travelers disembarked onto the streets of Boston.

Over her shoulder, Nina lugged a bag of clothes, including Francois' possessions. She stepped down the gangplank, glancing apprehensively for Jean Noire among persons leaving the pier, dearly hoping he was satisfied to have the pendant. Streets near the wharf bustled with warehouse workers and carriages retrieving new arrivals. She felt lost and alone. No one spoke to her and she could not understand words she overheard. Where was the avenue called Riverfront?

Without money for a carriage, she had to walk the neighborhood in search for the Inn of the Back Whale.

Not far from the dock, peals of laughter drifted out from a tavern's open door.

Setting her teeth, she summoned courage and headed inside to face a large room crowded with sailors and merchants shouting noisily in warm sweaty air. She scrunched her nose at the pungent smell of ale and edged over to the counter, where a barkeep moved back and forth, replacing empty glasses with refills. When he passed her position, she held up a hand.

*"Auberge du baleine noire?"*

The barkeeper looked puzzled and made an incomprehensible reply.

*"J'ne pas comprehende,"* she shouted above the noise.

Not far away, a gentleman looked up. He rose and came over to her with a smile. To the young girl's relief, he began speaking in French.

"*Bon jour*, mademoiselle. May I translate for you?"

"Oh, thank you, sir. I'm lost," words burst out uncontrollably. "I wish to find the Inn of the Black Whale. Do you know where it's located?"

He paused with a frown.

"The Black Whale? I'm sorry, young lady, the Inn of the Black Whale burnt to the ground a week ago."

# CHAPTER THREE

At London Dock, stevedores, watermen and stewards completed preparations for departure of the American Black Ball merchantman, *Oceana*, bound for Chesapeake. William and Elizabeth milled through Saturday morning's throng of passengers overseeing luggage transfers. A smell of tide and mews of circling gulls reminded Elizabeth her ordeal of a month-long sea crossing was about to begin. She agreed with its necessity and, despite days of mal-de-mer ahead, refused to sit idly at home and miss the voyage of a lifetime. But now, as she tasted salt on the incoming raw-edged wind gusting her face, Elizabeth cringed and shuddered at foggy mists swirling above the Thames' dark waters, whose looming obscurity seemed to underscore the uncertainty of this enterprise.

Near the crowded gangplank, William stepped away for a moment to purchase the latest London Times. He returned, intently focused on the paper, oblivious to jostling tourists surrounding him. As he came closer, she noticed a wrinkled brow. Without raising his head, he took her arm. "Lizzy, look at this!"

LADY CARLISLE DU MONTCLAIR
IMPLICATED IN FRENCH SCANDAL

Investigation into last month's disappearance of Lady Carlisle, widow of the founder of the Montclair Ship Line, Sir Lewis Carlisle du Montclair, has uncovered incriminating documents at her former residence, Rosewell Park. These papers suggest LC was involved in a plot to house American and French spies during the last days of war on the Continent. Evidence also implicated Sir Terrence Winthrop in these traitorous activities apparently conducted by the infamous French Ministry of Espionage.

“The whole mess is now out in the open," William groaned. “It's bad enough we're involved in a murder committed at Mayfair; this scandal will put the entire family under suspicion of treason. I would dearly enjoy getting hold of Sir Terrence and wringing his bloody neck!”

“Can it be true?” Elizabeth wondered. “Sir Terrence was a French agent, the individual behind the mission? It might explain why the Paris Magistrate didn't have a record of an Englishman detained at the gendarmerie.”

William scowled. “Of course it's true. Winthrop is probably the Faucon Deux.”

A boarding call announced impending cast-off.

He rolled up the newspaper, anger flaring in his eyes. It would be months before their return and a chance to track the man down. Nor was there time to consult a solicitor for advice on how to deal with the article’s insinuations.

Elizabeth could already sense gentle swaying of the ship as she climbed to the end of gangway. Below her, waters lapped in the shadows, its’ surface dotted with scum bobbing up and down. With a deep breath, she resolutely marched aboard ship, feeling the dread of a condemned prisoner.

“I fear this ordeal has fallen heavily on your shoulders," William observed from the rail. “The loss of Louisa, the disaster at our anniversary ball, and now the shame of harboring a conspirator within our household have struck at our family's stability. If we'd never met, you might have had a more peaceful life without calamity.”

“And I would have quietly grown old without challenge or interest. How dull! You cast too much blame on yourself," she replied. “We’re not even certain of Lady Carlisle's guilt.”

“Oh, I think there can be little doubt on that score. There again, I am responsible for inviting her to share our residence at Mayfair Hall," he added dourly.

“Well, I’ll give you that, but she is your only living relative," Elizabeth consoled. “I wouldn't have expected you to do less.”

Three weeks passed. Despite pleasant weather, Elizabeth suffered disorientation each day and remained within their quarters, giving William an excuse not to interact with other passengers. When he did emerge topside, he was certain every man condemned him by his glance. Women and children were hurried from his presence. Even the crew kept their distance from the outcast. He was now a well-known member of the 'notorious' Darmon gang of traitors. When they returned from America, would a hangman be waiting?

Elizabeth finally regained composure when the Oceana arrived in the calm waters of Chesapeake Harbor and was fully recovered by the time solid surface rested under foot in Baltimore.

"I'm afraid I haven't been much of a companion these past weeks."

William smiled with sympathy. "Nonsense. You've shown great courage. I, for one, could not have borne these weeks at sea with your malady."

"Well, I'm looking forward to the fixed surroundings of a hotel room," she said, trying to put the voyage out of mind.

William nodded. "We should get plenty of rest before tomorrow's ride to the Capitol. After we check in, I'd like to consult a local newspaper for records of ship arrivals dating back to the spring of 1814."

An hour later, they found their way into the office of the Maryland Gazette. It was a small, weathered gray stone cottage. Inside, a smell of ink and machine oil permeated the air. Three persons pushed and prodded arms of an old iron press situated behind a polished oak counter.

A bald gentleman with bristling grey whiskers and ink-stained blue apron noticed the visitors, before wiping his blackened hands. Upon hearing their request, he rubbed discolored fingers over a forehead already streaked with print marks. The pressman then went to the back wall and began searching stacks of paper. Returning with three issues, the clerk apologized for their infrequent publication due to wartime interruptions. They found a tottering table behind the press and began carefully leafing through pages of yellowed journals.

Only two ships managed to penetrate the British blockade during the time of interest: La Coquille and the Aurora. Both privateers carried cargos of soft goods and eight passengers. The issue dated February 28, reported a La Coquille voyager had been swept overboard. A young lad by the name of Francois du Hurst.

"Oh, how awful!" exclaimed Elizabeth. "The poor boy. It means Nina must have arrived on her own. I wonder if the servant girl completed their mission without him?"

William placed a reassuring hand on her shoulder. "Darling, she must have accomplished the task. We have the evidence in hand which proves she reached the Capitol and transferred the pendant's message to the Speaker of the House."

"Of course, my perceptive sleuth." She smiled mockingly. "Perhaps Aigle waited for them at the docks."

Afternoon sunlight changed to deepening orange color through the office's four-paned windows by the time they decided to return to the hotel.

Halfway up the stairway to their room, William noticed the door stood slightly ajar.

He motioned for Elizabeth to stop while he proceeded to slowly push it open. Within the faintly lit space, he could make out a floor cluttered with vague forms. He tentatively stepped inside, stumbling trying to find a lamp. When light finally cast through the room, they discovered contents of their luggage spread over the floor, drawers from the bureau pulled out and their bedding disheveled.

Elizabeth gasped. "William, notify the police!"

He kicked angrily at the pile of clothes. "Is there no place safe from those conspirators?"

Elizabeth took his arm. "Slow down. Do you really think French agents followed us aboard ship and this is their calling card? No one knows we're here. We've no quarrel with the Colonists. It's more likely predators who watch for wealthy tourists leaving the docks. This is probably the act of harbor cutthroats."

William calmed down. "I guess you're right. Let's straighten up and see if anything has been taken."

On the floor, near one of Elizabeth's gloves, William spied an unfamiliar object. He picked up a gold button with filigreed edges. "Look here. This doesn't look like something left behind by a common thief!"

Having put the room in order and finding nothing missing, they thought better of seeking police involvement, which might slow their investigation.

A cold, clear morning greeted the couple's departure in a hired carriage as they set out on a thirty-mile ride to the American congressional buildings. White clouds billowed in an azure sky. Large black birds circled above densely wooded hillsides and meadowlarks boldly chirped from mossy branches. Golden sunlight danced off fluttering leaves and swaying long grass within passing fields. Rhythmic sound of the horse's trot provided a pleasing background for their open vehicle as it bounced swiftly along the road.

Elizabeth's spirits lifted with the fresh air. She smiled, appreciating the solitude. Fast movement caused the conveyance to rock side to side, and she swallowed with a familiar feeling of dizziness. Determined to persevere, she focused on her dress, a favorite outfit worn especially for their meeting with Speaker Clay. The gold gauze linen dress sewn with flowers of maroon silk complimented her brown, postilion-back jacket trimmed with matching colors in velvet. It belonged to her mother, and she always felt confident wearing it for business engagements.

An hour elapsed when two riders came into view on the distant path ahead.

William squinted at the newcomers dressed in farmer's coveralls with straw hats. They appeared to be in no particular hurry coming down the trail, heading toward Baltimore. As the images grew, William observed one carrying a pole six or seven feet in length, much like an ancient jouster holding a lance. The other possessed a flat board resting against his shoulder displaying several protrusions at the upper end.

Distance between them closed rapidly.

Just as the horsemen were about to pass, one rider abruptly crossed in front of their vehicle. The driver pulled hard on his reins, raising the horse's head and sliding the carriage to a stop.

"Watch out, you fools!" the chauffeur shouted, reaching for his whip.

Suddenly, one rider lunged at the driver with his pole, knocking him off the seat. William stood up to protest, when the other slammed their animal's rump with his board's protruding spikes. The startled horse reared and lunged forward at a gallop, throwing William back onto the seat next to Elizabeth. He desperately clawed at air, trying to climb forward and reach the empty driver's seat, but could not regain his balance.

Elizabeth screamed.

They raced at breakneck speed, careening though the woods, trying to grasp handholds, hanging on for dear life.

An empty field flew past, and ground began rising beneath their path. Within a blur of birch trunks, the course began to wind, swinging the carriage precariously from side to side, barely staying on track.

The road turned sharply.

Their carriage swung around on two wheels. A fallen tree trunk flashed into view, lying across their path. The horse charged up to it, desperately jumping into the air. It cleared the log for an instant before the carriage front wheels struck full force into the trunk. The impact brought the rear of the carriage upwards and flung its occupants flying over the fallen animal.

Elizabeth shrieked, plunging into a row of bushes twenty feet from the toppled cart. William thudded onto a grassy slope, rolled down the incline and awkwardly splashed in a small creek. The carriage crashed onto its side with a loud crunch, coming to rest on shattered wheels.

Soft silence settled over the chaotic remains.

Stunned, William lay waiting for the sky to stop spinning. Slowly, he moved his fingers in cold water and felt a white-hot pain stab his wrist. He moaned, sensing other parts of his battered body complain as he tried to sit up. Seeing his wife gingerly move a short distance away, he forced limbs to climb to his feet.

Elizabeth extracted herself from the bush's barbs, tearing fabric and shaking with rage. "Those bloody bastards! They tried to kill us!"

She looked in anguish at her clothes, torn and matted with mud. "Mother's dress! I've ruined mother's dress."

He gently placed a hand on her shoulder.

A grimy face turned toward him, covered with red scratches and a purple bruise on the forehead. William hugged his wife. Using fingers, he wiped dirt from scratches on her face. "It seems like the country is punishing us for trespassing."

"Listen, William, I don't care who's behind these attacks, I refuse to be deterred from our rendezvous with Clay," Elizabeth said, eyes as hard as winter.

He looked at her with a twisted smile. "I agree. As you say, this may be an everyday occurrence in a land where only the strong survive."

The Englishman went over to the trembling horse and unhitched it. After a moment's stroking the frightened equine, he turned.

"I doubt we've come halfway to the Capitol. We'll ride back to the driver and seek medical attention in Baltimore. Come, let me help you up."

The horse walked without complaint. They cautiously retraced their path, anxious to avoid a second encounter with the scoundrels.

Before long, they overtook their carriage operator on his way, walking back to civilization. Althoughed bruised and angry at the damage to their vehicle, he did not seem surprised at the encounter.

Once in Baltimore, they consulted an apothecary and proceeded to a local police station. In response to their grievance, the superintendent cautioned them to beware of highwaymen and war refugees laying siege to unsuspecting travelers. He promised to interview a local farmer whose sons were known for their pranks, but skeptical at the prospect of recovering payment for their losses.

The next day, William and Elizabeth attempted a second journey.

In spite of the Darmon's apprehension, their vehicle made the trip without incident.

They arrived at the government center to view a familiar sight.

As in France, major restoration activity had workers busily repairing wartime damage and erecting new structures. Masons, carpenters and supply wagons crowded bustling city streets, while a stream of visitors paraded in and out of official buildings.

Passing in front of the freshly painted White House, Elizabeth leaned over the carriage door. "My word, I see the Colonials have just about repaired their wounds three years after the Treaty of Ghent. Perhaps now, they'll curtail their imperialist appetite."

Inside the Capitol building, William discovered Congress in session and received word Henry Clay would not be back in his office until mid-afternoon. With some time to wait, they chose to visit the French consulate to see if the presence of a French girl had been recorded during the spring of 1814.

A stiff gentleman with a thin mustache answered their inquiry with a stack of papers. William and Elizabeth divided up the pile and began leafing through messages, bills and newspaper references to French citizens. Some notes dated back to the turn of the century and a few were only fragments of original documents. After ten minutes, Elizabeth encountered a familiar name in an old newspaper clipping:

Fire destroyed the Inn of the Black Whale last night. Police have reason to suspect arson. Just before flames broke out, an unidentified individual ran from the building. When the conflaguration was finally doused, firemen uncovered a badly charred body within the rubble. Next to it, lay a gold watch engraved with the name Megras Aigle, a Paris Emissary reported missing five days earlier.

"The date precedes Nina's arrival by a week," Elizabeth noted. "So Aigle could not have been at the docks to meet her."

William frowned. "She must have gone to see Clay on her own."

Elizabeth unfolded a small pink sheet of paper. Her hands began to shake. "William, take a look at this!"

She held up a consulate request for audience with H. Clay dated March 1. Under the approval stamp lay the signature of Terrence Winthrop and his daughter, Nina.

Comprehension flared in her eyes. She drew in a breath.

"So, he was here in America four years ago! He must have taken Aigle's place to ensure Bonaparte's letter got passed on. It certainly confirms his French allegiance. I can't believe he worked against us all that time. Maybe, he came to our house to silence Louisa and, later, escaped with Lady Carlisle."

William's eyes narrowed, trying to frame his thoughts.

"I have another theory. Don't forget that three weeks after this fire, a response was sent to Fouche signed by Aigle. Suppose Aigle killed the real Sir Terrence and assumed his identity. He knew Colombe was coming, so he waited for her at the docks and proceeded with the exchange using his new name."

Elizabeth's eyes widened. "So our friend of the past two years is actually Megras Aigle, a French spy who purposely left his watch with Sir Terrence's remains?"

William leaned back in his chair, regarding the ceiling beams.

"Could this impersonation have gone undetected in London? I don't recall his having any family, but what about the home and servants belonging to the original Sir Terrence?"

Elizabeth nodded. "Of course, it's possible he never retook the former Winthrop residence and only used his new identity in Kent where he became our acquaintance to find out who delivered the false message and caused their plan to fail."

They thumbed through remaining material without finding anything of interest.

The couple thanked the concierge and left the consulate. Following a brief meal, they returned to the American politician's office .

An hour passed before a secretary escorted the couple into the statesman's room. Henry Clay rose from his desk, giving a conciliatory smile.

"My dear Mr. and Mrs. Darmon, welcome to America. Please sit down."

The tall, raw-boned gentleman spoke in a smooth voice. His dark blue coat and faded tie displayed the wrinkles of a day's work, but his sinewy frame portrayed youthful vigor of an outdoorsman, reflecting his upbringing on a Kentucky homestead.

"You have my sympathy for the recent loss within your household," he offered. "But I fail to see what the government of the United States can do for you."

Elizabeth's mouth dropped, surprised at his knowledge of their affairs.

"It's this subject which brings us to you," William replied, reaching into the pocket of his waistcoat. "We found a note with your signature near the body of Louisa Hurst."

He withdrew the pendant and placed its message on the desk.

Clay leaned forward and stared at the paper without comment. He stood up and walked over to a window. Looking out at the nearby street, he seemed lost in thought. After a long moment, he shook his head with resignation and returned to the brown leather chair.

He smiled thinly at the English visitors.

"So my reply never reached Bonaparte. We lost the entire mission because our French contact never knew where to rendezvous!"

Elizabeth took a deep breath. "We think another message may have arrived in its place, directing the agents to a supposed landing near Hastings. Meanwhile, Dover received British troops and our warship, Essex. A trap was set for your privateer."

"Who else knew your ship was bound for Dover?" inquired William.

The statesman sagged back into his chair. "Well, now the events are well past, I suppose there's no harm in giving you some details.

"Only Commodore Rodgers, Secretary of War Armstrong, myself and, of course the ship's crew knew the plan. When Commodore Rodgers reached the English Channel without resistance on a voyage the year before, we decided there was opportunity for a first strike in the fall of 1812. We began thinking of ways to demonstrate our ability to strike at your shores and thereby convince the Royal Navy to dispatch fewer ships abroad.

"Early the following year, a French Agent known as Faucon Deux contacted me and suggested a similar mission, offering assistance once our men landed. We met several times. On one visit, a woman accompanied him. Ultimately, she was to carry my response to Bonaparte in the east of France."

"What was the woman's name?" Elizabeth asked, arching an eyebrow.

"Why, Faucon Une. Their true identities were never revealed. They seemed a pleasant enough couple. The gentleman looked a bit rotund with a small scar on his left ear. I'm told after the aborted landing, he took to drink."

William nodded. "The description fits Arthur Hurst. And was the woman short in stature with red hair?"

"I believe so."

Elizabeth smiled triumphantly. "His wife, Louisa. They were in it together!"

William pressed. "By what means did Bonaparte's original request arrive?"

Clay tried to recall the visit. "Another agent, identifying herself as Colombe met with me here. She was very young and could not speak English, but an older gentleman accompanied her to translate."

William's eyes brightened. "Would you describe them?"

"I recall the man was about my height, graying hair, a little older than myself. His most prominent feature was a long nose, bent as if previously broken."

"Sounds like the Sir Terrence Winthrop we know," Elizabeth acknowledged. "And the lady?"

"She was maybe seventeen. She didn't speak except to confer with this Winthrop in French. Slender girl, about your height with pale complexion, short blonde hair and large brown eyes."

William glanced quizzically at his wife. "Doesn't ring a bell. Did they mention a boy with whom she traveled, Francois du Hurst?"

Henry Clay frowned. "Why yes, now that you mention it. Winthrop said she told him a sailor calling himself Jean Noire threw the lad overboard. She said he took a pendant from the boy, but it contained a false message. Fortunately, she hadn't seen the blackguard since."

William shot up as if stung by a bee. "Jean Noire? I know that name! In English, Jean Noire is John Black."

Elizabeth clutched her husband's arm. "John and his wife Estee were at our ball the night of the murder."

William spread his hands. "So, you received a message from Colombe asking for a landing at Dover. She didn't know it was really a false message, and John Black now had the real one. Your response confirming a Dover landing was returned by Louisa, or rather Faucon Une. But by the time it got to Paris, Fouche had received a different message from Bonaparte and sent Arthur to wait near Hastings. But someone on our side had to have seen your reply to know where to set the trap."

William rubbed his chin. "Did the pendant ever leave your possession before passing it to Faucon Une?"

Clay shook his head. "We used a drop-off at the Hotel Franklin. I placed the pendant in an envelope and left it with the desk clerk by the usual procedure."

William scratched his head. "Then access may have occurred at the hotel or during Louisa's trip to France. Do you know her means of travel?"

The statesman gazed out his window once more.

"We provided her with the fastest ship in America's fleet, a new type of yacht employing a steam engine combined with sails. It crosses the Atlantic in under twenty days. The *Savannah* is presently in the Mediterranean drawing a lot of attention. It put to port at Marseilles where Faucon Une was to proceed directly to Castle Philippe. I heard no report of an intervention."

Moments later, Clay requested a conclusion to the meeting to accommodate a busy schedule. The pair thanked him for the interview. He, in turn, invited them to Ashland, if they ever visited Kentucky. He also offered an invitation to a cotillion to be held at the

White House the next day's eve. Honored by the opportunity to sample the best of American society, the Darmons graciously accepted.

Leaving the Capitol, William pondered.

"When Black took the pendant from Francois, he should have read a request for a landing at Dover, since Nina said the boy carried a false message and the archive roll contained Bonaparte's letter to Fouche requesting an intended Hastings landing. Instead Black got the correct Hastings request.

Elizabeth paused. "It means the children may have inadvertently switched the messages. My God, you mean fifty Americans perished because of a child's mistake?"

He frowned. "But if Black was a British agent, he would have returned to England to make sure a trap was set at Hastings. Why did he think our troops should be deployed at Dover?"

Elizabeth scratched her head. "Since the request was addressed to Clay, he probably knew enough to go to the statesman's office and wait for Nina. Afterall, what was important was how Clay responded to Bonaparte's request. For all he knew, Clay might turn the general down.

William nodded. "Somehow, he had to intercept the return message.

"So he tailed the Speaker to the drop-off. He may have opened the envelope at the hotel and read the message before Louisa retrieved the package. I doubt he'd risk going after the pendant once it came into the possession of an experienced envoy like Louisa. And, being English, Black would not want to wait until she arrived in France before intervening."

Elizabeth nodded. "It explains why Nina never saw him again. Black was now after Louisa."

***

The next day, the English couple spent time preparing for the White House gala. Elizabeth looked forward to meeting the President at his new residence. Her enthusiasm for large parties sent her to the finest milliners in Baltimore. William also expressed an interest in developing future business prospects for the import of American cotton.

Shortly after dark, their carriage arrived at the expansive two-story structure. Warm moist air of a languid summer's evening hung closely over their open transport. Fireflies darted among bushes on the White House grounds as they pulled up a circular driveway off Pennsylvania Avenue. Bright light streamed from all ten ground floor windows and sounds of ballroom music could be heard. A smartly dressed liveried servant helped them from their carriage and led them by a colonnade up steps to the North Portico. Elizabeth held William's arm as they maneuvered by a number of guests mingling in the Entrance Hall, crossed a polished marble floor and passed between majestic marble columns lining Cross Hall.

She paused to adjust her white gloves at the elbow and gave a final approving inspection to many folds in her teal satin dress. A glance at the corridor's white marble walls and vaulted ceiling arching gracefully overhead made her realize, despite the ambiance, much of the interior remained unfinished. From where she stood, the south portico still needed repair. William mentioned that architect, James Hoban had been hired to rebuild the executive mansion in 1815, but two years later, President James Monroe took residence despite its incomplete condition.

With a nod toward her husband, she resumed advancing over a red carpet to the largest room of the manor, the Public Audience Room at the east end of the building. The hallway resplendent with floral decorations and pastel colors of lavish gowns became crowded near the entrance to the East Room.

When the Darmons finally squeezed inside the spacious room, they gazed at the splendor. In front of them, yellows, powder blues, pinks and various shades of white spread among stiff black suits of attending gentlemen and blue-coated servers. Over two hundred guests attended in honor of the French ambassador.

Above their heads, signs of repair stood out. Walls showed bare plaster and windows sat unadorned, mantles displayed simple painted wood, and the floor consisted of raw boards. An ornamental anthemion frieze, highlighted with gold leaf on a black-flocked background, provided ornamentation near a large portrait of George Washington rescued by Dolly Madison from war's destruction.

Elizabeth began conversing with two women of her age. William feigned attention while gossip exchanged regarding President Monroe's latest attempt to furnish the White House. He had placed an order for mahogany furniture from Pierre-Antoine Bellange for the oval and state dining rooms. The president's agents, an American firm of Russell and La Farge in LeHavre, however, informed the president mahogany was not appropriate furniture for a Saloon, even in private gentlemen's houses. Instead, they shipped fifty-three carved and gilded pieces with crimson silk upholstery.

William excused himself and wandered off toward the ambassador.

He passed two gentlemen engaged in subdued conversation and overheard a few words spoken quietly in French.

"...fifty British uniforms have been sent to Ottawa..."

William stopped, intrigued by Frenchmen concerned with uniforms of his countrymen. "Excuse my intrusion. Can you direct me to the Ambassador?"

The shorter barely paused, absently waving to his left.

William regarded the individual. Beneath dark shoulder length curls, his pale face displayed a meticulously trimmed mustache and goatee. They both wore blue military-style coats with tight white trousers and knee-length stockings. Gold buttons accented the dress uniforms.

"And may I have the pleasure of learning your names?" William asked.

The gentleman glared as if annoyed by a persistent gnat. "LeClair and Perchant. Please excuse us."

William bowed curtly and strode off, hearing one mutter, "English scum."

The evening wore on with William drifting between conversants and frequently rejoining his wife for the latest revelations. A toast to the Ambassador preceded an encounter with Henry Clay, who introduced them to President and Mrs. Monroe. A brief discourse of mutual compliments concluded with another visitor's introduction and the Darmons stepped away.

As midnight approached, William stepped outside to discretely approach carriage drivers sitting patiently for their masters. After several encounters, he found the driver who ferried the two Frenchmen. Hotel Franklin was given as their address. Elated, William returned to Elizabeth.

A short time later, the Darmons expressed gratitude to their host and hostess before leaving for accommodation at a local hotel.

The next day, William and Elizabeth set out to visit the Hotel Franklin.

William's encounter with LeClair and Perchant, who seemed to be up to no good while residing at the Hotel, suggested French agents continued to use the facility. Perhaps a tie to Louisa's death remained.

Elizabeth identified herself to the Hotel clerk as a LeClair acquaintance. She learned his room number and the absence of a key suggested he stepped out. Help with some luggage outside gave William the chance to retrieve the hotel's master key.

When Elizabeth made her way upstairs, she discovered William waiting at LeClair's doorway. Hearing no sound within, they slipped inside.

A well-worn room contained a bed, bureau, table and chairs and large wardrobe. Within the latter they found a coat missing a button which matched the one found at their Baltimore hotel. Further search revealed no papers nor clues to their intentions. As they turned to leave, sounds of approaching footsteps came from the hallway. In panic, they looked for another way out. Finding none, they froze as the door opened to reveal the surprised expressions of LeClair and Perchant. "*Quoi...*"

William lunged forward, attempting to push them aside, but the Frenchmen quickly subdued him. Perchant withdrew a pistol and directed the Darmons to stand by a wall away from the door.

"Why have you invaded our privacy? Or are you still seeking the Ambassador, Monsieur Darmon?" LeClair sneered.

Elizabeth clutched William's arm.

He held up the button. "We're looking for the person who burglarized our hotel chamber. We found this. I believe it matches the one missing from your coat."

LeClair burst out laughing. "Am I to understand you broke into our room to confront us with a missing button?"

A soft knock came at the door. Perchant opened it to another tall gentleman. LeClair glanced over his shoulder at the visitor. "Bonjour, Megras. We've caught two thieves going through our possessions."

The gentleman smiled at the hostages. "I see. You must be the English couple who attended the White House ball last night. Aren't you the Darmons?"

William suppressed an urge to throw himself at the person. "Are you a part of this gang of thieves?"

"I am Megras Aigle of the French embassy."

Elizabeth gasped. "Aigle? We surmised you to be a gentleman we knew as Sir Terrence Winthrop."

"Winthrop? I do not know this name."

She frowned. "Weren't you involved in a fire at the Inn of the Black Whale back in 1814?"

The diplomat shrugged. "Black Whale? I've heard of that tavern, a place of intrigue during the war, frequented by spies and cutthroats. I believe the former Aigle met his end there."

Elizabeth frowned. "Former Aigle?"

"Aigle, or 'Eagle' is a code name used back then. A few of us still carry the appellation for amusement. I am Megras, Eagle of our flock!"

She nodded. "I see. Why did your agents burn down the Inn?"

His eyes narrowed. "We claimed no responsibility. Given the numerous incidents of destruction propagated by you English, I think it more likely to be the handiwork of your countrymen."

William looked puzzled. "We came here to investigate the murder of Louisa Hurst. I believe she was an agent of yours formerly known as Faucon Une."

Aigle shifted uncomfortably. "Word of Madame Hurst's demise

has spread. She was sympathetic to our needs from time to time during the war. Her loss is regrettable. I assure you we had no part in the crime."

"Did you ever meet her?"

"Before I took my position, we, how do you say, 'moved in different circles.' Only the highest levels knew the role of this English lady."

"You mean Fouche?"

"Precisely."

"And you had no involvement in courier activites here at the Hotel, particularly for an American raid on Parliament requested by Bonaparte?"

"Mon Dieu. I 'ave never heard of this, I assure you."

"Why should we trust your assurances?" William exploded. "Last night, I overheard LeClair, here, plotting to send British uniforms to Canada!"

Megras shot a glance at the Frenchman, who wrinkled his nose slightly.

"It is a delicate issue," the emissary said. "We have been supplying Canadians with British uniforms to help allay their fears of further American invasions. Parliament cannot afford the expense of re-enforcing the Provinces and your British generals refuse to supply uniforms to anyone outside their own militia. We do it quickly, using remnants left in these former colonies. The procedure benefits England by giving the appearance of additional regimentation protecting your territories. We make a small profit, but you can understand the need for secrecy from our American friends."

William harrumphed. *Was it all a misunderstanding*? "I guess we owe you an apology."

The Frenchman laughed, reflecting on the humor of ill-founded suspicions. Eventually, the Darmons were released with wishes for success in their investigation.

Uncertain what to believe, the couple returned to Baltimore and decided to take a respite from their pursuit before setting sail for London.

On their last night of sightseeing, William and Elizabeth strolled the shoreline, enjoying now-familiar surroundings. Cool breezes off the bay felt good after a hot seafood dinner. Two hours of wandering brought them to a small tavern a block from their lodging.

They sat at a corner table while a few patrons quietly conversed near the bar, paying no attention to an almost empty room. William settled back, relieved to call an end to their time abroad. "Well, my dear, in four weeks, your contest with the sea should be over for good."

Elizabeth smiled. "It was a price to be paid. We're a little closer to the truth, but heaven knows what's in store for us at Mayfair."

William pounded the table. "I can't wait to get my hands on Winthrop and Black."

She gently placed her hand on his. "I don't know what to feel. On one hand, the French agent who was our enemy treated the servant girl with kindness. On the other, Black, trying to foil a traitorous plot, ruthlessly threw a young lad overboard."

A server appeared at their table. "Allo. May I bring you something warm to drink?"

Hearing the accent, William glanced at the blonde haired woman. He paused, looking into hazel eyes while she waited for their order. "Nina?"

"Do I know you?"

Elizabeth's mouth fell open.

He grinned broadly. "No, but we cannot express our satisfaction at finding you at last!"

They spent the evening discussing the Darmon's investigation. William paid a sizeable sum for the barkeep to keep Nina at their table. As their accounts reached events of the day, he paused. "And you never saw Jean Noire again?"

She shook her head. "I think 'e was satisfied to have recovered Francois' pendant. I kept close to Monsieur Winthrop. When I explained my situation, we opened the pendant and saw the message was addressed to Monsieur Clay. 'E got us a meeting, and I passed on the pendant. 'E also found a place for me to stay 'ere in Baltimore."

Elizabeth frowned. "So you weren't asked to carry any more messages back to the Castle?"

"Oh no," the girl replied. "Without Francois, I had no ties there. It seemed better to remain in America until the war was over. I got this job and began learning English."

"Did Winthrop ever mention an agent named Aigle?" asked William.

She turned her head toward the door. "I had no further meetings with them. Monsieur Clay said my task was done, and 'e would make all further arrangements for the delivery of his response."

"What happened to Winthrop?" Elizabeth posed.

Nina shrugged. "'E told me he had business in England. 'E left the country a week later. I believe 'e intended to visit 'is relative there, an aunt named Lady Carlisle."

# CHAPTER FOUR

A series of unexpected events disrupted Charles Bagwell's well-ordered life.

While the Darmon's were away in America, a summons arrived at Bagwell Manor. John Black requested a meeting at his London flat, near Parliament Square. Charles hesitated. He only just met this person at the Darmon ball, and their brief conversation convinced Charles he lacked the demeanor of a gentleman. A day's ride to face the scoundrel would not be pleasant, but the proposed rendezvous could have something to do with his sister's murder, and he did not intend to ignore a possible lead.

Following overnight lodging at London's Hampton House, Charles called upon Black early the next morning. The man gave an address of a three-story apartment situated a mile north of the Square on Martin's Lane. It was a lower class neighborhood with barking dogs, street hawkers and soot-covered brick buildings shoulder to shoulder along a cobblestone street five blocks west of the Thames.

He stood on the front step surrounded by foggy mist and banged an iron doorknocker until the latch sounded. The short, stocky fellow answered with an expression of curiosity. His weather-beaten pockmarked face crinkled when recognition crossed his eyes. He wore casual clothes, a drab flannel shirt and dark blue trousers, which made Charles wonder if the meeting had been forgotten.

"Mr. Bagwell, welcome. Please come in."

Black waved him across a tattered brown carpet to a pair of doeskin-colored winged-back armchairs in front of a garden window. The diminutive furnished parlor comprised the flat's first floor with a polished maple stairway leading to other rooms above. Charles paused on the threshold, not quite willing to give up his last chance to avoid the interchange, but he needed the man's information.

A flicker of amusement crossed Black's face as he watched his visitor draw in a breath and come leadenly over to join him. “May I extend my condolences once more for the loss of your sister. Louisa and I were good friends.”

“Indeed?” Charles replied. “I don't recollect Louisa ever mentioning you.”

“I've done business with the Hursts for years,” Black went on. “However, our exchanges were of a confidential nature.”

“So you say," Charles responded with ill-concealed insolence.

Without comment, his host abruptly rose, left the room and returned carrying tea service. After placing a tray with cups and plate of scones on the table between them, he began pouring the steaming liquid. “Look here, I'm in need of a favor. I've decided to take you into my confidence. I'm in the trade of manufacturing gunpowder.”

Charles' eyes widdened. “Gunpowder? You were selling explosives to my sister?”

“Patience, Mr. Bagwell," Black said, smiling wryly. “Let me fill you in on some background. I built my company during the war. We use potash from kelp beds in Scotland. It's superior to wood ash and more readily available in times when wood is needed for other purposes such as building ships. The ingredient is used in the production of explosives at my factory on the south coast.”

“You furnished ammunition to the Royal Navy during the war?” Charles asked.

“My service to the Crown was vital then, but in time of peace, I make derivatives available to all sorts of customers," he admitted.

Charles frowned. “In other words, you arm any nation that wants to build an arsenal.”

“We make a living whether or not our clients are on a list approved by the Ministry of War," John Black acknowledged.

Charles raised an eyebrow. His instincts about the man seemed on target.

“Alas, with the end of the war and this recession in Europe, markets have all but dried up,” the entrepreneur continued.

He took a sip of tea and downed a cookie.

“Recently, however, prospects brightened with a sizeable order from the Canadian colonies. They request munitions for cutting a canal between Ottawa and Kingston. According to John By, a waterway around Chaudiere Falls would permit travel on the St. Lawrence River all the way from Montreal to Lake Ontario without exposure on the American side. Construction requires earth removal over a span of thirty miles, hence I've been asked to export twenty tons of explosive to the frontier."

Charles whistled. "But what has this to do with me?"

Black lowered his voice. "Transporting gunpowder aboard ship isn't popular with most captains. Until recently, we've used the Montclair line. However, Lady Carlisle has abandoned her husband's commerce, and the police are looking into her business practices, every manifest is open to question."

"She's disappeared," Charles confirmed.

Black leaned back in his armchair, staring intently at his visitor. "Three weeks ago, I received a letter. She desires to quit her residence in England until the furor subsides."

Charles jerked upright. "You've been in contact? Do you know where she's hiding?"

"Up in Edinburgh somewhere. The note mentioned a family cottage."

Bagwell's cheeks flushed. "My God, that's my place! I could be accused of harboring a criminal."

Black pursed his lips. "If arrangements could be made for my exports and her travel to Canada, she'd be out of there in no time. I've come to you because of your ties to the family and your impeccable reputation."

Charles swallowed and reached for another drink of tea.

The businessman's gaze never left Charles. "There's a ship, the *Merryweather* due for departure to Halifax next Saturday. Authorities are watching for her attempt to leave the country, but with your influence, you could arrange passage for my wares and my mother. May I impose upon you for this service?"

Charles slowly exhaled. "Why can't you do it yourself?"

"My dear man, I'm already suspect in Louisa's death. The police would never let me leave the country, nor would a captain since I'm tied to the explosives. You, however, are above suspicion and simply doing a favor for a friend."

Charles considered his request. It sounded easy enough, and if he could help William's aunt get out from under the war scandal, it might be best. William suggested she might have gone into hiding to flee a killer. She had not been charged with any crime, so he would not be doing anything illegal.

He looked squarely into the man's eyes. "You must see to Lady Carlisle's safety. Whatever you may think, she's my friend's aunt and a bit fragile at her age."

Black smiled pleasantly. "Of course. You may rest assured I'll see that her Ladyship has the best accommodation. One more thing, please be discreet about this. We cannot risk her apprehension prior to departure."

Discussion turned to details of container deliveries, bills of lading, and money transfer. Black provided Charles with a note of credit to be deposited following the vessel's departure. After a drink to their success, Charles left for the Montclair Shipping Office.

A clerk reviewed the proposed manifest with routine disinterest.

"Thirteen containers of tea from the LCM Factory and two passengers in your service. May I have the names of your representatives?"

"John Glass and Lady Wilhelmina Glass," Charles replied.

The clerk wrote the names in a ledger with careful hand. Charles paid transportation charges with his own letter of credit.

"All cargo must be on dock by noon of the day prior to sailing. Passengers are welcome to board any time during the day of cast off," the attendant advised.

Leaving the Office with midday hour approaching, Charles decided to dine at a nearby public house on the waterfront. He smiled at the beautiful day. The sky had cleared. Pleasure boats and strings of barges moved gracefully on the Thames. Closer to shore, numerous merchantmen swayed at their moorings, waiting for cargoes to be off-loaded or carried onboard.

Taking a small corner table at the rear of a noisy room, he settled back, satisfied his mission had been accomplished. He ordered a pint of favorite ale, reminding himself there would be no telling the Darmon's of these events. Knowing William, he would want to confront the authorities head on, demanding retractions and exposing Lady Carlisle to more ridicule in what might simply be a misunderstanding. Fortunately, they were not due to return until after Lady Carlisle departed. His role in the affair was minimal, but he made a note to inspect the Edinburgh property to ensure Lady Carlisle left no evidence behind.

At half-past nine the next morning, Charles dressed to leave for Surrey. He looked forward to joining Emily who missed her sister's company. A tapping noise came at the door. He opened it to face two men with somber expressions, attired in gray suits. The shorter of the two exhibited plain features with curly black hair, close-knit bushy eyebrows and a florid complexion. He shifted uncomfortably in a tight fitting vest with buttons strained at bulges down to the stripped trousers of a city gentleman. Towering above him, the other individual stood painfully erect with a countenance suggesting some import. He appeared older the other, sporting white lamb chop sideburns and a jutting chin marked by a pale scar.

"Charles Bagwell?"

"Yes?"

The taller gentleman stepped closer. "Mr. Bagwell, I am Michael Gravis of His Majesty's Ministry of War. This is Chief Inspector Matthews of the Metropolitan Police at Palace Yard. May we speak with you?"

Charles felt a prick on the back of his neck. He stepped backwards, allowing them to enter. His pulse began to race and suddenly felt sick. "What's this about?"

The official scowled. "I believe you reserved passage for John Glass aboard the Merryweather. Is that correct?"

Charles nodded weakly.

"May I ask how you're involved with this gentleman?" Gravis asked.

"I hardly know the man," Charles stammered. "He requested help to secure transport for some construction materials."

"I see. And you decided to do this because….?"

Charles began to fidget. "It seemed like a noble cause. He said he was unavailable to purchase the tickets himself."

"Look Bagwell, things can go badly for you," Inspector Matthews interrupted, his voice edgy with impatience. "We've got men out on Martin's Lane watching Mr. Black's apartment. We know you called upon him yesterday and then went directly to the Montclair Shipping Office at London Dock. Unless you can prove the identities of your fares are none other than John Black and Lady Carlisle, we must arrest you for providing a false application and interfering with a murder investigation. The murder, by the way, of your own sister, former French agent Louisa Hurst. You'd better come clean."

Dark waters pulled Charles into an abyss.

"See here, my sister was not a spy. This is preposterous! What evidence do you have to support such a claim?"

Mr. Gravis withdrew a folded paper from his pocket. "We found this at Rosewell Park."

Charles took it in both hands, shaking convulsively. Beads of perspiration formed on his forehead. He retreated to the edge of his bed, keenly aware of their scrutiny as he tried to focus on scrawled penmanship.

*Faucon Deux*

*Since Louisa is abroad, another courier will bring you details of the landing. I am confident you will concur with my choice of messenger.*

*Lady Carlisle*

*3 April 1814*

Charles looked up wretchedly. "Who is this Faucon Deux?"

Gravis watched him carefully. "It's apparently a French code name, used by an agent whose alias was 'Falcon number two'. He was involved in a plot to have Americans land at Dover during the war, but the Essex took care of them in short order."

Charles winced.

At last he sighed. "Black said he'd been contacted by Lady Carlisle with a request to leave the country. He said he'd take care of her. She's my brother-in-law's aunt, for God's sake."

Gravis shot a glance at Matthews with a thin smile.

He turned toward Charles. "Thank you, Mr. Bagwell. Let me assure you, if you cooperate, we do not intend to place you under arrest."

A flicker of surprise crossed Charles eyes. His dry mouth disappeared. "You don't?"

The policeman shook his head. "We've come up with a plan to avoid a crisis with serious consequences."

Gravis went over to the window and looked out as if to make certain no one else stood within earshot.

"Over past years, Mr. and Mrs. Black have worked for me from time to time to counteract French espionage."

Charles shot up. "Are you telling me he isn't a suspect in Louisa's death? All this business about his running an explosive factory and helping Lady Carlisle was just deception?"

Gravis shook his head. "The story is part of his cover, but the factory is real."

"Why didn't he just tell me he was working for the Ministry of War? I would have gone along without hesitation."

"We were testing you. We weren't certain of your loyalties given the recent exploits of your relations."

The agent put a hand on Charles shoulder.

"Let me explain. A while back, we received information something big is unfolding in the Canadian Provinces. Black attempted to infiltrate a band of conspirators, but just as he was getting close to Lady Carlisle, the incident at Mayfair Hall sent her into hiding. We believe Arthur Hurst may have recognized him from an incident dating back to the war."

Charles frowned. "Black said they had done business together."

He nodded. "And they have, as spies working against each other."

"But why involve me?"

"Hurst sent word he wants to meet with John in two days," Gravis announced. "We could intervene, but it would tip our hand. We want you to be present at the meeting to forestall any outburst against our agent. We must know his intentions. If he's suspicious of Black and intends to inform Lady Carlisle, then we must detain him."

"And how do we do that?" Charles asked numbly.

"A signal from you at the window will alert us to move in and apprehend the French agent."

Charles' eyes narrowed. "But what if he's already sent word to her and Black's cover is blown?"

"Then Black will have to leave the place any way he can. We'll have to stage an accident later to remove him as a threat to their plot," Gravis concluded.

Charles brightened. "Is that why you're loading explosives on board the Merryweather?"

"Explosives are Black's ticket into the conspiracy, but if he's suspect, we'll have to take measures to keep the Merryweather from reaching Canada."

Charles looked up with a wry, twisted smile.

"Will you help us then?" Gravis asked.

He could not afford to back out. "I suppose I really have no choice or you'll think me a French sympathizer. By the way, are the Darmons involved?"

"They're not, as far as we can tell," Gravis answered. "The pair is off in America looking for your sister's killer. The culprit's identity is unknown, but I assure you British agents weren't responsible."

John Black and Charles sat quietly in the first-floor room of a tri-level flat waiting for the arrival of Arthur Hurst. Unlike Bagwell, the British agent seemed unmistakably calm, content to silently peruse the Times. Charles, on the other hand, paced the floor, imagining all sorts of difficulties which might arise during the meeting.

He paused, glaring impatiently at the newspaper which hid the agent's face.

"What if Arthur shoots us?"

Black lowered his reading material. "Calm down Mr. Bagwell. We've been over this. He's your brother-in-law, remember? If he suspects nothing, open the curtains and stand at the window. If he's onto us, open the curtains and stay out of sight."

A rapid knock resounded. Black raised his frame and leiasurely crossed to the entrance while Charles quickly retreated to a chair.

Arthur Hurst's imposing figure filled most of the brightly lit entrance.

"So, John, we meet once again!"

An unusually sober face frowned upon seeing his brother-in-law. "Charles, what on earth are you doing here?"

Charles rose stiffly.

"John invited me to hear new information concerning Louisa's death. He suggests you weren't so drunk as it appeared the night of the Darmon's ball."

"Now wait a minute!" Hurst growled. "If you think I killed my wife, you're way off the mark. I wasn't anywhere near her room that night. I assure you wine was far more interesting than the conversation. You know those Darmon affairs. You'd be better off pursuing this gentleman here, a ruthless child killer."

Black raised a cautioning hand. "Settle down. My actions during the war were a service to the Crown. I'm a businessman and cannot afford to lose a country's good will."

Hurst returned to the task at hand. "So, I hear you're selling gunpowder. A pity you can't see fit to supply French ships with the products you broker."

"I'd rather do business with the devil!" Black retorted. "I know full well my factory at Hastings was the target of your invasion back in '14. Americans may have thought otherwise, but I believe Bonaparte was out to cripple Britain's main source of powder."

"Well, you took care of that," Arthur lamented. "Many died, including an innocent French boy who happened to be my nephew. I should kill you, here and now."

Black did not flinch.

Instead, his face contorted with contempt. "It wouldn't be advisable. I've received quite a sizeable order for explosives from the Canadians. Lady Carlisle informed me of the shipment's purpose. If you expect delivery, I must be a part of the operation."

Hurst looked sharply at Black. Hatred etched his eyes and his lips clenched so tightly their edges became colorless. For a moment, only the soft ticking of a hallway clock broke the silence.

"Why should you care what use it's put to?"

Black shrugged. "Actions that produce conflict serve me well. In peacetime, lack of customers threatens my company's existence. Americans manufacture their own materials, but I can still make money off the Canadians as long as Parliament keeps its nose out of my business."

Arthur relaxed a bit, eyes remaining fixed on the agent.

"So, you want to be part of the undertaking? Well, perhaps we can use your services. There'll be reward enough for all if it succeeds."

Charles walked over to the window. He pulled open the curtain. "See here, this talk borders on treason. I will have no part in it!"

He could see Gravis waving on the far side of the street where thirty agents stood ready to converge on the apartment. The assault was called off, and men began retreating to their carriages.

Black frowned. "Let's go upstairs and relieve Mr. Bagwell of his trepidation. Charles, wait here until our discussion is ended."

The two men disappeared upstairs.

A moment later, Black rumbled back down, scowling at Charles.

He spoke barely above a whisper. "Call back the agents! He hasn't told us what he suspects or what he's said to Lady Carlisle."

Charles froze, petrified. "But it sounded like he has no suspicions."

"So why act rashly? Your mistake could be fatal," Black seethed. "Now get out there and tell Gravis to remain at their positions!"

Quietly, Charles slipped outside.

He spotted Gravis and ran up to him, waving his hands. "The signal was wrong! Get the agents back."

Gravis stopped and gestured his men to return. "Tell Black if we attack, we'll meet back at the Ministry and proceed with the alternative option."

When he reentered the flat, Charles spied Black coming

downstairs once more.

The agent smiled with relief. “We're safe. The man suspects nothing. I'm to proceed with Lady Carlisle to Canada.”

Charles stopped. “My God, I just told Gravis to get ready for an assault!”

Black grimaced. “I only said your signal was premature. I'd better get out there. Go upstairs and occupy Hurst 'til I return.”

Black rushed out into the hallway and promptly collided with a large cleaning lady who had just reached the top of the entry. The impact pushed her backward. The two tumbled down the steps, landing in a heap on the walkway.

Charles ran to the window to see Black’s motionless body while the woman struggled to her feet. He laid sprawled within a pool of blood.

A loud voice bellowed from upstairs. “Bastard!”

Charles raced up to the third floor and found Arthur Hurst sitting at a desk, rummaging through drawers. He clutched a piece of paper in one hand, shaking it with rage as he looked up at Charles.

“Businessman, hah! This man, Black, is a British agent! Here's the proof of his duplicity. Where is he? It's time to put an end to the vermin.”

Charles gasped in shock. The charade was unraveling! He tentatively leaned toward the desk, reaching for the note. “What do you mean? What evidence?”

Hurst glanced down at one of the drawers. He reached inside and picked up a ledger.

“Wait a minute. Here's something else.”

Charles' eyes darted toward the window, knowing Black lay outside, unconscious and defenseless. Quelling an urge to run, he pretended to be curious at the discovery. Slowly, he edged around behind the man to look over his shoulder. What should he do?

Desperately his eyes searched the area until he spied a letter opener.

In one motion, he grabbed the dagger and plunged it into Arthur's back. The rotund body jerked upwards, his back arched and dropped the notebook. He tried to reach the knife, but instead, slumped forward on top of the desk.

Charles stood trembling. What he had done to his sister's husband?

He made for the stairs, leaping down steps three at a time and flew out the doorway.

He hit the pavement in one jump, barely noticing Black's absence, and sped across the narrow street to the safety of the agents.

An hour later, Charles sat quietly in his room at Hampton House.

Agents had escorted him with little conversation. Now he stared out the window, recalling past life with Arthur.

Once more, someone called from outside. "Charles, it's Michael Gravis."

He did not feel like speaking to the man who caused his unthinkable action. "Please go away. I'm not well."

"John Black is dead."

Charles' mouth dropped. He unlocked the door, looking anxiously.

"I saw him fall on the steps when he ran to talk to you. He was gone when I came out so I assumed he completed his mission. How could he be dead?"

"Apparently, Hurst had an accomplice."

Charles frowned. "A cleaning woman came up the steps just as Black left to see you. He ran smack into her, and they ended up in the street."

"When Black came out, she probably assumed the worst," Gravis said. "We found him on the ground with his throat cut after she disappeared in an alley a block away."

Charles sagged onto his bed, drained of energy. He dearly wanted out of the mess. "So, what now?"

Gravis regarded him solemnly. "We'll proceed with an explosion aboard the Merryweather. A forged message from Fouche is on its way to Lady Carlisle, instructing her to sail instead from Plymouth. Estee Black has her under surveillance up in Edinburgh."

A cold shiver ran down Charles' back, reminding him she was at his cottage.

The agent sighed. “I doubt the old woman would trust a new agent to accompany now.”

He strolled over to the small window and gazed out once more. “Black must have had good reason to remove Hurst at this point.”

Charles winced. “Excuse me. I was the one who stabbed him. Hurst found some evidence revealing Black was your agent. He was about to hunt him down. I had to do something; I thought your man lay helpless in the street.”

“You probably saved the trouble of a hangman.”

Gravis turned from the window to face Charles. “But there's still the problem of infiltrating this organization and finding out what they’re up to. Our plan was to have someone with Lady Carlisle. Someone she'd trust.... "

The official waited patiently with eyes challenging Charles.

“If by some chance you were also on the ship, she might enjoy the company of a family member.”

“Me?” blurted Charles. “I'm not a spy. I wouldn't know how to act or how to prevent their operation. Besides, my wife is home alone. It's absolutely out of the question.”

“These are desperate times," the agent responded. “Another war, and I fear our country won't survive. We're losing ground to America in world commerce. England depends on trade for stability. I have a letter addressed to you from Edward, Duke of Kent. Please read it.”

Charles sat up. “A letter to me? The brother of the King of England is even aware of my existence?”

Slowly, he read the message imploring him to take this action on behalf of his fellow countrymen.

He pondered.

Finally, he cringed hearing his words. “What do you want me to do?”

“Thank you, Charles,” Gravis replied, reaching to shake Charles’ hand. “We don't have much time. Return to Surrey, and tell no one of your involvement. Once news of the Merryweather’s destruction reaches you, proceed to Plymouth. Give Emily some pretense for an absence of two to three months. The East Wind sails in three weeks.

That should give you plenty of time. Estee will remain in Edinburgh to see if any other French agents turn up; we don't know who else Lady Carlisle has contacted."

Charles nodded woodenly.

"Come with me to headquarters," Gravis added patiently. "I'll brief you on what we know. Believe me, you've made the best decision."

# CHAPTER FIVE

As their ship headed for open water, the Darmons leaned on a rail watching the coastline recede. Elizabeth slowly inhaled sea air, smelling fish and tar with a feeling of queasiness growing sharper each breath.

William's hair danced in a biting breeze laced with sea spray. He smiled with satisfaction at sun-washed hillsides slowly shrinking on the blue horizon.

"We've had an eventful two weeks. I believe it's fair to conclude John Black is now the primary suspect for Louisa's murder."

Elizabeth lifted her gaze to meet his. "His presence at the time of her death and the fact he has the same name as the rogue on board La Coquille are unlikely to be coincidences."

Looking at her bright eyes and flushed cheeks, he felt a sudden uneasiness.

"Well, he's guilty of at least one of the murders, undoubtedly the boy Francois. How many Jean Noires can there be?"

"What if John never intercepted Clay's response?" Elizabeth wondered.

William shrugged. "Well, even if he missed it, he knew enough of the American plan to forge a note that would convince Fouche to send Faucon Deux's men to any landing spot."

Elizabeth considered his words. "But, he would still think the privateer was headed for Hastings, and we know the trap was set in Dover. So he must have seen Clay's reply at some point."

William rubbed his chin. "Most likely at Hotel Franklin. However, if Louisa delivered the confirmation, why did she have it in her possession years later?"

Her expression changed. "Well, the French don't seem to be holding a grudge against her for not delivering it. Or, do you think Aigle was lying?"

“I don't know if anything he said is true," he said, curling his lip. “It's just too convenient to believe the former Aigle died in a fire while holding a watch engraved with his code name. But if Megras Aigle survived, why didn't he show up for Nina’s arrival?”

William sighed. “It's easier to think Aigle exchanged identities with Terrence Winthrop, and hence did show up.”

Elizabeth shook her head. “All these coded identities! Let’s see: Colombe means Dove of Peace; Faucon is Falcon; and Aigle is Eagle. All are types of birds, if that has any significance.”

William frowned. “If we believe this new Aigle never heard of Sir Terrence, what role could Winthrop be playing in all this?”

“And, if he wasn't working for the French, why help Nina get her message to Clay?” added Elizabeth.

He scratched his head. “Well, Clay indicated no familiarity with Sir Terrence, he may have simply been a good-natured bystander.”

Elizabeth scowled. “Who just happened to be at the wharf when she arrived? And why would he claim a relation with Lady Carlisle?”

“Well, suppose the French lied to us," he speculated. “They know the original Aigle assumed Sir Terrence's identity. The French spy goes after Louisa at our party because she changed Clay’s message herself! Maybe she, too, was an agent of the Crown and simply delivered a counterfeit missive.”

Elizabeth's eyes narrowed. “But if she altered it, why keep the real message all this time?”

William chuckled softly. “Maybe she saved it as a souvenir of her most devious handiwork, only to have the pendant recognized at our ball.”

“Can you imagine the intrigue that night?” she reflected. “Sir Terrence catching up with Louisa and Arthur, then John and Estee Black arrive, and finally Lady Carlisle. And we thought it was just an anniversary celebration!”

He grinned. “We were just innocent onlookers.”

During a moment’s pause, she tipped her head as her stomach gave a sudden lurch. Grasping the rail with white knuckles, she fought distress. “Do you believe the French are really selling British uniforms to the Canadians?" she managed hoarsely.

He turned his palms upward. "Why not? The war's over. How else could the French agents benefit from such an arrangement?"

"Maybe they're planning an assault on our former colonies disguised as English soldiers."

"I doubt they could raise enough of a force to be more than a minor annoyance to the Americans," William replied, noticing her pale complexion.

"I need ginger root," she said with a look of apology. "I fear it's time for me to retreat to my bunk."

A cold and dreary afternoon greeted the Darmons when they reached port in London. Although anxious to return to Kent, proximity to the Black residence demanded an immediate visit. They flagged a hansom and ten minutes later, pulled up at the flat not far from Parliament Square.

They climbed steps in front of the three-story apartment. Elizabeth noted darkened windows above. They knocked repeatedly without a response. To their surprise, the door was unlocked and they went inside.

Gloomy weather did not provide much light.

They stood by the door surveying an empty room, hearing clip-clops of horse traffic on the cobblestones.

William let out a breath, sensing stillness on premises which perhaps stood vacant for sometime. He went over to the window and lit a lamp. Furniture surfaces appeared free of dust, and a three-day old London Times indicated Black may not have been absent for very long. Near the front door, a potted fern lay on its side, suggesting he left in a hurry. They had to be on guard for his return.

"This silence is nerve-wracking," Elizabeth whispered. "Why are we tiptoeing if the flat is deserted?"

A creaking noise sounded overhead.

William put a finger to his lips.

They tread softly to the stairs and quietly climbed to the upper levels. Two bedrooms took up the second floor. Nothing of significance stood out.

The pair made their way up to a third floor loft. Their lamplight spilled onto walls of books, a leather chair between two dormer windows and an expansive desk.

Elizabeth gasped.

Amid stacks of papers, a large body lay slumped onto the desktop. A knife protruded from his back. They rushed over and lifted the corpse back into the chair.

“It's Arthur Hurst!” William exclaimed.

“Poor Arthur," Elizabeth said. “What’s he doing here? He must have been searching the apartment and didn't hear an intruder come up behind him.”

“I doubt anyone could have entered this room without notice. The attacker must have been someone he knew," William muttered as he felt through the dead man's pockets.

She shuddered. “A relative maybe?”

“More likely we can chalk up another victim to Black," he answered.

Elizabeth stared at the ashen face, frozen forever in surprise. “When do you suppose this happened?”

“The body is rigid. He's lain here awhile, maybe days.”

Elizabeth noticed his right hand clenched in a fist resting on shards of glass from a broken lamp. A tiny paper fragment showed between the man’s fingers.

“What's this?” she asked, removing her glove. She gingerly touched the man’s cold palm. With her thumb and forefinger, she tried to pry pudgy fingers apart, but the large hand refused to open. She grimaced and slid her hand under his manicured nails. Pressing upward, she gradually pulled the stiff fingertips away from the paper.

William watched her efforts. A wadded piece of paper with blurred handwriting tumbled onto the desktop.

*John:*
*I've followed Lady Carlisle from the interment at Liverpool to a cottage*

*near Edinburgh. I await your instructions at the McDougal House in Leith.*

*Estee*

Elizabeth's eyes widened. "She's been hiding in Charles' summer cottage!"

William gave a determined look. "If Black killed both Hursts, Lady Carlisle may be his next target. He must be aware of the newspaper's account of her helping the French invaders. We have to get up there as fast as possible. There may be still time to prevent another murder."

They left London before nightfall.

Two days of hard riding brought the Darmons to Scotland where they spotted the small stone house set apart from others on a street not far from cliffs overlooking the river, Forth of Firth. Late afternoon fogs obscured most of the bank below, and on the hilltop, an evening draft began to rise.

Halting their carriage a short distance away, the couple anxiously climbed out and began sneaking toward the residence.

William gently held Elizabeth's arm. "I remember spending a week here with Charles ten years ago. His mother left him the place. He comes up now and then to peruse Edinburgh's libraries."

She paused. "Such a quaint domicile and peaceful location."

"There's a magnificent view when fogs lift," he noted. Seeing no movement behind the front windows, he motioned to Elizabeth. "Let's go around back."

They peered through a rear glass. The rooms looked unoccupied.

William moved to the back door and forced it open. Inside, the pair found a small kitchen well kept except for a plate on the table holding a half-eaten piece of cheese. They crept to the hallway. Window rattling resounded in the front room. William glanced uneasily over his shoulder through the kitchen panes at blowing tree limbs. Without speaking, he pointed to the front parlor.

Peering around the doorway, Elizabeth spied several pieces of clothing scattered on the floor and a chair lying on its side.

“Isn't that Lady Carlisle’s dress?” whispered Elizabeth.

William nodded and cautiously stepped into the room. He bent over the articles.

A curtain next to the bay window rustled.

“William, behind you!”

A tall thin woman emerged cradling a two-barreled pistol. “Please don't move.”

“Estee, where's Lady Carlisle?” Elizabeth blurted.

Her expression changed as she recognized the visitors. “Mr. and Mrs. Darmon, I thought you two were overseas. What are you doing here?”

“Estee, what in God's name is going on?” William demanded. “We found your note in Arthur's dead hand. Has John killed the Hursts? What have you done with my aunt?”

The woman flinched in surprise.

A look of contempt came over her gaunt face. Hazel eyes flared and her narrow jaw became rigid. “French spies, both of them! Traitors deserved worse than they got for their crimes.”

William winced at her icy tone, which grated on one's ears. Her forcefulness was intimidating and called to mind an evil spirit such as Lilith or Irish banshee. “But my aunt… The war's long over. Why are you insisting on this revenge?”

“Your aunt!” she spat. “Worst of the lot, an adherent of continued French subversion! Who do you think helps Fouche and his infamous *ordre du espion* now Bonaparte is out of the way? Even as we speak, our provinces lay open to plunder and it's the Montclair ships which make it likely to happen.”

William flushed. “Wait a minute, my aunt is no traitor. You’re terribly mistaken!”

“We've been trying to infiltrate her organization for years," Estee scoffed. “She was just beginning to trust John when your party took place.

"So you followed Lady Carlisle here, after you killed Louisa?" Elizabeth asked.

"We had nothing to do with that. The last thing we wanted was to tip our hand by killing one of her agents. After the ball, she ducked out of sight until I spotted her at the funeral. When I approached, the lady requested help to leave the Isles. With the scandal at Rosewell Park, she no longer has control of her ships. I suggested John could make arrangements to get her out of the country."

"Out of the country….! Please, I must speak with her!" William pleaded.

"You're too late," Mrs. Black sneered. "She left to join my husband in London. In three days, they'll set sail for Halifax aboard the Merryweather. Once in Canada, he'll make sure she leads him to the rest of her spies."

"But these people should be brought to trial for their crimes. It's not your place to carry out their punishment," Elizabeth admonished.

"Treason doesn't merit a court of mercy by old men who've already forgotten treacheries of the past war!"

All at once, William threw himself at Estee.

The gun went off, blasting away pant fabric on his right leg as he fell on top of her. They crashed down onto the room's brick fireplace. Estee's head struck a rough edge and she instantly went limp.

Elizabeth rushed to the sprawling bodies. "William you're bleeding! Let me help you."

He groaned, trying to stand up.

She pulled him to his feet. He steadied himself against the hearth, looking down at a growing stain covering his trouser. Raging against pain, he slammed his fist on top of the mantle. He stopped and gaped at Estee.

Elizabeth reached down to touch her face. "My God, she's cold as ice. There's no pulse."

William grimaced, feeling his lower limb being torn from his body. "Bloody hell, I didn't mean to kill her."

Elizabeth reached under his arm. "I know. Can you manage to the carriage?"

“I think so. There's an infirmary back down the lane.”

Inside a plain brownstone two-story hospital, the nurse escorted William into a white-walled examination room while Elizabeth waited outside.

After an hour, she was permitted to enter. William lay on a bed propped against pillows. His leg was wrapped in a splint, and a three-inch wide bandana wound around his head. He looked at her with a twisted smile as she came over to embrace him.

“Dearest, I'm in reasonable health, except for a leg bone broken by the bullet's impact. I've informed the doctor of Estee’s death at the Bagwell’s House.”

“Oh, William, I'm so sorry about your leg. You must rest now," she said.

His brow furled. “There are only three days until my aunt is to leave London. We have to try to intercept them.”

The doctor frowned. “Mr. Darmon, I wouldn't recommend a hasty journey in your condition.”

William winced again, attempting to pull himself off the bed.

Elizabeth brightened. “Perhaps, I can secure a boat of some kind. We can sail to London within two days.”

The doctor shrugged.

William nodded. “Sounds like a good idea! We might just make it.”

A few minutes later, she left for the Port of Leith to search for a seaworthy vessel.

Dockside of the Firth, estuary of the River Forth teemed with berths, seamy fishermen, and outfitting shops that included sail makers, ironmongers and chandlers. To her dismay, Elizabeth discovered most berths lay empty and only a single vessel larger than a dinghy was found tied at the wharf.

“Aye, she don't look like much, but f'r o'er twenty-odd years I’ve fished t’ese waters. Been to London in 'er too, not two years past," a grizzled seaman offered.

Elizabeth’s face contorted, aghast at the boat’s appearance. The smelly thirty-foot scow had rotting deck planks and a dirty sail with numerous patches. Paint peeled from sides of a small cabin just large enough to hold its captain, and the barnacled hull suggested a vessel well past its bountiful years.

"Well, maybe. Let me look around some more."

"I 'magine she's ta only one in port, what with fishin' season at hand. We c'n be ready by first light on the morrow," he muttered in a toothless grin.

Elizabeth sighed, grateful to have found something.

In fading light, she turned to go back to their rented loft in a nearby public house. Chilly blustery air made her eager to join William in their warm room. Striding through cluttered streets, she paid little attention to heavy clouds building above. She wound her way between heaps of timber and huge stone blocks amassed along the roadway. A large dark structure towered ahead. A sign out front announced construction of a wartime memorial called Waterloo Place.

Heavy mist created early morning dreariness the next morning. Their captain greeted them with heavy coats, boots, and slippery black hats. Several boxes of provisions stacked aft of the scow's tiny cabin. The boat stank of fish, and aged planks creaked as they climbed on board. William took a seat behind the cabin and propped his leg on top of a nearby crate.

Once freed of its mooring, the vessel slowly drifted out from shore, floating on soft lapping ripples through enshrouding fog. Occasional cooes of passing gulls and warning clangs from a distant buoy interrupted the calm. Cold dampness made Elizabeth thankful for the heavy coat as she huddled next to William. He shifted in discomfort, but gave a reassuring smile whenever she looked to inspect his condition.

The craft glided with the current. Shoreline hills loomed into view, and disappeared within the haze in a dreamlike setting.

William wondered out loud. "I wish we could have resolved Aunt Catherine's role in all this. How can she still be involved with French espionage at her age?"

Elizabeth shook her head. “Maybe Fouche's men have taken over Uncle Lewis' shipping line.”

“What has she to gain by this?” he asked with rising frustration. “Rosewell Park is long gone, and why should she concern herself with the politics of France?”

Elizabeth shrugged. “She's such a strong-willed person. Forgive me, but her demanding behavior will not change after a lifetime’s indulgence.”

“I know. I know. By the way, how are you feeling? For your sake, I wish we could have traveled by road instead of sending the carriage back to London.”

She looked uncertain. “The river's fine, but I'm not looking forward to reaching the bay. You know me. I think sea travel is dangerous and usually sickening.”

Their boat began to pick up speed. She poked her head around a cabin corner and tapped a window next to the old salt. “How long ‘til we make open water?”

The fisherman sipped from a tankard. He turned toward Elizabeth, his face nearly buried under heavy clothing. He wiped the forward glass, peering into the swirling veil ahead as if he made out an unseen visage. “Won't be long ma'am. We 'ardly need a sail in this current, but I 'spect a bit o' weather to be a wee bothersome.”

Mist turned to light rain before the vessel began pitching, a sign they were moving into the North Sea. Elizabeth settled back, leaning against her husband's shoulder, breathing deeply. Resolutely, she concentrated on another subject. “Darling, are you certain we're on the right course?”

William smiled. “We must trust a man who knows the sea.”

She frowned. “I mean are you convinced Lady Carlisle actually is a French spy?”

“Perhaps my uncle did have dealings with the French," William observed. “But other than providing housing during the war, we've only Estee Black's conjecture she continues to support a subversive cause. We’re no longer at war with France, for God’s Sake. Let the past go. The Blacks are insane!”

Elizabeth nodded. “They cannot be acting for the Crown at this point. There can be no excuse for murder.”

“Aunt Catherine may have decided to hide because of publicity concerning the old events, but there’s no evidence of treasonous intent," he added firmly.

“So why is Black following her?” she asked. “If she’s off to Canada, maybe there’s a connection with what Aigle told us about selling our uniforms for Canadian security. It sounded like a harmless enterprise. He could be off on a wild goose chase thinking there's a conspiracy going on.”

The boat rocked more violently. Sea spray splashed them with the bow’s rise and fall. Water streamed over planking. Rolling waves grew three feet high while the boat worked its way further from land. Wind shifted, blowing gusts and rain that pelted them square in the face. Splashing and howling drowned out the hull’a groaning protests.

Clinging to her husband, Elizabeth’s fear heightened every minute and she fervently yearned for the voyage to be over. Her body shuddered and heaved the contents of her stomach across the deck. Sky spun dizzily overhead. Desperately, she fixed her gaze on the cabin, hoping to find reassurance on the captain’s face. She could no longer see through the splattered glass. She dug fingers into interstices between the cabin’s planks, but the wild pitching would not let her stand up. The mast complained with each sway and waves pounded with increasing force against their slanting deck.

A huge geyser crashed on the port side. When the descending spray cleared, they were dismayed to see a six-foot piece of railing had disappeared.

“The boat is disintegrating!” Elizabeth cried.

“Hang on!” William yelled.

With her help, he looped a rope around her midsection and tied them both to a short beam at the edge of the ship's hold. Despite the lifeline, the frightened pair slid sideways to portside, then starboard, over and over.

“I'm getting sick again," she warned. Her pale lips parted and vomited. Her body wracked with convulsions, leaving her limp and exhausted.

Swells nearly ten-feet tall towered on all sides. Their craft struggled up to the top of crests and plunged down into a pit of dark foam. Each time the bow dove into the valley, its timbers protested loudly and the deck immersed under a flood of sea.

"William, I can't take any more of this!" she pleaded weakly.

Words were barely out of her mouth when a gigantic wave tore sideways at the hull, nearly turning the vessel on its side. Elizabeth shrieked as a wall of water smacked their bodies against the railing. When the boat righted, the cabin had vanished along with the old seaman.

"We're going to drown!" Elizabeth yelled.

Over their heads, the mast snapped. The upper piece narrowly missed William before taking a chunk of siding into the water. Icy wind whistled harder, threatening to sweep the refugees from their twisting, lurching perch. They clutched each other, gulping for air and praying what remained of the boat stayed afloat.

With half the deck torn away, the mid-section rose to another crest among endless swells and gorges. Once more they plummeted downward.

"Oh, my God," William's terrified voice came above the roar as their craft dropped bow-first, from a height of twenty feet.

The impact came like an explosion.

Elizabeth plunged deep below the surface in a swirling maelstrom of frigid gray turbulence. Current carried her further and further into darkness. Desperately, she clawed at the liquid, trying to stop the descending flow.

She slowed without sense of up or down, only cold pressure crushing the life within her. For an instant, she hung, suspended in an amorphous world of dimness. Searing pain tore at her lungs as if they would burst.

Elizabeth felt herself being pulled upward by the rope around her waist. Surroundings brightened, she found herself immersed in a cloud of foam. Hgher and higher she rose through murky fluid.

Suddenly, she burst into a blast of cold air. Coughing and spiting, she gasped air amid churning water around her head. Above, stormy skies sent a myriad of drops splattering onto her face. She flailed at the ocean with leaden arms, her body numb, trying to stay afloat through sickening rolling tide.

A few feet away, a dark form bobbed within the swells.

A piece of boat decking pulled at the rope, still tied to the hold section. She grasped the line through the heaving current. Scrambling onto the floating section, she clung to the beam, pressing her head against dripping wood, panting from exhaustion.

After a moment, she noticed a knot of rope on the opposite side, straining as it slid over its mooring. William's line! Behind it, rope stretched over the deck into the water. She jerked up to her knees. Not five feet from the deck's edge, a bloated coat floated face down.

"William!" she screamed and lunged for his line.

Despite pitching, Elizabeth pulled her husband's waterlogged body onto the raft.

She turned him over and lifted his head out of the water. With rising panic, she peered at the palid face and closed eyes. Her fingers rubbed the cold, flacid skin of his cheeks.

"William, don't die! Please don't leave me!" she cried.

Desperately looking for help, she fought a feeling of hopelessness. The slanting raft was already halfway under water, and turbulence continued to send inches of water streaming over the portion sticking out from the waves. She began to tremble uncontrollably, crouched next to his side, squeezing his chest despairingly.

She moved his head against her chest and found blood streaming down his neck from a dark patch of matted hair behind his ear. With her left hand, she pried open his mouth to help him breathe.

A wave splashed on top of them, throwing their bodies against the hold. When foam subsided, he began to cough, spitting out water. Eyes fluttered open, and stared with a glazed expression. Tearfully, she clutched his shoulders to hers as they rode over the top of another swell and plummeted into a cavernous trough waiting on the other side.

***

Stormy winds subsided by evening, and swells diminished, but pitching and rolling persisted through the night.

When morning finally came, exhausted survivors lay chilled-to-the-bone on their irregular piece of boat, floating with half of its boards below the surface. They drifted without means of control as waves lapped against their limbs, spreading over the slanting hulk. William lay propped on Elizabeth's lap, alert, but with legs numb and too weak to move, facing sunrise.

Under brightening sky, no sign of land appeared in any direction.

Elizabeth watched the featureless horizon, feeling alone in the vast expanse of waves.

She began to cry softly. "It doesn't seem fair; after all we've come through, now to be lost at sea. Are we going to die out here?"

William looked up at her wearily. "Stay calm, Lizzy. Current will take us south to shipping lanes near the Thames, or at worst, to the Continent. We'll see land soon."

Hours passed slowly.

By mid-morning, William struggled to sit up despite an aching head. Cold water splashed them, but the warming day offered welcome relief, and a calm sea did not sink their raft further. He drifted in and out of consciousness, often awaking in pain to see Elizabeth staring out to sea, willing some sign of rescue.

Around noon, Elizabeth's eye caught a glint on the horizon. She squinted at flashing, dancing waves, wondering if it was her imagination. Another bright spot came forth.

"William, look there!" she said, pointing to the distance.

He opened his eyes and followed her outstretched arm to the tiny square of a ship's sail. With her help, he struggled to his knees on their tilting deck.

Gradually, the image enlarged to a full, three masted merchantman.

"Oh, yes! It's coming right at us!"

Elizabeth climbed next to him. They began shouting and waving.

The ship veered slightly south of their position, but it headed near enough to make out three tall masts with billowing sails.

"What a beautiful sight!" William exclaimed. "At last, an end to this misery!"

The barquentine heaved to and fro, slicing gracefully through the waves.

William shaded his eyes. “I can see her name just below the foresail. M…R…H…ER ... MERRYWEATHER!”

“My God! It's her ship!” Elizabeth shouted excitedly. “We've caught them just in time!”

It closed to within a half-mile. Figures could be seen moving on deck as the vessel forged at nearly twenty knots. By the time mizzensails came into view, it became apparent the ship was not changing course.

Merryweather did not come about.

Anxiously waving, they watched the craft recede without acknowledgment.

Hearts sank.

Two hours after the encounter, the Darmons spotted a smaller sailing ship. They were taken on board a yawl, and the captain turned his boat back to the Thames.

From the sea, they were taken to medical facilities in London and, after a week's recuperation, returned to Mayfair Hall. Using a cane, William hobbled about, looking forward to a month or two of relative inactivity.

Never had Elizabeth been so thankful to be at home in Kent.

Two days following their return, a messenger sent by William to the Montclair shipping office climbed the steps to Mayfair Hall.

“I found John Black’s entry on the passenger manifest of the Merryweather," he reported. “But there was no record of Lady Carlisle. She probably sailed under a different name.”

Elizabeth wrung her hands. “If not for the storm or a more prodigious current, we might have intercepted them. We came so close, but the ship sailed by without even slowing. I imagine they've congratulated themselves on a successful escape.”

“You haven't seen the latest Times, then?” The courier asked, unrolling a copy.

WRECKAGE OF MERRYWEATHER SIGHTED

Yesterday, fishermen aboard the trawler *Marie* reported finding remnants of the ship Merryweather floating twenty miles southwest of Plymouth Port. They found fragments charred and splintered, suggesting an explosion occurred aboard the vessel. No survivors were located.

"No!" Elizabeth exclaimed. "It can't be true. Lady Carlisle is lost?"

She embraced her husband.

William slumped into a chair. "My poor Aunty. An explosion! Could it have been sabotage?"

Elizabeth stared out a large window at their fishing pond. "Perhaps Fouche knew Black's murderous intention and decided to eliminate him without regard to sacrificing another French sympathizer. This brings an end to it all."

"I suppose with the Black's out of the way, justice has been served," William remarked woodenly. "Francois, Louisa, Arthur and Aunt Catherine, all French sympathizers, and all victims of the fanatic John Black."

# CHAPTER SIX

William resumed the business of estate management. Despite discomfort, he limped restlessly about the manor and could not seem to settle into a daily routine. No word came from the police regarding the murder investigation, and William's discontent grew each day with a nagging feeling the crime had not yet been completely resolved.

Elizabeth sat on a grassy slope leading down to a pond twenty yards from the front porch. A warm summer afternoon had ducks swimming languidly, back and forth. She relished the tranquility with a pang of regret at day-to-day activities less worrisome without Lady Carlisle's frequent censure.

In front of the main house, William sat propped against the railing reading a book with his leg perched atop a cushion.

Suddenly, he slammed the volume shut. "This is no good. I can't concentrate. I'm going mad just sitting here. Why hasn't someone from the Palace Yard come to tell us the case has been closed?"

Elizabeth rose at the outburst, shaking her head.

"William, why can't you be satisfied with peace and quiet? Your leg needs time to heal, there's nothing more we can do."

He gave her a challenging look. "How can you be content? All we have is conjecture. We still don't know why the pendant's message wasn't delivered. We conveniently blame John Black for this mess and maybe we have a motive for his killing Louisa, but what about Terrence Winthrop's role in all this? Will we ever know the whole story?"

His wife shrugged, trudging over to the verandah. "You and your loose ends! Some things never get resolved, we must get on with our lives."

William wrung his hands. “It’s hard to let go.”

“I have an idea,” she announced. “How about a carriage ride to Surrey? We haven’t visited the Bagwells in months, maybe they can give us some news.

Emily greeted the Darmons enthusiastically. “It's about time you two got out of your hideaway! Charles isn’t here. He left for Plymouth the day after we heard about the Merryweather. He wanted to help search for survivors.”

William grimaced. “I should have made the trip as well. If it wasn’t for this blasted leg...”

“We are so sorry about your loss, William. I wish we could help somehow,” Emily consoled.

Elizabeth tried to smile. “Thank you. Has he sent word on how things are going?”

Emily shook her head wistfully. “An express arrived the day after he left, but it was addressed to him.”

William frowned. “Might I have a look? If it concerns the wreck, I might yet be of some use.

“Of course,” she replied and went into the study to retrieve it from Charles’ desk.

For a moment, he stared at the envelope's handwritten address wondering if its arrival was only a coincidence.

“Open it. It could have a bearing on his actions.”

*Dear Charles*

*The Lady has arrived in Plymouth and awaits departure for the Canadian Provinces on Saturday the 25th aboard the East Wind.*

*Yours truly,*

*Chief Inspector Matthews*

"I don't understand. Is Charles working for the police inspector?" Emily asked, peering over William's shoulder.

William's mouth dropped. "The Lady has arrived in Plymouth? Departing for the Canadian Provinces? Can it be Aunt Catherine? Estee said it was her intention. My God, maybe she wasn't on the Merryweather after all!"

"I don't believe it!" Elizabeth blurted in disbelief. And Charles is helping her escape? Maybe it wasn't coincidence Lady Carlisle fled to his house in Edinburgh."

After a long pause, William frowned. "He's working for Matthews, not the French, so I guess there's no question of his loyalty."

Elizabeth folded her hands. "Conceivably, the wreck of the Merryweather was no accident. Estee said John was trying to infiltrate a French espionage gang using your aunt. Is it possible Lady Carlisle lured Black on board to have him blown up?"

"John Black may not be the rogue spy we thought," William conceded. "I guess he could have been acting under Ministry's orders. It may be fair to conclude he and Estee were after the former spies for reasons that had nothing to do with revenge for their wartime exploits. If you're right about those uniforms, France may be trying to instigate another war between our Commonwealth and the Americans. Both our countries are nearly bankrupt, and France would benefit from our financial ruin."

Elizabeth placed a consoling hand on his arm. "If Black was enticing Lady Carlisle to take him to the Provinces, Louisa may have recognized him as a British agent at our ball and tried to warn her."

William's expression became grim. "If the murder had nothing to do with the pendant nor Napoleon, maybe she was silenced to protect this new conspiracy."

Emily's brow wrinkled with worry. "The letter implies Charles is involved in countering the French operation. Is he to go with her to Canada?"

William anxiously limped back and forth across the marble floor.

"We must prevent Aunt Catherine from leaving the country or we shall never get to the bottom of this. All these events revolve around her, and I don't know if Charles will try to stop her. There are still three days 'til East Wind sets sail, a fast ride might get me there just in time."

Elizabeth glanced at his leg. "Are you up to it? The journey to Plymouth isn't an easy one. You think you have the stamina for a two hundred mile gallop over the countryside."

"The leg's not healed," he acknowledged. "But, I can ignore the aching and you know I'm an excellent horseman."

His pace slowed, once William reached London road. Wagons and foot traffic crowded the main path and recent rain left muddy hazards within bordering fields. He dared not stop. An hour's rest could be the difference.

At Camberley, the way cleared a bit, but the road narrowed, which caused delays when on-coming carriages challenged for the same space. A midday supper on Friday was the only respite he permitted himself. Despite the lack of opportunity to maintain a full gallop, he kept a steady pace and paused only long enough for his horse to drink from streams and ponds.

An interruption occurred near the town of Shelborne on Saturday morning, sixty miles east of Plymouth. A wagon rested on its side in a ditch. An old woman stood helpless, watching a gang of thieves rummage through her possessions. The situation could not be ignored. William had little difficulty dispensing the villains, but retrieving the woman's belongings and getting the cart upright took nearly a half hour.

Finally satisfied, he sped off, his body ached with fatigue.

At last, Plymouth shore came into view. He stopped on a rise. Afternoon sun shone brightly on two and three story block buildings with pointed roofs and slender chimneys along cobblestone passageways stretching down to the docks. Across Mill Bay toward Mount Edgecombe, yachts in full canvas dotted the waterway and frigates nestled at moorings while tiny figures serviced their cargoes.

He gazed at fortifications of the citadel across the busy harbor before spotting the sails of a large three-mast ship making its way out of the harbor. His heart sank. He urged his mount down the hill toward the waterfront. By the time his mad dash through the avenues brought him to the passenger loading area, the wharf was nearly deserted.

William climbed from his horse and ran to water's edge.

"Aunt Catherine why have you done this!" he shouted in frustration at the diminishing sails. It did no good. His shoulders slumped in resignation.

A voice came from behind him. "'Ave yer missed the East Wind, mister?"

William turned to see an rough looking tar dressed in a tattered woolen sweater and shapeless blue trousers. His weather-beaten face held a bristling beard and crinkled cheeks, and when he spoke, parted lips revealed mostly gaps in place of teeth.

"I've missed my aunt," William remarked paying the inquisitor a half-glance. He became suddenly impatient to find Charles, and scanned the surrounding dock. "She's run off with some French cohort. Did you happen to see an elderly English woman among the passengers, perhaps with a red-haired gentleman about my height?"

The salt took out a clay pipe and tapped it to remove dottle.

"I do believe I did. The old lady was 'elped up the gang' by a young gent as tall as you and 'ad curly hair."

William took a deep breath. "And did he sail with her?"

"Well, I ne'er saw 'im get off. Oh, and you might be interested in one more t'ing. J'st as they made to lift the gangplank, another fellow comes running up in a big 'urry. I could tell 'e was military from my service with the Dragoons before the Colonial Wars."

"And what did he look like?"

The seaman scratched his chin. "Older, 'ad light hair and a crooked nose."

William gulped. It was a fair description of Sir Terrence Winthrop.

Five weeks passed. Shortly after departure of the East Wind, Michael Gravis visited Emily and Elizabeth at the Bagwell estate. He confirmed Charles had been asked to accompany Lady Carlisle to Canada on a mission for the British home office, but would not supply details. He said his agent John Black had been killed in the act of murdering Arthur Hurst, and, since both Black and Hurst were dead, it seemed the most likely suspects for Louisa's murder had met a just fate. Therefore, as far as her death was concerned, the metropolitan police considered the case closed.

Upon William's return, the Darmons invited Emily to stay at Mayfair while Charles was abroad. Although he did not agree entirely with the Ministry's pronouncement, William reluctantly agreed to remain at the Manor and wait for news from his brother-in-law, since the two persons who could shed further light on the issue, Lady Carlisle and Sir Terrence Winthrop were both in America.

Each day, William strolled through his gardens, anxiously anticipating daily delivery of the Times. When it arrived, he scanned every page for news from the Colonies. Besides concern for his aunt, he worried Charles might meet an unthinkable fate. Yet no mention of French activity nor Canadian hostilities appeared.

One morning as he sat looking longingly at his lush grounds, realizing how much he missed Charles and their frequent shooting forays, rapid hoof beats of an approaching rider echoed in the distance. Hurried pace meant a significant piece of news on the way. The horseman quickly came into view, galloping up to William's veranda where he dismounted and walked quickly over to the landlord.

"Have you heard the news?" the rider asked, as he handed William the rolled paper.

"News? No, I presume it's in this issue of the Times."

"The American Vice President has been kidnapped!"

William gave the man a gratuity and tore open the paper as the messenger rode off. The headline read:

VICE PRESIDENT TOMPKINS KIDNAPPED
PRESIDENT MONROE OUTRAGED

Yesterday, while on his way to a dedication of the newly

> founded city of Pittsburgh, Vice President Daniel P. Tompkins and his party were ambushed by a company of British infantry. Three Americans were killed in the fracas at Landers Creek. The abductors were last seen moving north towards Lake Ontario. President Monroe had planned to attend the ceremonies, but at the hour of his departure, Speaker Clay called him to the Capitol and Vice President Tompkins agreed to take his place. An American fleet has set sail for the St. Lawrence to prevent the invaders from escaping to open water.
>
> President Monroe issued a warning to the British government that this provocation may lead to further military action. Reprisals could mean a resumption of conflict between the two countries. King George IV denied British responsibility. Instead, he accuses France of conducting subversive activity designed to create contention between England and America. The king offered full support to the Americans in apprehending the kidnappers.

"My God, what have they done?" William exclaimed, rushing to find Elizabeth.

The outlaws made good time on a trail through woods in Western New York. Dense foliage provided cover, and thick undergrowth would slow any pursuit. Well-trained men moved without conversation at the brisk pace of practiced woodsmen despite their bulky uniforms. Within the column, blindfolded Tompkins struggled against a stiff cord binding his wrists and a rope yanking him along the twisting path.

After nearly ten hours of sustained march, Charles experienced trouble keeping up with the procession. He dearly wanted to shed his heavy disguise, but was told the charade had to be maintained. Between dodging branches and lumbering through clearings, he reflected on his successful infiltration into the clandestine group. Lady Carlisle hadn't shown surprise at their encounter aboard the East Wind. She understood his business occasionally took him abroad. She did scold him, however, for his absence from Emily and accepted no excuse for leaving her behind.

The Lady expressed interest in the Darmon's reaction to her disappearance and their discovery of her French sympathies. Charles simply reported William did not pass judgment on her wartime activities. He and Elizabeth were consumed with determining the identity of Louisa’s killer. She agreed the villain should be brought to justice, but offered no insight to his identity. Charles added for her benefit, his income might benefit from a French marketplace and hinted there could be added benefit to the Montclair line. She seemed convinced he was not a threat to their plans.

As to her compassion for France, she spoke of the chaos leftover from the war. The old leadership had returned following Napoleon’s defeat, but rival factions vied for control. The country was on the verge of collapsing into a feudal state. She believed only Bonaparte could reunite French citizens and restore political freedom enjoyed by the British and American communities.

Over the course of the three-week interchange, Lady Carlisle took him into her confidence. Charles was outraged at the planned abduction, but he knew the Ministry was counting on his portrayal of an eager recruit, so he accepted her invitation with an agreement to have minimal participation in the actual events.

Interception near Pittsburgh came off with flawless precision. Charles observed the action from a hilltop two miles away. From Pittsburgh, a week's traverse north led them towards Lake Ontario and a rendezvous with Lady Carlisle who waited on shore with a small party of Iroquois. The final destination was kept secret from him. He presumed the band would seek a French held area of Quebec far from the American border until concessions could be extracted for Tompkins' return.

The gang moved stealthily onward on a path carefully chosen to avoid known settlements. Five hours rest was permitted each night without campfire until they were roused to break camp before first light.

Late one night, Charles lay on top a blanket provided in his backpack. He stared upward through trees at a canopy of stars, wondering how Emily must be coping back home. He felt isolated, far from familiar surroundings. A nagging memory carried him back to the East Wind. He remembered seeing the face of Sir Terrence Winthrop. Was his presence a coincidence or was he following them? The gentleman kept his distance throughout the voyage, and boarded another ship in Halifax. Perhaps he was on his way to the American Capitol to alert fellow conspirators of the planned abduction and effect the last minute substitution of Tompkins.

The next morning, Charles ate rations and resumed the march northward. Anxiety grew each passing day. His British citizenry would do him no good if the other conspirators found out he was an agent of the Crown. And that was nothing compared to his fate if the Americans intercepted their flight. He was, in fact, exactly what their uniforms pretended to be, a British spy kidnapping an American statesman.

Daily marches ended at sunset on the seventh day when they arrived at the shore of Lake Ontario just west of the Genesee River. Two mid-sized schooners quietly floated one hundred yards out. Lady Carlisle greeted them grimly and immediately began directing a boarding strategy. Charles and fifteen of the company were ferried to the lead ship, while the rest, including Tompkins followed with Lady Carlisle. The forward ship was to proceed across to the Canadian shore where they would enter the St. Lawrence River flowing eastward. Between Kingston and Montreal, they would be most vulnerable within sight of New York settlements.

Once underway, Charles sighed, relieved to be free from American territory, if only by a few miles. He especially appreciated a rest from the forced march. He sat on a barrel near the craft's stern feeling the bite of cool air as the two ships cut through calm, dark water.

In fading twilight, a lookout spotted the encampment at Kingston, their vessel still a mile offshore. Charles grinned, they crossed the Lake without encountering either American or British ships. There would be no stopping them now.

He moved to the sailor at the helm. “Will it be difficult to navigate the River in darkness?”

The young sailor nodded. “I've done parts of the Saint Lawrence several times, but we can only pass the Long Sault rapids in daylight. If we meet no interference, our boats should reach Montreal in two days. It's another day to Quebec City. There, the River widens and allows smooth sailing all the way to the Strait of Belle Isle in another five days.”

Charles flinched in astonishment. “Strait of Belle Isle? Are we taking him to open sea?”

“Aye.”

Charles scratched his head in darkness. Were they taking the Vice President back to France? The charade of British troopers would then be pointless. Only a destination in the Isles could further incriminate Parliament’s role in the abduction, but who in England would welcome such a hostage. Who indeed? With a sinking feeling, Charles glared at Lady Carlisle’s vessel behind them.

A distant thump made him jump. Seconds later, a whizzing sound preceded a whoosh of splashing water on the port side. A cannonball impacted only twenty feet from their ship.

Another sailor ran up pointing to a black silhouette emerging from the St. Lawrence tributary. A large ship closed directly in front of their path.

“It's the *Niagara*," someone shouted.

“Time to perform our mission,” the wheelman replied.

“Heave about!” he yelled to the crew.

Their schooners listed heavily in the sharp turn. Terrified, Charles grappled for a handhold.

The Niagara closed to five hundred yards.

Charles’ small craft began sailing southward, slowly picking up speed. The warship tailed after, apparently unaware of the trailing ship, which stayed well behind. As the schooner made towards the middle of the Lake, a second missile hurled into the forward mast rigging high above deck. A spar cracked loudly, then toppled, crashing into aftward sails and creating a tangled mess of sails and rope plunging toward the water.

The schooner slowed, no longer able to outrun the oncoming frigate.

A third and fourth barrage took apart most of the forward section and sent billowing showers of bright embers up into the night. Remaining crew members dove overboard while Charles desperately looked for a refuge. His ability to swim to shore in dark waters seemed dubious, but preferable to the raging inferno around him. He grabbed the railing and leaped into blackness below.

Splash of cold water stunned him. He began thrashing, trying to swim away from the flaming target above. A floating piece of decking nudged his hand. Clutching it, he furiously kicked away from the disintegrating craft. He glanced over his shoulder in time to see what was left of the ship disappear below the surface.

Niagara came closer, only fifty feet behind. Charles prayed he would be missed in the darkness. Torches glowed brightly, held by sailors stretching out over the railings, while searching for survivors in black and yellow waters below the hovering ship.

A small boat was lowered over the side. When it splashed into the water, oarsmen shouted, pointing in his direction. Charles froze, paralized with fear; he could never swim fast enough to escape. All he could think of were the captain's last words... "Time to perform our mission." They were a decoy! Lady Carlisle saw he was placed on the lead ship to divert the Americans. No wonder she'd taken him into her confidence, he was the final evidence of British involvement in their carefully executed plan.

Three weeks after Emily and the Darmons learned of the kidnapping, news of Charles' arrest reached Mayfair Hall.

Elizabeth desperately pulled her husband to her. "William, he'll be hanged for certain! Is there no possibility of the Ministry's intervention?"

"I am afraid Whitehall cannot reveal his mission nor his ties to the Crown. He may be safe for a while. It would do no good to execute someone whom the Americans think could provide a bargaining chip for Tompkins' release. A trial won't be held until after the whole incident is resolved."

"If we could only expose the French culprits!" Emily lamented. "It might save his life."

William grimaced. "Exposing the French would also tie a noose around Lady Carlisle's neck. The Americans are so incensed, it will be difficult to stay out of another war."

Elizabeth met his eyes, worry etched on her face. "Might we contact Henry Clay to use his influence to spare Charles?"

William pondered. "He might be sympathetic. Especially, if he were convinced of French treachery in the kidnapping, but he could not afford to have his sympathies become public. On the other hand, if he thought we would use the pendant as evidence of his tie to Bonaparte, he might try to help us arrange an escape for Charles."

Elizabeth pressed on. "And the speaker's call for the last minute substitution of Tompkins might also appear suspicious, even tie him to the kidnappers. It can hardly be seen as coincidence in light of his participation with French espionage during the War. I wonder if Clay can be linked to LeClair and Perchant. They were both at the White House the night we attended."

"That's circumstantial at best," William cautioned. "The deaths of Faucon Une and Deux removed his only direct connection. But LeClair and Perchant might well be involved in the kidnapping. They were supplying British uniforms to someone. They must be the ones used to provide the British disguise. Maybe Charles knows the larger plan which might further implicate Clay in the kidnapping."

Elizabeth frowned. "We're probably the only persons Charles can trust to confide such information."

William looked distressed. "You think we should journey to America again?"

She groaned.

"Lizzy, you should remain here with Emily and be spared the ordeal of another spell at sea."

He could see sadness overcoming her, but relief in her eyes.

The following morning, William set off for London to book passage for Baltimore. Emily also left for her residence in the neighboring shire to spend a few days attending to her estate. Elizabeth found herself alone in Mayfair Manor with only servants to provide conversation.

She tolerated two days of house bound chores before restlessness overtook her. She requested a carriage. It was time to inspect their property known for its well-kept and diverse landscape.

An open transport bounced over miles of private roads that occasionally disappeared within fields of long grass. Feeling free of confinement, Elizabeth closed her eyes to sense fragrances of autumn within cool air.

A mile north of the manor, her driver reined the horse to a bluff with an excellent view to the west, overlooking an expanse of countryside all the way to a Militia encampment near the village of Langdon twenty miles away. Elizabeth gazed into the distance for nearly an hour, content to appreciate the beauty of Kent. Eventually, hunger pangs could not be ignored and the open-air venture ended.

The next morning, she arose with a headache. She descended the staircase to breakfast while mentally postponing several activities. One task could not be put off. Elizabeth looked forward to Emily's return later in the day, and her room must be readied. Taking her usual place at one end of their long dining table, she began sampling a soft boiled egg and toast with strawberry jam.

Servant Thomas Reynolds entered, bowing respectfully. "This note just arrived from the Bagwell house, madam."

Words written in a barely readable scrawl read:

*My mistress has fallen and is unable to move. Please come at once.*
*Jonathon.*

Elizabeth stood up and called for her outer garments. "Send for Doctor Gracepool in Langdon! I'll meet him at the Bagwell's."

She made the trip to Surrey at breakneck speed. Rushing through the entrance, she called and narrowly avoided tripping over several bags stacked at the foot of the stairs.

At the top of the steps, Emily started down.

She looked surprised. “Elizabeth? I was just about to leave for Mayfair.

“Emily! Thank God, you're all right! I came as soon as your message arrived.”

“What message?”

Elizabeth tried to recover a normal heartbeat while handing over the note.

“This is a forgery. Why would Jonathon play such a mean trick?”

Elizabeth stared blankly at her sister. “Oh no, we must return to Mayfair at once!”

They rushed to the carriage.

In seconds, they were racing down the road back to Kent.

Three hours later, the two women climbed Mayfair’s front steps and entered the Great Hall. The manor seemed deserted. They called without a response.

“Where is everyone?” Emily remarked. “Look, there's a note.”

Elizabeth snatched it up.

*Madam, we are being escorted to the Militia encampment at Langdon. We have been arrested for treason.*

*Thomas Reynolds*

Within minutes, they were on the road again headed towards Langdon.

Clouds gathered overhead by the time they reached town an hour after leaving Mayfair Hall. Their carriage pulled into the campground where uniformed men appeared to be running in all directions.

Elizabeth called to one of the soldiers taking down a tent. “Where's your Captain?”

The guard appeared hesitant. “We are closing up camp. The Captain's already left for London.”

He turned his back, picked up the canvas and hurried off.

Elizabeth called after when a second soldier commanded him to halt twenty paces away. In misting afternoon gloom, she could not hear their conversation. The officer then took hold of the man's arm and glanced over his shoulder at them. Elizabeth quickly looked away, stunned at the sight of Perchant, the Frenchman confronted at the American Capitol.

"French agents are here in Langdon!" Elizabeth exclaimed under her breath. "We must return to the Manor and dispatch a letter to Whitehall!"

At her signal, their driver turned the carriage around.

Rain began to fall by the time they passed the village square. Soon, the road turned into a muddy trough. The driver tried to make time as best he could.

The journey seemed endless.

Emily fidgetted. "When do you suppose they arrived? Is this the Perchant you think is involved in the American Vice President's kidnapping?"

Elizabeth could only nod her head. "I can't imagine why they've come here of all places."

"And why have they taken your servants from Mayfair?"

The carriage slowed. Elizabeth leaned out in the window. "What is it?"

"There's an accident ahead, ma'am" the driver yelled.

Elizabeth peered at the road, trying to see with cold rain stinging her face. She made out the shape of a buggy lying on its side thirty yards away. A body lay sprawled in a ditch next to it.

Their carriage moved closer.

"It's Doctor Gracepool!" Emily exclaimed.

With some difficulty, the driver and ladies managed to lift the body into their closed vehicle. The driver could not right the buggy because its' left wheel had been shattered, so he released its horse. Emily retrieved the doctor's medical bag and their conveyance turned around. The carriage sped off, back toward Langdon.

Shivering and dripping, the sisters gaped at Gracepool's ashen face, lying motionless against the opposite seat. Elizabeth nervously rubbed his hands.

Emily sighed. “If only I'd come an hour earlier to Mayfair, this accident might never have happened.”

“Emily, you are not the least accountable," Elizabeth admonished. “I was the one who requested the doctor come to Surrey.”

She gave Elizabeth a concerned look. “Do you think the false note is connected to the kidnapping?”

“Someone wanted me and my servants out of the house. They were taken to the encampment where Perchant and who knows how many Frenchmen are posing as our soldiers. What do you think?”

Emily clenched her fists fretfully. “And now, they’re breaking camp for London. What can they be up to??”

The muddy road proved less passable on the way back to Langdon. Darkness fell by the time the doctor’s wife and son carried him up to his bed. Nothing more could be done until morning. Mrs. Gracepool insisted Elizabeth and Emily be given hot soup while the driver sought their accommodation at a local inn.

Late at night, in an upstairs room, Elizabeth paced the floor. “Somehow, we have got to get a message to Gravis. This delay could be tragic. If Perchant recognized me, they may have cleared out before the storm hit.”

Emily put hands on her sister’s shoulders and met her eyes squarely. “Surely, wherever these criminals have gone, the storm has them indisposed too.”

Sounds of commotion erupted downstairs. Footsteps clamored on the steps, a moment later urgent banging came at their door.

Thomas Reynolds' son, Robert stood dripping in their doorway.

The tall strapping lad, not yet eighteen, hesitated, uncertain whether to enter. “Excuse me, ma’am, I've been trying to find you. Soldiers came this morn while you were away. I hid in the livery and watched them take everyone from the house. I didn't know what to do. Then, I saw you and Mrs. Bagwell return. Before I could get to the building, you'd climbed back into the carriage. I called, but the driver didn't stop.

“An hour later, two more carriages show’d up. I couldn't believe my eyes. Lady Carlisle stepped out of the first one with three gentlemen! Behind them, four others climbed out with a prisoner blindfolded and tied at the wrists. They all went inside the house. Since you'd left in the direction of Langdon, ma’am, I crept out and came here.”

The ladies gasped.

“Oh my God,” Emily blurted. “Lady Carlisle! They’re holding the American Vice President hostage at your manor!”

Elizabeth set her teeth. “Robert, go downstairs and get a quick bite to eat. When you’ve finished, come back up here. I will have a letter for you. You must ride to London tonight and deliver it to Michael Gravis at Whitehall in London. This is a national crisis. We’re counting on you to get through as fast as you can!”

After the door closed, Emily's voice rose an octave. “They've got control of Mayfair’s grounds. The town Constable can’t possibly extricate them. Gravis has to send troops.”

Elizabeth agreed. “But, news of Tompkins at Mayfair is so incriminating, he may have trouble believing we aren’t conspirators in the affair.”

# CHAPTER SEVEN

Charles Bagwell looked despondently at his dismal surroundings. Locked in a cell at Fort McHenry near Baltimore, he shivered at the thought of being America's number one enemy. Without battlements of the fortress, local residents would have gladly lynched him. American prosecutors traced his movements back to Surrey, and even knew of his acquaintance with John Black, a known British spy.

His only chance for vindication lay with homeland's Ministry of War, but Americans were not about to listen to pleas from the perpetrators of this outrageous act. If the kidnappers were apprehended, the conspirators might confirm his casual involvement, but Lady Carlisle wasn't likely to be much of a character reference. Gloomily, he supposed Emily had heard the news and hoped Michael Gravis would give her the true story, which she could pass on to William and Elizabeth. But what could they do when the two countries were gearing for war? It seemed hopeless.

Clanking metal bars interrupted his dejected thoughts. A young guard appeared and asked if Charles would permit a visit by Megras Aigle. Desperate for distraction, he gave an affirmative nod, and the door was unlocked.

A tall, thin distinguished looking gentleman entered.

"Mr. Bagwell, please let me extend my sincere condolence for your circumstance."

"Who are you?" Charles countered, rising from his cot.

"I am Megras Aigle, attaché with the French Embassy."

Charles felt his anger rising. "It's about time you got here. Look here, you people created this mess, what are you going to do about it?"

Aigle sat down on the cubicle's single chair, carefully placing his hat on his lap. "We have been following your involvement in this deplorable crime. I believe the Americans have acted rashly and should not blame you for this unspeakable deed."

Charles returned to his cot, lacing his fingers about a knee. "Well, you'd better get me out of here or I'll blow the lid off the whole operation!"

Aigle's eyes narrowed. "Alas, impatient Americans want some kind of justice whether or not it's miscarried. We will continue to share their grief and do what we can to help them find a resolution."

"My country knows exactly who's responsible for the abduction, and you can rest assured the guilty will be punished," the Englishman responded, his voice quivering and hands trembling.

The diplomat let the remark pass, apparently unmoved.

"In the face of such overwhelming evidence, I fear, at the very least, England will be barred from trade with America. Economically weakened, she may become only a satellite of European commerce. I'm told you have an interest in doing business with France. Should you find a way out of here, you might consider moving your industry to the continent."

Charles glared at the envoy, gripping the cot's frame until knuckles turned white. He could not believe the man's condescension.

"Thank you, but I prefer to seek residence in a country which isn't on the verge of descending back into a medieval monarchy."

Aigle smiled thinly. "Our revolution was not without consequence. Political factions fight for the right to lead France to its ultimate destiny. Perhaps the Ultraroyalists will succeed in removing outdated policies of Louis XVIII. You may condemn our methods, but, on the other hand, can you afford to turn away the only person in America who doesn't want to see you dead?"

Charles paused. "Are you suggesting I have a choice in my fate?"

"We have influence with certain American politicians. If I were to let it be known you joined this gang of British outcasts to conduct espionage for France, it might convince them your intentions were not anti-American. We could request your release into my custody. I have an agent in Baltimore who can secure passage aboard a ship to France."

Charles looked dubious. "How can a statement from you have

such impact or, for that matter, be taken as truth? What proof could you offer?"

Aigle reached into his pocket and withdrew a small object. "I have in my possession a pendant used for message transport during the war. See the markings on the back? Inside is a request from Henry Clay for our agents to support a troop landing at Hastings."

"The Darmon's have a similar message requesting help for a landing at Dover. It also has Clay's signature," Charles replied, puzzled.

Aigle nodded. "This is the one delivered to us in Paris. We acted, believing it to be genuine. It caused the loss of the entire expedition."

Charles looked perplexed. "Is this a forgery, then?"

"The signature appears genuine," the diplomat said with an edge to his voice. "Which suggests Clay, himself, may have made the switch."

Charles remained confused. "But why? Did he have second thoughts about the strike?"

Aigle lowered his voice. "We have reason to believe President Madison discovered the covert operation and advised Clay his political future could be jeopardized by involvement with Bonaparte's espionage activities. If the action succeeded, it would have enlarged the scope of the war. America couldn't afford to invade Europe in Madison's eyes. It's well known the President's primary concerns were to maintain this country's independence and prevent unjust treatment of American seamen."

"So Clay wrote a second message after the first one was already on its way, sending his own troops to their deaths at Dover?"

Aigle spread his hands. "It would appear that way."

Charles frowned. "The other message was found at the Darmon's Manor when we discovered Louisa's murder. Do you know how it got there?"

"We don't know why it turned up after all these years," the Frenchman answered. "It's possible someone carried the pendant, Louisa recognized it and confronted her killer."

Charles settled back on his cot. "So, you're going to suggest Clay approve my transfer to your custody or else he'll be exposed for subverting a wartime mission."

Aigle stood up and straightened his coat. "Such revelation would cost us a powerful ally. We would expect compensation for your extrication, a service performed, which we will specify once you've left the country."

"It will cost me my birthright, as well," Charles countered. "Only a few persons will ever know I wasn't really a French spy."

"Are you agreed?"

"Given the alternative, I will abide by your terms."

"*Bien*," he smiled thinly. "In a few days, you'll be informed of the details. Once we have you within the Embassy, an agent will escort you to our ship."

William Darmon arrived in Baltimore to discover headlines of the Maryland Gazette:

BAGWELL CONFESSES TO BE FRENCH SPY.

EMBASSY CONFIRMS INFILTRATION OF BRITISH CONSPIRACY.

HOUSE SPEAKER ACKNOWLEDGES UNDERCOVER WORK.

William read and reread the news, but its' contents did not change.

In small print, he learned Charles was to be released into French custody until the true kidnappers were brought to justice. William could not fathom why Charles would admit to such deception. Surely, the Ministry would prove his innocence once the real villains were apprehended. He began walking to the nearest livery, determined to speak with Charles once he was out of prison.

A boisterous crowd assembled outside Fort McHenry as time drew near for Charles to be transported to the French Embassy. Animated discussions flourished among onlookers, many incensed at the French revelation, believing it to be a sham. Some regarded Bagwell as the mastermind behind the abduction. Others believed he should have prevented the kidnapping if he really was a spy. Arguments led to shouting and shoving among farmers and shopkeepers, outraged housewives and sailors on shore leave.

Backed up to the gate, a black paddy wagon waited to take the captive an hour's ride to the ambassador's residence located a mile from the Capitol.

William elbowed his way to an inconspicuous spot near the waiting carriage.

At last, the gate parted and soldiers emerged.

Bystanders pressed forward. Bodies jostled William first forward and then squeezed him backwards as guards pushed to clear a path. For an instant the mob quieted when Charles appeared. His hands were manacled between two blue jacketed guards who stepped forward shoulder to shoulder.

Shouts broke out from the mellieu: "Traitor!" "Kidnapper!" "Assassin!"

Bystanders near the procession reached out to grab at the prisoner. "Give us back the Vice President!" "How much did you pay to get out?"

Hostility increased with each step towards the police vehicle.

Bodies pressed forward.

William felt panic, sensing the growing force of a mob out to hang his brother-in-law. Just as Charles reached the rear of the transport, William called out. The prisoner glanced over in his direction. For an instant, fear in his eyes was replaced by relief. Then he frowned and shook his head as the door closed behind him. The driver didn't hesitate. The wagon lurched forward parting anxious citizens.

A moment later, the horses passed through the crowd and disappeared down the road.

The assemblage began to disperse.

William retrieved his mount and took off after the police escort.

Keeping well back, he wound his way along the path he and Elizabeth took months earlier. Disappointed at not having gotten closer to Charles, he frowned, uneasy at his friend's reaction to his presence. It suggested Charles thought he might jeopardize his situation with the French diplomats.

A similar crowd filled grounds surrounding the French Embassy.

Following the prisoner's arrival, his escort passed inside a fence fifty feet to a red painted door of the official's residence. Two uniformed guards stood by the front gate, and armed policemen kept the throng's perimeter ten feet away from the fence.

As night fell, the group did not decrease despite the cold. Torches were lit. Only a few gave up their vigilance.

William remained among the individuals, pretending to be another concerned witness, and speaking as little as possible lest his accent betray him. Several persons eyed suspiciously. He wondered if Americans were hostile to all foreigners at this point.

By midnight, William decided his presence was not doing Charles any good, so he left for a local hotel, resolving to see Henry Clay the next day.

A loud knock at the door awakened William from deep sleep.

At first, he tried to ignore the banging, but it would not stop. Grudgingly, he rose from the bed, staggering sleepily in the direction of the pounding. On the other side of the door, someone urgently called his name. "Mr. Darmon, Mr. Darmon."

William reached the handle and opened the door. The Hotel Capitol clerk gaped at him in an agitated state.

"Mr. Darmon, they burnt it to the ground! There's nothing left!"

William tried to regain his senses. "What are you talking about?"

"The French Embassy! Last night a mob set fire to it. Your friend Bagwell could not be found. The whole country's looking for him!" the clerk stammered.

William abruptly came fully awake. He turned to gather his clothes and pulled on his boots. "What are the police doing about it?"

"They insist it's no longer their responsibility. If he's captured, I'm sure they won't interfere if he's strung up."

"I must get to him. I've got to find those French agents. Get me a horse!"

His first thought was to try the Hotel Franklin, the infamous French hangout. Upon arrival, he felt dismayed to find the place completely deserted. Papers littering the lobby, suggesting a hasty departure. Upstairs, no one responded. Hotel occupants appeared to have abandoned their residence in the face of rising sentiment against their harboring the notorious Bagwell.

William scratched his head. If Aigle, Perchant and the others went into hiding, what hope did he have of finding Charles? He thought of Nina. Perhaps the agents still used her as a lookout on the Baltimore waterfront.

In minutes, he straddled his mount, racing towards the edge of town.

Within an hour, he pulled up at the tavern he and Elizabeth visited five months earlier.

Groups of men carrying clubs and knives milled about the streets, angrily accosting strangers as they came into town. Cautiously he dismounted and hurried inside. Nina was not at her post. After a brief discussion, the barkeeper remembered him and managed to come up with the girl's address for which William paid another sizable fee.

The direction took William through narrow streets of aging, crowded buildings, many in need of repair. His path frequently diverted when he spotted vigilantes up the avenues. At last, he arrived at Nina's two-story building, nine blocks from the Inn. Inside, he found her apartment at the end of a dark hallway on the second floor. He knocked softly. A cough came from inside.

From behind the door, a barely audible voice hoarsely whispered. "Who is it?"

William identified himself, and the door opened a crack. Nina peeked out. She pulled it further open and waved him quickly inside. He stopped suddenly, gawking at the figure standing behind her. Charles!

They hugged. William could sense the man's relief.

"I worried your coming might jeopardize my escape," Charles recounted. "French agents are in complete disarray There's a ship in the harbor waiting to take me to France. If I can get there, it's the only way out of this manhunt.

William smiled. "You've had enough of this espionage business?"

He shook his head. "You understand Whitehall directed I become part of the kidnapping? Your aunt is behind the whole thing. They've taken the Vice President out to open waters. I think they mean to take him back to Rosewell Park and further incriminate Parliament. She set me up to take the blame as a decoy. An agent named Aigle suggested I become a confessed French spy to keep from being hanged. When this mess is resolved, I only hope I can return to England with my honor intact."

William looked at him curiously. "Emily received a letter from the Duke of Kent, thanking you for your service. I doubt you'll have trouble restoring your good name in the English countryside."

Nina took his arm. "But why did your aunt do this? What has she to gain?"

"I can't imagine," William said. "Her sympathies toward the French are well known, but to participate in such an outrageous act against the colonies and cast blame on her homeland is just unthinkable."

Charles grimaced. "And I was left to take the consequences."

William glanced out the window. "There's time enough to speculate later. Right now, we have to get out of here. I suggest Nina go to the waterfront and locate a skiff for us to get out into the harbor. Once you return, I'll leave first to distract any pursuit."

A half hour later, the two men exchanged clothes and William began making his way to the wharf. It wasn't long before a voice alerted others to his presence in the streets.

William began running to further attract attention.

A nagging doubt arose in his mind as to the wisdom of trying to elude denizens on their familiar ground. Every street seemed to hold more residents anticipating his flight.

He found himself in the middle of a block with angry hordes approaching from each end. His head jerked side to side searching for a way between buildings. He swallowed hard, put his head down and dashed up to a doorway. Slamming a shoulder into the portal, he burst through into a living room, startling two ladies into dropping their teacups.

William flew by and jumped out a rear window.

In the rear of the yard, he leaped over a four-foot fence and slumped to the ground, panting in an alleyway. A few seconds respite ended with a gunshot from the room he just exited. A fence post splintered two feet to his right. Unseen dogs began barking as pursuers piled into the back yard.

Time to abandon the plan of going back to Nina's. He would have to run straight to the wharf.

Another shot rang out shattering a stone in the building to his left.

He flung himself headlong down the narrow lane.

Six blocks of running brought him in sight of the water. It seemed as if half of Baltimore was chasing him, shouting and firing shots into the air. Despite dodging pedestrians and weaving his way around wagons, the mob of pursuers closed fast, less than fifty-feet behind.

He darted down a sloping pathway towards the harbor.

At the end, horsemen and carriages crowded in front of his path. Puffs of gun smoke erupted. William didn't stop. He sprinted forward barely able to keep his balance. Faces of outrage became clearer as he charged headfirst into the multitude. He smashed into a bystander and staggered forward amid outstretched, clutching hands. Twisting and turning, his momentum carried him across the roadway to a railing beside the water. With his last ounce of energy, he threw himself over the edge and dove underwater.

For an instant, he felt safe within murky surroundings. Then, dull thuds of bodies hitting the water made his adrenaline pump even harder as he swam for his life.

Dark hulls of boats in their moorings loomed ahead. They could be helpful for evading pursuers both above and below the surface. He surfaced to gasp air between boats and plunged back underwater. His arms ached and cold water sapped his strength. Soon, better swimmers than he would be closing in. He could not keep up the chase for long.

Several hundred feet from shore, he spied Charles rowing feverishly out to sea. He pitched underwater, held his breath for as long as possible, then broke the surface and swam a final race to the small craft. He could still hear shouts from shore, but saw no one nearby in the water.

He reached the boat.

Charles grasped his arms, pulling him on board.

They rowed furiously toward the French vessel. Its crew already scurrying to set sail, apparently alerted by a swarm of boats heading out from the wharf. The schooner began to move by the time the two men maneuvered alongside. Two seamen reached down and lifted them onto the deck. After several minutes, increasing speed outdistanced pursuit. Their ship was well on its way down Chesapeake Bay.

Two weeks later, on a calm, moonlit night, Charles and William stood by the rail looking out. Luminous, ghostly waves gave an eerie peace to the vast expanse and softly pitching hull. A stiff breeze smarted, carrying sea spray blustering gently on their faces. They discussed events of the past months including the deaths of Arthur Hurst and John and Estee Black.

Charles sighed in the darkness. “William, I remember a conversation between John and Arthur while in London working with the agents. Black presented himself to me as a businessman who helped the war effort as it benefited his business. I don't know if it was his cover or not, but Black suggested the actual motive behind the planned invasion of 1814 wasn’t to raze Parliament, but rather, to destroy his gunpowder factory at Hastings.”

William grasped the railing in frustration. “The trouble with the American involvement both now and then is that we never know who's charge. Was it Bonaparte, Clay, Fouche, Aigle, my Aunt, or even Terrence Winthrop? Whose the real culprit?"

"Could the wartime events be somehow related to the kidnapping?" Charles wondered. "Louisa's death and the pendant appear to be keys to both occurrences."

William's voice challenged. "Clay responded to a request from Bonaparte forwarded by Fouche's agents. The Hursts tried to implement the plan. Louisa and Lady Carlisle helped out, but it all came to naught."

Charles nodded. "The mission of the pendant was bold, but was Parliament really within reach of only fifty men? Aigle suggested Clay may have had second thoughts, and he could have been the one who deliberately sent a wrong message to Fouche."

William paused for a moment. "Really? Clay seemed genuinely shocked when Elizabeth and I showed him the Dover message which never made it to Faucon Deux."

"It could have been an act," Charles replied with an edge to his voice. "To cover up his sabotage of the mission."

"So now, we have a kidnapping. Bonaparte is in exile, the Hursts and Blacks are dead, and my Aunt is somewhere directing traffic. I can't accept this was her idea. France may be the beneficiary, but why would Louis XVIII take a risk of being blamed for the action. Economic sanctions would follow and a coup would be inevitable."

Charles shrugged. "Maybe it comes down to Fouche, but what has he to gain? Is he working for King Louis, Bonaparte, or one of the other factions trying to control France?"

William sighed. "And it still doesn't bring us any closer to the murderer. Some believe Louisa intentionally delivered the wrong response and hence, became a target for revenge. Surely, she would not have betrayed them on her own, and why keep the correct message in her possession all this time?"

"Conversely, if someone else brought the pendant to your ball and the confrontation led to her death, why bother after all these years?"

Charles observed.

“An odd thing is neither the English, French nor American agents claim any involvement in her demise.”

“Unless someone is lying,” Charles added.

William’s lips tightened. “My bet is on the French.”

“Well, we may know soon enough," Charles remarked, drawing a rough woolen coat around his neck. “In exchange for this transport, I've agreed to perform a service for the French government. I suspect we're about to be delivered to the Minister of Espionage, himself, Joseph Fouche.”

# CHAPTER EIGHT

Two sisters hurried up to a small desk just inside the entrance to Metropolitan Police Headquarters. The marbled office stood among Ministry buildings north of Parliament Square on a block becoming popularly known as the Scotland Yard.

"Excuse me, my name is Elizabeth Darmon, this is Emily Bagwell."

The receptionist, a young man in his twenties, sat perfectly erect, neatly dressed in a gray suit. Well-manicured hands deftly shuffled papers stacked on the desktop in front of him. When he heard the name Bagwell, a bored expression changed to interest.

Elizabeth grabbed the edge of the table, waiting for her heart to stop racing. "We've fresh information regarding the recent American kidnapping..."

The official rose and waved her silent. "Wait here a moment."

He retreated through a nearby door into the next room. A few minutes later, he reappeared with an older gentleman who gave a thin smile.

Chief Inspector Matthews bowed. "Madam Darmon, Madam Bagwell, good to see you again. My man says you have news. Permit me to escort you across the way to Whitehall. Mr. Gravis will be most interested as well."

Two blue-jacketed officers joined the Inspector, and the party of five walked briskly between buildings.

Gravis welcomed them in a large conference room with more gentlemen entering each minute.

Gravis introduced the pair to assembled agents and turned solemnly to the women. "Let me assure you, Mrs. Bagwell, your husband's movements are being carefully followed. Once all the conspirators are in custody, a full disclosure will be forthcoming. We've already determined these perpetrators passed through the Strait of Belle Isle..."

Elizabeth interrupted. “They're here at Mayfair Hall! My servant witnessed two carriages arrive yesterday with Lady Carlisle and Vice President Tompkins. We also discovered an encampment of thirty Frenchmen disguised as soldiers near Langdon. The detachment has since left for London, having removed servants from my home.”

Agents leaped to their feet, barking orders. The room cleared within seconds.

In under ten minutes, men clustered outside on horseback while Elizabeth and Emily sat with Michael Gravis in a carriage. Every available guard was pressed into service. Up front, Inspector Matthews gave a sharp command and their carriage lurched forward. The procession moved out at a fast trot, clattering down London’s narrow cobbled streets to the surprise of local inhabitants.

After three hours, Matthews drifted back to the carriage and spoke to Gravis through a window. “We're getting close now. The men will take positions around the main building. It should be dark within about two hours and give cover so we can close in.”

Elizabeth leaned out the carriage window. They were beginning the long approach to the Manor. Wisps of smoke rose in the distance. catching her attention

“Is there a fire on the grounds?”

Emily peered out. “It might be a campfire of some sort.”

“No, it's too big. Look at the haze over the trees.”

Their carriage rounded a curve, giving them a view of the premises. Smoke poured out front windows of the main building.

“It can't be!” Elizabeth gasped.

She stared in disbelief as the carriage approached.

By the time they reached a rise opposite Mayfair’s front entrance, tongues of fire projected from downstairs openings in the main structure. Intense heat kept the men from coming close to the steps.

Elizabeth jumped from the carriage and ran shrieking toward the arched portico.

“My house! My house! Who has done this to my house?”

Two agents took off after her. They pulled her back as she struggled wild-eyed, trembling on the verge of hysteria. The inferno roared upwards, turning the salmon colored exterior into ugly black scars over each window while smoke spewed into a towering column.

Agents stood, watching the huge blaze consume Mayfair manor.

Emily put her arms around her sister. Together, they cried, witnessing the manor disintegrate before their eyes. Through front windows Elizabeth glimpsed furniture blazing and pictures blacken on the walls. She tried to remember details of each room to preserve its memory.

A huge section of the east-wing roof collapsed inward, sending showers of cinders lofting into a sky already darkened by oppressive black smoke. Elizabeth shut her eyes and recalled her first sight of Mayfair, beautifully situated among rolling hills and woods. Her first year there was blissful, not simply because of the wealth it entailed, but for the haven of solitude it offered to all who visited. William's grandfather rebuilt the east wing of the ancient structure sixty years earlier. His family knew no other residence.

Another section crashed inward with a thunderous bellow. Elizabeth remained rigidly in front of the holocaust with tear stained cheeks, refusing to return from her reverie. And the parties! Where else, in all England could such festivity be enjoyed? The roof over their ballroom was coming down! She mourned the passing of their link to a bygone era. Some day, by heaven, Elizabeth promised, they would recreate it.

As if Emily read her thoughts, she turned to Elizabeth. "Poor William, he knows nothing of this!"

The conflagration continued lighting nearby grounds as evening twilight advanced. Destruction persisted for hours. Agents were joined by townspeople from Langdon who saw smoke from twenty miles away. They formed bucket lines from the pond in front and managed to save three adjoining buildings.

By dawn, Elizabeth and Emily were covered with soot that rained down on bystanders through most of the night. The two women sat together on a small hill, hugging each other and recounting good times.

A smoldering stone shell seethed wisps of smoke into the air.

Near the edge of a pathway leading to the livery, a commotion arose. Emily got to her feet. Some fifty yards away, two agents pushed a man in scarred clothes toward Gravis and Matthews.

Elizabeth followed her sister, hurrying to a growing crowd of tired firefighters. The prisoner was streaked with soot, two angry welts marred his chin and forehead.

Elizabeth recognized him. “Terrence Winthrop! What on earth are you doing here?

She stopped, remembering his past. A fury grew within. “You're part of this conspiracy, aren’t you? This is on your head! I hope you pay dearly for this disaster.”

“Hold on ma’am,” Gravis interrupted. “This is American agent, Robert Hayes. He's been tracking the kidnappers at the behest of the American government.”

“It’s true,” responded Hayes. “I set the fire to drive the criminals out of their hiding. Two of my men recovered Tompkins. Three of their party are dead down the road over there behind the livery, but we couldn’t stop the rest along with Lady Carlisle from escaping into the night.”

Elizabeth’s jaw dropped, incredulous at his words. Her eyes flared, unable to control her rage. “You burned down my house to drive them out?”

“We were out numbered and would never have recovered Tompkins,” he answered matter-of-factly.

“You might have waited for our assistance,” Gravis replied. “Or did you think despite our assurances, we Brits were a party to the kidnapping, and this misconception gave you the right to extract revenge on English property?”

Hayes shrugged. “It may have been rash, but considering the severity of the crime and threat of war between our countries, events dictated we move swiftly. Americans will not stand still for such transgressions against our leaders. I can promise you the revelation of French culpability for this deed will serve both our countries.”

Elizabeth settled down. “So, all this time you were pretending to be English? I guess it explains why you weren’t recognized as a British citizen in the gendarmarie, and why you helped Nina, a French ally during the war.”

Hayes smiled. "I spied against Britain during the war working under cover as Terrence Winthrop, an English gentleman. After Clay decided to abandon the strike of 1814, I delivered a pendant to our contact working with Lady Carlisle. We intended to leak the identity of the Dover landing site to your English agents."

She nodded. "So, you helped the French envoys deliver the message directing the Americans to use Lady Carlisle's manor for a rendezvous."

"Yes, but I never had dealings with Louisa Hurst."

"Yet, after the war, you continued your disguise as Terrence Winthrop."

He looked at her squarely. "When the war ended, I was assigned to keep the activities of Lady Carlisle under advisement. LeClair and Perchant were also under our surveillance. For awhile, we believed you Darmons were part of the plan because of your relation to Lady Carlisle."

Elizabeth's eyes widened. "You were at our anniversary ball to spy on the conspirators. You were the one who killed Louisa Hurst!"

"Now wait a minute," he protested. "I had no quarrel with her, I told you I never met the woman. You can rest assured the American government had nothing to do with Madam Hurst's death."

Emily interjected, "Now the Vice President has been recovered, I hope these French culprits will be exposed and my husband's name cleared."

Hayes shook his head, "When word reaches the United States of the French involvement, I'm afraid one confessed spy will be in serious trouble. Your husband, Mrs. Bagwell, will need full support of the British government to convince anyone he hasn't gone over to their side."

Elizabeth suddenly felt very tired. Her body numb and senses dulled from the ordeal of the past night, she nodded woodenly at Emily's suggestion they return to the Bagwell residence in Surrey.

During the carriage ride, Emily talked on while Elizabeth drifted in and out of consciousness. Elizabeth smiled sleepily at her sister wondering where she got the energy to keep rattling on.

Emily, chortled. "It's over! The crime has been resolved and Charles will be coming home soon."

"Bloody Americans, Bloody Hayes, Bloody Clay," Elizabeth mumbled.

Emily nodded, suddenly reminded of how devastated her sister felt. "Imagine, all that time, Hayes working for the Americans..."

Despite closed eyes, Elizabeth kept muttering. "He burned down our house.... just trying to drive them out...."

They both drifted to sleep with swaying motion of the carriage.

An hour passed. Elizabeth woke to Emily's shaking her arm. "Lizzy, I have an idea," she blurted. "What if Mayfair wasn't burned down to drive out the kidnappers?"

Elizabeth tried to focus on her words. "What? What're you saying? Hayes confessed it."

"Suppose it was done by the kidnappers to cover up their presence at the Manor. Maybe Robert Hayes didn't set the fire at all."

Elizabeth shook her head to brush away mental cobwebs.

"Why would he take the credit for it? That would mean he lied and is in league with the kidnappers."

"Perhaps he was closer to your Aunt than he admitted," Emily countered. "Afterall, he delivered a pendant to Lady Carlisle during the war and newspapers said there were papers discovered at Rosewell Park, linking both Lady Carlisle and Winthrop to the French."

Elizabeth paused briefly before answering. "Americans were allied with the French against us at the time. That's no reason to think Hayes is now part of the kidnapping conspiracy, and why would Aunt Catherine burn down our house, for God's sake?"

Emily persisted. "But, why did the kidnappers come to Mayfair? Surely, there are more secure places. Why risk a trip to Kent, unless something at the Manor was important to them, something they would burn rather than risk discovery?"

"Perhaps they just needed a large place to house thirty men, and Lady Carlisle was already well acquainted with the grounds," Elizabeth answered, annoyed at Emily's flight of fantasy. "They probably expected William to be drawn overseas to rescue Charles."

Emily countered, "But the soldiers never stayed at the house. They encamped near Langdon, and removed your servants from the facility."

Elizabeth stopped. "Speaking of the servants, where are they? Thomas' note said they'd been placed under arrest and taken to London. I hope there's truth in that. Gravis must find them quickly. Poor Thomas."

"Lizzy, please," Emily said with an edge to her voice. "I still can't see why they would come to Mayfair. Surely, a barn somewhere near the coast would offer enough space and less risk of attention. Could it be related to Lady Carlisle's abandonment of Rosewell Park two years ago? Maybe there was another reason for her appearance at your home."

Elizabeth let out an exasperated breath. "Emily, this is preposterous. Next you'll say the kidnapping was staged just so the American Vice President could come to England and meet with King George at Mayfair Hall!"

The absurdity sounded almost plausible and sent them into thoughtful silence.

Elizabeth was too tired to think any more.

She sighed with relief when their carriage finally arrived at the Bagwell Manor. Emily became preoccupied with the accommodations, engaging in only minimal conversation the rest of the day.

The two women slept soundly all night.

At daybreak, feeling refreshed, they decided to return to Mayfair to look through the ruins for dear artifacts which might have survived the maelstrom.

Upon approach to the Manor, the sisters found deserted grounds except for a few animals; dogs and horses that returned to their home despite the absence of servants to care for them.

A stiff breeze greeted their descent from the carriage; portending winter's approaching chill. Elizabeth could hardly bear to look at the blackened remnant hulking like the carcass of a huge animal.

At the entrance, Elizabeth came to tears once more. She clung to the frame and sobbed. Straightening at last, she took a deep breath and resolutely proceeded inside with Emily.

Within the shell of the main building, they faced a surreal scene of charred timbers jumbled with piles of plaster and broken pottery. All the familiar surroundings had been painted with a slate colored brush under the blue canopy of sky, absent a roof overhead. Eerie stillness pervaded despite faint sounds of air buffeting outside. A stench of burnt wood and swirling ashes assaulted their nostrils making it difficult to breathe.

They gingerly stepped through rubble scattering a cloudy haze.

After awhile, the ladies drifted apart, each trying to make sense of charred objects and poking under ceiling pieces.

By noon, they worked their way to opposite ends of the main floor. Gray soot covered Elizabeth's hair and her clothes and hands streaked with black. She wandered aimlessly in a malaise as dreary as her surroundings, stepping over a broken marble statue while toting a box of a few precious ornaments.

"Lizzy, come here!" Emily shouted.

Elizabeth revived from her stupor and began picking through wreckage over to Emily. Beyond a pile of beams, she suddenly viewed a crater in the floor created when the upper floor plummeted onto the main level.

Fifteen feet below, Emily looked up from the cavern waving in dim light. "Down here! You won't believe what I've found."

Her mouth dropped. "Where did this come from? I never knew there was a basement under the main floor."

Elizabeth carefully climbed down with increasing wonder at the hollow area under the house. At the bottom, she squinted into darkness at a huge space cluttered with wreckage and storage crates.

Emily held up a sword encased in its scabbard. "Look at this!"

She pointed to an inscription where ashes had been wiped away. It said Bonaparte.

Elizabeth gulped. "Where did this come from? I don't remember William mentioning he owned a sword."

She glanced down at pieces of singed clothing scattered among the ashes.

Attached to a few of the tatters lay filigreed buttons like the one they found in the American hotel. Two black pointed hats stuck out between nearby crates, dented but still intact. None of the apparel looked familiar. She tried to think where in the house these items could have been hidden. Had they fallen from upper stories or stored under their feet all this time?

Continuing their search through the newly discovered room, Elizabeth spotted unfamiliar furniture buried under layers of plaster chunks. The style wasn't anything like she would have picked for the house. Had they been here since before she married William or did Lady Carlisle bring them from Rosewell Park? Why wasn’t she told of this?

She stepped to a large bureau resting partially on its side and began pulling the drawers. A wooden box rattled at the rear of one. Emily came up as she lifted the varnished container from its hiding place. While Emily looked over her shoulder, Elizabeth wiggled the cover until the lid finally came open. They gasped at the contents.

Inside, eight pendants displayed the Bonaparte inscription.

# CHAPTER NINE

Cold, gray winter greeted the French schooner as it heaved into port at Le Havre, one hundred kilometers from Paris. Charles and William trudged down a gangplank, knowing they were not free to return to England. Instead, a carriage waited, ready to conduct them the remaining distance to Paris Headquarters of the Ministre Du Espionage.

Three hours waiting inside a small anteroom ended when a blue suited receptionist escorted them into an enormous chamber furnished with large paintings, baroque chairs of blond wood, a gray marble table, statuary, and an immense mahogany desk.

Charles stepped woodenly toward the seated Minister, anxiously wondering what fate would be imposed in exchange for escape from the Americans. Two soldiers stood at attention behind the short gentleman who conversed to one side with another individual wearing a powdered wig, blue coat tails and white stockings. Their escort gestured them to halt.

Joesph Fouche turned to the two travelers. "Welcome, mes voyageurs. I trust your journey went well. Monsieur Darmon, I am pleased you've come as well to 'elp Monsieur Bagwell repay 'is debt. Monsieur Bagwell, I trust you are now prepared to perform a small service for the government of France."

Charles straightened his coat and nodded. "I am in your debt for rescuing me from that horrible circumstance."

"Yes, those conspirators left you in the lurch, so to speak," the minister replied. "I 'ope the guilty will soon receive just punishment for their unspeakable crime."

Charles' brow furled. "You do? Wasn't it your plan to have Americans cast blame on England for the kidnapping?"

"Not at all. The abduction wasn't authorized by 'is majesty. It is going to 'arm our relations with both countries when the culprits are apprehended and found to be French citizens."

William stared in disbelief at the Minister. "It was your agent, Aigle who got Charles here. He was working with Penchant and other conspirators."

He smiled thinly behind the desk. "Aigle is one of my agents. 'E keeps me informed of their activities and arranged for you to be brought 'ere at my request."

Charles looked puzzled. "Why, then, did this gang abduct the Vice President and dress like British soldiers?"

Fouche extended a hand. "Please sit down. I will explain."

The pair settled onto two directoire side chairs.

"In France today, there are many who wish to control our country's destiny. My office is besieged with rumors of secret societies. Many of these groups incite demonstrations and plot to remove key members from government. The situation might be called desperate. It is 'ere that you may be of 'elp.

"One group in particular, retains a fanatical devotion to Bonaparte and would restore 'is regime, if 'e were not regarded as an outlaw by the rest of 'umanity. Their members include a few individuals of wealth both 'ere and in your country. While it is not realistic to think there's any chance of the Emperor's return to power, the faction continues to plot against 'is adversaries, which include Louis XVIII."

William sighed. "Why haven't you brought them to justice?"

"It 'as been difficult to infiltrate their organization," Fouche continued. "'Owever, we 'ave one contact who tries to keep me informed of their movements. This person 'as learned of a meeting to be 'eld 'ere in Paris three days from now. Assuming your concurrence, 'e will see to it you're invited as men of influence who might be useful to their cause. All we ask is that you determine their intentions so we can catch them in an act of lawlessness. By removing their leaders, France will finally be rid of these traitors and you'll be free to return 'ome."

"So we only have to attend this one meeting as interested

bystanders?" Charles responded.

William gave a shrug of resignation. "What do these people call themselves?"

The other gentleman stepped forward. "They are known as *Le Nid*, or in English, 'The Nest'."

It was nearly 1:00 AM when William and Charles set out to meet Fouche's contact. They followed narrow streets through a lonely Paris suburb under a moonless sky. Pitch black alleys without window lights suggested the community had retired for the night. Sounds of crunching footfalls echoed loudly as they walked cautiously to the appointed rendezvous address.

"I can't see a thing in this light," Charles whispered. "Are you sure we're on the right street?"

"I hope so," William replied quietly. "God only knows what could jump out at any moment."

"I'm glad you came with me," Charles said.

"Shhh. I think someone's standing over there in the doorway."

A low voice resonated to their left. "Beegwell?"

"Yes, with Darmon." Charles replied.

"Come. *Le* meeting *est* upstairs, *au premier etage*."

A barely discernible form knocked softly on the door behind him.

It opened without a light inside. They could sense, rather than see, a large figure standing in the doorway, beckoning them. They squeezed by his bulk, into a diminutive space permeated with cloying odor. The door clicked shut. In complete blackness, the individual brushed past and began lumbering up stairs at the rear of the room. Charles and William felt their way after.

At the top of the stairs, a sentry softly tapped at a door down the hallway.

Orange light spilled out.

Inside the spacious room lit by several small lamps, William observed thirty people sitting in silence on five rows of benchs. Many appeared well dressed and a few wore military uniforms. They faced a portly gentleman dressed in dark waistcoat over lace cuffs and turned up collar. From a podium, he appeared medium in height sporting wide mutton-chop sideburns and a bushy mustache. He turned papers in front of him, barely glancing up when they entered. The Englishmen kept their heads down while edging to an empty space to sit.

The speaker regarded his audience and began addressing them in French.

"Failure of our plan will not deter us. We shall not rest until he is among free men. It is the right of every Frenchman to choose under which regime he lives."

A voice came from the audience. "Why did the American President refuse our request? What about their debt to us from the war?"

The speaker looked pained. "He would not acknowledge us as rightful representatives of French citizens. President Monroe said America would not deal with hostage takers, and therefore, not trade for his release. He condemned our action and said we would be treated as renegades by lawful countries."

Another voice from the crowd asked, "Are we suspect by evidence left behind?"

The speaker's manner improved a bit. "Nothing of an incriminating nature survived the fire. The men we lost carried no identity papers. We had planned to leave the hostage behind and move to a more remote location. Remember, he was blindfolded until entering the Napoleon Room. Were it not for the fire, Madam Carlisle could have returned to the premises without much fuss."

William suddenly straightened. "Madam Carlisle! My Aunt? What's he talking about? What fire?"

Charles tried to keep him from drawing attention. "Shhh, keep your voice down. We're here only to listen."

Questions continued. "What has become of our unit?"

In reply, the leader pointed to a cloaked individual across the room. "Most of them have returned to the Continent. Thomas paid off the servants."

The hooded figure nodded as William stretched to see his face. "It's been taken care of."

William scrunched his nose. "He sounds like Reynolds, my manservant!"

"Sit down!" Charles commanded as forcibly as he could. Heads turned in their direction.

The man in front continued. "It's unfortunate we must abandon the English front for now, but the destruction will not sit well for some time. All operations will be conducted from Paris until newspapers forget the loss of Mayfair Hall."

William gasped. He jumped to his feet.

"Loss of Mayfair Hall? Loss of Mayfair Hall! You bastards burnt down my home? I'll wring your bloody necks!"

He lunged forward.

Charles just missed grabbing his coat. Several large men stepped into the aisle, blocking William's charge.

After a brief skirmish, William lay pinned to the floor under their weight.

The speaker stepped from behind the podium and stared down at William. "Your home? Who might you be?"

Despite his position, William struggled, raging out of control. "I'm William Darmon. Mayfair Hall is my home! If you've harmed my wife or my family in any way, there won't be a place on this planet you can hide."

"Darmon? Monsieur Darmon! What are you doing here? I apologize for the loss of your residence. I can assure you no one in your household was harmed. We never intended to destroy it unless it became necessary to abandon the project."

Thomas Reynolds joined in. "Master Darmon, sir, we acted under direction of Lady Carlisle. When authorities discovered our presence at the Manor, we fled for our lives, knowing the crime we'd committed was a hanging offense."

William relaxed a bit. "What were you doing there in the first place? Why was it necessary to burn down the Manor?"

"Monsieur Darmon, allow me to introduce myself. I'm Sage

Hibou, leader of this group. Let me explain what we intended by this action."

"Please do," William replied as his captors lifted him onto a seat of the front bench. Other participants also settled back.

"We members of Le Nid support principles of Napoleon Bonaparte, a great leader who installed a government for the people, won by our Revolution thirty years ago. His Code Civile replaced a ruthless, self-indulgent monarchy that oppressed French citizens since the Dark Ages. As you know, our leader is now imprisoned on the Isle of Saint Helena in the South Atlantic, and the old policies have returned to France under the despot Louis XVIII.

"If you remember, on the fifteenth of July 1815, Bonaparte surrendered on board the *Bellerophon*, expecting the British government to allow him passage to America or possibly asylum in England, as Paoli received in London. Instead, he was treated like a dog! Lord Liverpool wanted King Louis to hang him.

"During his days at Plymouth, Count de Las Cases, a member of our group who is with Bonaparte now, came up with a way to force the Americans to permit an exile in their country. The plan could not appear to have French involvement or else our group would certainly have been eliminated.

We began to assemble a force in Canada, making slow progress, but the Emperor had great hope for our success. We enlisted help from Lady Carlisle who offered a hiding place for the hostage which would be above suspicion."

"I gather from your earlier remark the Americans refused to cooperate, despite capturing their Vice President," William observed.

"President Monroe would have nothing to do with us, and now the gentleman is on his way back to the United States."

"But what of my property? Why did you burn it?"

Hibou nodded. "When Lady Carlisle abandoned her residence at Rosewell due to careless use of the pendants, she stored many of our artifacts in your basement including several of Bonaparte's favorite uniforms which we hoped he might wear again someday. When our presence was discovered, we could not leave evidence of Le Nid behind so we set a fire in the basement. Once we fled the premises, Reynolds took care of the other servants under condition they not return to Mayfair."

"Excuse me," Charles interrupted. "What do you mean, 'misuse of the pendants'?"

He reached into his pocket and retrieved a pendant identical to the one William had in his possession. "Members of the Society carry pendants like this one with Bonaparte's inscription."

"You mean all your members carry these things?" William asked.

"Of course," Hibou said. "They are replicas of containers used to pass messages from Napoleon during the war. We use them as a kind of recognition code. We even place copies of some of the famous missives inside."

"Such as Clay's response to Bonaparte to invade England?" William finished.

"Given the target, it's one of the most popular."

"What happens now your plan has failed?" Charles interjected. "Will you give up the idea of a more pleasant exile for Bonaparte?"

Hibou expressed surprise. "Absolutely not! Unfortunately, it's now critical we rescue the Emperor as soon as possible. A new Governor has replaced Admiral Cockburn on Saint Helena. He is ruthless and insensitive to the health of our leader. Letters from Las Cases have disappeared, and rumor has it the Count will soon be deported to the Cape. It is an intolerable situation."

"But what can you do?" William asked with a frown. "Your little group cannot remove King Louis and reinstall Bonaparte on the throne."

Shaking his head, Hibou opened his palms. "All we wish to do is transport Bonaparte from his despicable surroundings to a place where he, as any exile, can live out the remainder of his days in peace."

Charles rubbed his chin. "There must be an entire garrison stationed on the island to prevent any escape."

The leader of Le Nid took a deep breath. "We intend to mount a direct assault on Saint Helena and provide our leader with a ship to sail to the country of his choice."

# CHAPTER TEN

Elizabeth and Emily listened to wind howling in icy blustery night air outside the Surrey mansion. A blaze roared in the fireplace while they unpacked musty boxes of decorations for upcoming Christmas holidays.

Eight weeks passed since the Mayfair fire. The ladies revisited the ruins many times, but little else was found. In the absence of servants, caretakers were hired in Langdon to look after the animals and board up remaining structures. No further word came from Palace Yard regarding the missing help or the whereabouts of Charles and William after the Vice President went back to America. The women worried over their husbands. Presumably, hangings had not yet taken place.

A knock came at the manor door.

A caretaker announced a gentleman who identified himself as Paul Reme, husband of Josette.

Elizabeth rushed to the entrance. A grey haired gentleman stood grasping a thick coat tightly about his neck with calloused hand. Above windblown skin of bristled hollow cheeks, his eyes stared hard and steady.

"Pardon Ma'am," he spoke in a wavering voice. "Would a Missus Elizabeth Darmon be about these premises?"

She took his arm. "Monsieur Reme, how good it is to see you. I am Elizabeth. I'm sorry we never got to meet in Paris. Please come in and warm yourself by the fire."

After taking his coat, they helped him to a seat by the hearth.

He rubbed his hands near the flames. "Thank you, ma'am. Your English winters threaten a man's constitution."

Emily bit her lip at his appearance. "May we get you something to eat? I'll have Sarah bring you a bowl of soup."

Mr. Reme nodded. "Thank you kindly, ma'am."

"And how is your wife?" Elizabeth asked. "Does she still work at the Ministry?"

He smiled. "She is well, thank you. Josette told me of your quest to find this 'ere Columbe du Paix."

He withdrew a folded paper from a well-worn vest pocket. "Three days ago, your 'usband came to visit us. 'E gave me this letter and asked it be delivered to you because 'e and Charles Bagwell could not leave Paris. 'E wanted to allay any concerns you might have over their well being."

"They're safe!" Emily exclaimed. "They're out of America, only two hundred miles away! What a relief."

Elizabeth took the letter and quickly unfolded three tightly creased pages. She took a seat close to a table lamp and began reading.

*My Dearest Elizabeth:*

*I am in good health. Both Charles and I left the American colonies for what I hope is the last time; at least for many years. Nina sent her good wishes for your continued happiness. Charles is also in good health, and we both wish it were possible to come home.*

*By now you have heard of Charles' pretence as a confessed French spy. It was done to escape a hangman's noose, and we narrowly averted tragedy at the hands of an American mob. Aigle provided a means of transport to the Continent, at a price. That price is servitude to the French Minister Fouche for one last operation that requires our presence here for a bit longer.*

*News of the Mayfair fire has reached me, which is why this letter was directed to the Bagwell estate. I am greatly saddened by its loss, and I fear the pain will be unbearable when I view the ruins. Alas, we must be content with memories for now, but I promise you my energies will be devoted to its restoration upon my return. That event and my longing for your presence will sustain me while we perform this project to which we are committed.*

*The situation in Paris remains chaotic. Indeed, if it were not for the good graces of Ms. Reme, this letter could never reach you. It is not clear who's leading the country. The monarchy appears to be losing more influence each day. Fouche directed us to spy on one of the societies opposing the French King. By no coincidence we have crossed their path before and your observation of many months past pertaining to fowl was more accurate than you imagine. Its leader's name is 'wise owl' and he's plotting to recover their most cherished 'egg'. I expect their chance of success to be quite small.*

*I have made little progress in resolving Louisa's role in the wartime assault. You will be surprised to learn there are more pendants about. It's possible one of this faction may be Louisa's killer, Lady Carlisle and our trusted servant, Thomas Reynolds are also involved. However, they will not participate in the forthcoming venture. Her location is unknown. You are probably closer to finding her than us.*

*Charles and I are saddened to miss the holidays with you. We hope to join you in a matter of weeks, at least before the warmth of summer comes again to the grounds of Kent. I trust you and Emily will do well in Surrey.*

*God be with you.*

*All my love.*

*William*

Elizabeth hugged her sister.

Tears welled up in their eyes.

After a moment, Elizabeth sighed thoughtfully. "I'm so relieved they're free of the Americans. Despite the Vice President's return, bitter feelings will probably linger until someone is brought to justice. I, for one, do not intend to go back there."

Emily reviewed the note. "Lizzy what do you make of this 'project' they must undertake?"

"It's puzzling, a society whose members are named after birds. It suggests Aigle and Faucon were operating separately from Fouche, and the government of France. Since Fouche directed our husbands to watch these people, they must be planning something of a threat to the current regime."

Emily frowned. "Yet, this Aigle saw to it Charles and William were delivered to Fouche."

"Perhaps he's a counter spy within the conspirators." Elizabeth said.

Emily glanced at Paul Reme. "Didn't William say its members carry Bonaparte pendants?

They must favor Napoleon, but he's incarcerated on Saint Helena."

"France is struggling with remnants of his rule," Elizabeth noted absently. "I see another bird has emerged, an owl. Perhaps we should contact Michael Gravis to see what he knows of a French society of bird people; and what is this cherished egg?"

Emily continued. "The eight pendants found in your underground room may have been left by members of that group. Or perhaps there's a club of English sympathizers who met with Lady Carlisle in your basement, carrying on with souvenirs to make them feel they're back in France. Do you remember any of her friends coming to Mayfair?"

Elizabeth drew in a breath. "I would have noticed a regular gathering. Servants would have found evidence of their presence unless they were members themselves."

"Then why store aritifacts in your basement? If the gang was preparing to kidnap the Vice President, what do French costumes have to do with it?"

"Maybe they planned to kidnap a French general next?" Elizabeth said, trying to smile. "He might feel comfortable with those items during a prolonged stay."

"Something to consider," Emily agreed.

Elizabeth moved closer to the fire. "Gravis didn't seem concerned about our discoveries in the ruins. He said the items might be more relevant to solving Louisa's murder than providing evidence of an international plot. Perhaps in light of this letter, he might be convinced it's worth looking into this latest project."

"And what about Louisa?" Emily retorted with a sound of desperation. "You don't seem to be any closer to finding her killer in spite of all your travels."

Elizabeth sighed. "You have a point. The killing may have nothing to do with either the pendant or the conspiracy. Perhaps we've been 'barking up the wrong tree'."

"But what other motive could there be?" Emily said with mild surprise. "I wonder if Inspector Matthews uncovered any clues during his interviews of your guests."

Elizabeth nodded. "We should visit him as well if we can get to London tomorrow, once this abominable weather subsides."

An idea flashed the back of Elizabeth's mind. Something to do with Lady Carlisle and Bonaparte. William inferred Aunt Catherine might be close by, but did he mean in Kent, London, or simply, she never left the country after the kidnapping? She sighed. It could be sorted out another day. Now, she would help Emily attend to their guest.

Elizabeth turned to the gentleman. "Monsieur Reme, you must spend the night so we can catch up on the latest news from Paris."

# CHAPTER ELEVEN

"Gentlemen, this is our objective," LeClair announced, pointing to a large map at the front of their upstairs meeting hall. "This is the Island of Saint Helena."

Murmurs subsided and a hush fell over the assembly of Le Nid's most able-bodied men. Thirty pairs of eyes riveted on the speaker with heightened attention. Many members bore scars of the American abduction fiasco, eager to prove their worth for a cause benefiting French nationalism.

Conversely, Charles and William cringed at the idea of a five thousand mile voyage and risk of never returning. The Englishmen huddled on a bench near the back of the familiar room. Over the past week, meetings were held each night, but only miscellaneous details had been discussed until now.

The new mission was about to be revealed.

Sage Hibou gave an approving smile from his seat next to the podium while Perchant and LeClair paced back and forth in front of the audience, answering questions and gesturing at the chart.

"He seems well versed in battlefield work," William whispered softly to Charles. "Perhaps a former ranking officer in Bonaparte's army."

"More he talks, the more plausible this operation sounds."

The Frenchman moved his pointer around a perimeter of the landmass.

"The Island is located fifteen degrees South of the Equator, almost two thousand kilometers west of the African coast. I remind you, south of the Equator means tropical temperatures of ninety degrees when we arrive. The Isle measures approximately sixteen by ten kilometers with a northern part consisting of a semi-circular ridge of mountains reaching heights of nearly one thousand meters at Diana's peak. It is the rim of a great volcanic crater.

"The south side is much lower with water-cut gorges stretching in all directions and widening into valleys three hundred meters deep as they approach the sea. Hillsides contain caves and lava rock formations, which can provide cover for our invasion from the North. There are important landmarks we must use to keep our bearings. Here is Ass's Ears, and there, Lot and Lot's Wife, and this feature is known as the Chimney. Cliffs two to three hundred meters high prevent most ships from landing on the east, north and west sides. The only practical place to make port is at the southern tip of the island in Saint James Bay."

"The leeward side," Perchant added.

LeClair nodded. "At the mouth of the Bay, is the settlement of Jamestown. The harbor may be crowded with ships. Merchantmen of the East India Company put in for fresh water and supplies on their way back from trading excursions in the Far East. I'm told several hundred vessels dock there each year.

"From the head of the bay, a narrow valley extends northward two kilometers. There are seventeen plantations here, giving the Island a population of one thousand, half of which are Negro slaves. The East India Company has also begun importing Chinese from their factories in Canton.

"From the valley, ground rises to a plateau in the northeast quadrant where we find the Deadwood and Longwood plains five hundred meters above sea level."

Perchant interrupted once more. "It's the largest area of level ground on the Island. Here is where the farm of Longwood is located."

"Where else would one expect to find an egg?" Charles muttered with an edge in his voice.

William put a finger to his lips.

The Frenchman drew in a breath.

"Las Cases informs us the farm consists of three main buildings with a heavy garrison of British regulars encamped here and here. Bonaparte resides within this low structure. It contains eight rooms. Count de Las Cases, Doctor O'Meara, and General Gourgaud have now departed from the island. That leaves only General Bertrand with his wife the Countess, Count Montholon and his wife, and the new Corsican doctor, Antommarchi who remain housed in the Longwood residence with our leader. Governor Hudson Lowe resides in another building.

After we free the Emperor, a unit will cross this open area and dispose of the tyrant persecutor."

Color drained from Charles' face. "This is a blatant murder of an English officer."

"All madness," William echoed under his breath. "They're going to take on an entire garrison with only thirty men to effect his escape!"

LeClair paused, looking squarely at William. "Any questions so far?"

A gentleman in the front row spoke up. "How many troops does Las Cases say there are stationed at the farm?"

"He estimates one-hundred and fifty. There are more at the fortress in Jamestown and some could be on ships in the vicinity," LeClair replied. "Anyone else?"

Perchant stepped forward. "We move to our plan of attack."

"Two ships of schooner class have been secured with the help of Lady du Montclair. The *Alouette* and the *Canari* will depart from Marseilles on the third of January under control of a handpicked crew. We have twenty-three British uniforms left over from our last operation. The Alouette will dock at Saint James Bay under the guise of a vessel piloted by a wealthy entrepreneur enroute to the East Indies.

"Here, Monsieurs Darmon and Bagwell will provide assistance. They will have no trouble passing as English merchants without concern for Napoleon. Fifteen of our party will pose as crew and porters. Uniforms and weapons will be concealed inside crates on board the Alouette addressed for Monsieur Suette Lemoins, a plantation owner with French sympathies who lives not far from the Longwood plains. The Count has informed him of our arrival next month. From there, we shall move to a rendezvous at Lot's Wife and meet the other half of our landing party, put on the uniforms and take up weapons."

William's eyes widened. He turned to Charles and spoke softly. "Fouche better get us out of here soon! I've no intention of going through with such an idiotic venture."

Perchant continued. "The second party aboard the Canari will land at the northwest edge of the island, much closer to Longwood. They will have a far more difficult passage, but the division gives us two chances for success. The group will scale these cliffs and make their way over mountains to the rendezvous, which should take place at midnight on the eighteenth of February.

"Disguised as British soldiers, we will approach garrison grounds from the North. If sentries are encountered, they will be replaced as long as at least ten of our company remain to reach a small house known as The Briars. This was the place where Bonaparte was first incarcerated for two months after he arrived on the island.

"At 0100, half the unit at The Briars will move under cover towards farm buildings. Once inside the main house, they will secure the emperor and escort him back to Lots Wife for a second rendezvous. The other men will move to the governor's house, slip inside, and ensure this man never again conducts ruthless persecution.

"All parties will rejoin at the rendezvous site by 0300 to begin retracing their path to the northwest landing location. During the previous day, Alouette will sail up to the Canari so both ships will await our escape. This way, any pursuit will not know which ship holds the Emperor. From the Island, we shall proceed southward, round the Cape and head to the Far East. It's likely the Emperor will choose to spend the remainder of his exile living in China.

Charles groaned. "Another decoy plan. I can guess who will be stationed onboard the ship without the Emperor."

LeClair glanced around the room. "Are there questions on this phase of operation?"

Another voice came forth. "Are we likely to encounter British frigates at sea once the job is done?"

"Our schooners are fast and small in size which should help evade detection. When news leaks out of Bonaparte's escape, a major naval search will surely begin. By then, we should be close enough to India and within reach of China. Once we reach Canton, there should be no difficulty blending in with merchant traffic."

William's patience was wearing thin. Fouche or no Fouche he wanted out of the hair-brained scheme. "Hold on, Charles and I cannot be a part of such protracted operation."

LeClair glanced at Hibou. The leader rose, scowling at William. "Once we've cleared the Cape of Good Hope, we will put you ashore and you can return to Capetown. From there, it should be possible to secure passage back to your beloved England and we shall never meet again."

Side discussions broke out among onlookers.

Hibou nodded at LeClair and Perchant. "We're done here for now. Tomorrow, I suggest you all return here and begin packing supplies and uniforms for the trip to Marseilles. Good night to you."

The assembly shuffled out.

Charles turned to William. "We have a week to make the trip to Marseilles. Let's hope Fouche stops the mission before we have to board those ships."

William nodded. "We're not exactly prisoners, but I haven't convinced anyone we support the society's cause. They never leave us alone, and we can't leave the building. We might overpower the doorman, but escape would prevent us from fulfilling our obligation.

"I'm also reluctant to leave the group because a murder suspect could be a member of the Societie de Le Nid. At least four of it's members were present at our ball, Lady Carlisle, Louisa and Arthur Hurst, and Thomas Reynolds."

"You think your servant, Reynolds killed Louisa?"

"He might have seen the pendant and feared a member of their gang would be recognized."

"Hardly a motive for murder."

***

The next morning, a burly guard named Raymond escorted the English pair across town to purchase canvas wagon covers for the trip. During their errand, Raymond revealed himself as Fouche's agent and suggested their venture include a report to the Ministre du Espionage. William also requested a brief stop at the Ministre des Etrangeries.

At the latter institution, William located Josette Reme and gave her a letter addressed to Elizabeth while Charles occupied the French agent with a glass of wine at a nearby brasserie. Raymond did not object to the letter once assured it posed no threat to their covert activity.

Fouche's encounter did not go well. The Minister refused their request to break off before the mission got underway. Fouche did not yet have sufficient evidence to tie Le Nid to the American kidnapping and would not intervene to stop the rescue of the former emperor. The Society's new plan did not pose a threat to the regime of Louis XVIII. If Napoleon chose to spend the rest of his life in China, so be it. Such exile would not permit a return to France within the diminishing time left to His Majesty. The attack would be a crime perpetrated against an English garrision. Fouche would hardly try to prevent an incident embarrassing to the British navy if it proved they were unable to hold their former leader.

Of course, if the death of governor Lowe could be tied to a French conspiracy, consequences might be entirely different. The British would certainly insist on eliminating a faction capable of rescuing Bonaparte as a danger to civilized society. It would also be difficult to prevent further foreign meddling in French politics and perhaps its economy with sanctions imposed by the country's trading partners.

Thus pressured, a fragile French government might collapse; creating further disarray, possibly conducive to Bonaparte's return to power. It was an odd situation. The danger of Napoleon's escape was not from his political plans, but rather from Parliament's reaction to an attempt to rescue the man. Such reaction might result in his return from exile, exactly what England wanted to prevent.

Consequently, William and Charles received no indication they would be relieved of their obligation to continue spying any time soon. William considered sending a message to Michael Gravis to ensure a trap was set on Saint Helena, assuming there was enough time to send British ships to the South Atlantic. However, he hesitated, knowing it would probably be the end of both he and Charles, sunk by a British frigate or killed by a soldier's bullet at the British garrison. Resigned to the perilous undertaking, they left the Ministre for their temporary quarters.

The novice spies spent the next day helping others pack for the journey to Marseilles. Raymond was nowhere in sight. When they asked Hibou, his only comment was that he left the operation and would not be on board at the time of their departure.

Prior to the following sunrise, the squadron moved out. William and Charles rode with two members in the third wagon, which carried food, medicine, uniforms and guns.

Weather turned fowl, worse than usual for the time of year in southern France. Wind blew icily and rain fell much of the time, making progress slow over muddy roads. The Englishmen longed for the warmth of their Manors, wondering how their wives would spend Christmas without them. Elizabeth's parents usually visited their once proud estate together with younger sister, Victoria. Emily would invite Charles' sister, Madeline and neighbors for a celebration. A glass of warm ale would have been welcome as the gang persevered into a driving downpour.

After four days, the column arrived in Marseilles. Morning fog replaced the rain, while sounds of horses hooves on cobbles echoed off waterfront buildings. Smell of tide became strong in air which stung their cheeks.

Wagons pulled up at docks in sight of the two schooners swaying on an ashen sea below a slate-colored sky. Men climbed out of their wagons, buttoning pea jackets against damp, edgy weather. They found no other shoremen at the dockside, only a rhythmic sound of waves slapping against a decaying pier and seagulls mewing in the air.

"You two up front, come help unload," A tall member called from the back of their cart.

They began carrying crates onto the ships.

"I don't think I can go through with this," Charles said softly. "Let's just get out of here and go home."

William frowned. "If we fail to meet our obligation, Fouche will send agents after us, even to Surrey."

"He didn't uphold his part of the bargain."

"If we do nothing, our troops will die on Saint Helena," William countered. "Do you really want them to succeed?"

"I suppose not," Charles replied, shuddering at waves churning out in the bay. In the distance, a string of barges bobbed up and down, fighting the swells.

"Besides, a holiday in the nice warm tropics might do us good."

Charles looked dubious. "No one will return alive. Better to leave now than die on a foolish expedition!"

William remained calm. " Le Nid will not be put to flight. If we go along, we can eliminate of most of its members which may include Louisa's murderer."

Charles looked incredulously. "You see us coming back from this mess?"

William lifted a box into an open maw of the ship's hold.

"Don't give up hope. Perhaps in Jamestown, we can seek asylum once our role has been played. Or maybe, Elizabeth and Emily will figure out our destination and tell Gravis. Troops of the garrison could be alerted to our presence among the assault force and avoid their killing us outright."

"A pleasant thought," he responded sarcastically.

# CHAPTER TWELVE

Two schooners slipped quietly out of the port of Marseilles.

William stood next to the helmsman posing as owner of the Alouette while Charles ostensibly directed the Canari. William's ship carried ten society members, including Hibou, all uniform disguises and weapons. They had begun their four thousand mile voyage on a course for Saint James Bay. Charles and twenty-one team constituents were charted for anchor on the north side of the island.

Under good wind, the vessels traversed eight hundred miles southwest to the Straits of Gibraltar without incident. They had no trouble leaving the Mediterranean and subsequently, picked up a westward trade current toward the middle Atlantic. Passengers appreciated increasingly warm weather as the ships gradually freed themselves from winter's grip.

For two weeks, the two transports sailed southward, paralleling the African coastline at an average speed of ten knots. As brown smudged sky over the Sahara gave way to lush growth and afternoon storm clouds, progress slowed. At Port Guinea they took on food and fresh water. Shortly thereafter, they entered the Doldrums near the Equator where all wind ceased.

For two days, the ships floated listlessly under a warm tropical sun.

Marauders and seamen kept themselves occupied playing games and singing songs. A piper played, which led to spontaneous dancing, and society members joined in. By mid-day, heat drove everyone into the water seeking relief. The Canari pulled to within one hundred feet of the Alouette. William shouted a few words to Charles across the gulf between them.

On the second day, inactivity became intolerable to William.

Exasperated, he approached his Captain at the helm. "Will we still make landing at James Bay on the sixteenth of February?"

The sailor smiled, staring at the horizon. "Wind should pick up within a day or two. It always comes eventually. We're better off now than in three months when storm season begins."

William remembered that temperature differences between land and water usually produced daily breezes near shore. "Wouldn't we be better off tacking closer to the coast?"

He shook his head. "We need the stronger wind out here, and shorelines can be treacherous. We're due west of the mouth of the Congo. Riverboats sometimes venture out, and tribesmen have been known to waylay craft closer in. We're over five hundred kilometers from land, so you needn't worry. Have patience."

William left the helm. He wished Charles were onboard. Society members kept their distance from him, still distrusting his motives. He disliked being treated like an outsider and sighed with resignation, glancing up at a sagging shroud overhead.

Hibou sat with two other seamen near the bow, and William made for the small group.

"Monsieur Hibou, what will happen if we're late in arriving at the Lemoins plantation?"

Sage Hibou looked up at him. "We'll adjust the timetable accordingly before the ships separate. Suette is currently in India. He has no family, so the main house is unoccupied. Only a caretaker and workers are present at the farm."

"So you have no concern when we arrive at the island?" he said awkwardly.

"Once the Canari anchors north of the island, the clock will start ticking. We have until midnight on the second day to carry crates from Jamestown to the Lemoins property, unpack the weapons and uniforms, and rendezvous at night with the others."

William looked dubious. "But we could be stalled here for some time."

"The only consequence would be if word got out and a pursuit were on the way. Once we get close to the island, if no frigates are sighted, our mission won't be stopped."

He heard an edge to Hibou's voice, but wanted to continue the conversation. "Do you think men aboard the Canari will have trouble scaling the mountain formations?"

The leader watched William shuffle uncomfortably.

"We're all in excellent condition. Your friend Charles can testify to it from his march in America. In less than one week, we hiked three-hundred kilometers through all sorts of terrain. I'm confident this climb will be less of a challenge."

William sat next to the Frenchman with a smile. "Are all of your Society such able-bodied men?"

He leaned back and laughed. "We have a number of Englishmen among us, old men and women. Don't you remember Thomas Reynolds and Lady Carlisle?"

Pausing, he looked squarely into William's eyes. "But of course, you're still trying to find the killer of Louisa Hurst. We, too, would like to know the identity of this culprit. Let me assure you the society of Le Nid condemns this murder of one of our dear constituents."

William gazed out at a dark blue horizon. "I've heard such declarations before. If I'm to believe them all, no one in my house could have done in poor Louisa."

Hibou put a hand on his shoulder and lowered his voice. "Our group does have enemies, monsieur. Loyalty to Bonaparte is founded on his democratic principles. The *Code Civile* provides freedom we thought won by the revolution. Those supporting the monarchy oppose such forward thinking. These politicians are not necessarily militant, but there is one group of fanatics which wouldn't hesitate to use violence against us. They call themselves Ultraroyalists."

William straightened. "Is this faction much of a threat?"

A worried look crossed the Frenchman's face. "*Mon Dieu, oui.* Many are wealthy landowners who have a high stake in preserving their position within the regime. With vast holdings, these gentlemen have the power to eliminate any opposition. Adversaries have died trying to limit their influence over King Louis. You have such men in your country. I have observed that gentlemen of great wealth such as William Crullage have a bond of conservatism. Perhaps among your friends there are some who have ties to the Ultraroyalists."

William jerked his head up. "Crullage? William Crullage? By a strange coincidence, his son, Jack is a friend of Victoria, my wife's sister. If I remember correctly, he attended our ball the night of Louisa's death. You think he might have a connection with the Ultraroyalists?"

Hibou pursed his lips. "I only know of the gentleman. You may have more insight than I. Gentlemen with large resources generally cross paths in the world of commerce.

William nodded. "You may have given me some help there."

During the remainder of the afternoon, William mentally reviewed a list of business acquaintances who might be thought to favor Ultraroyalists. Crullage remained at the top of the list, although Jack was only a friend of Victoria and his politics were unknown.

By afternoon of the third day, the two ships drifted sufficiently southward to begin tacking a westerly breeze. Their yachts gained speed to everyone's satisfaction.

The next morning, a mile separated the two French ships when another vessel came into view off the starboard bow. Twin masts of a northbound ketch hove closer as the passengers watched, anxious the encounter could arouse suspicion. A flag at the stern identified it to be of Italian registry, and the vessel sailed past without slowing.

On an overcast morning, thirty-three days and three port calls after leaving Marseilles, the Island of Saint Helena finally rose on the horizon. Passengers took turns looking through a spyglass at rugged cliffs on the approaching northern edge. The yachts drew close together, sailing straight up to the rugged coastline.

Per plan, Canari dropped anchor and hovered in front of a rocky cove, one hundred yards off shore.

With a nod to the hour, Hibou and William signaled Charles, and Alouette tacked away. Soon, the second schooner drew out of sight around the cliffs, making its way south while Le Nid members aboard the Canari began loading rope and tackle into a small dingy.

Countdown to rendezvous had begun.

When the last of the attack troops ferried ashore, Charles settled back with a skeleton crew on board, pretending to be a wealthy tourist with a bent towards naturalism. Charles began sketching adeptly while scanning for birds and flora to add to his compositions.

Beneath looming overhangs, the society's detachment prepared for assault on the steep rock face. As expected, they found no sign of a British lookout due to the difficulty of making port anywhere on the island besides Saint James Bay.

When Alouette entered the harbor an hour later, rain began falling. Storms frequented the tropics at this latitude, usually lasting most of an afternoon. The downpour made transfering cargo to the docks a nightmare. One society member slipped while helping off-load crates. Instead of falling into the water, he landed on top of a small boat and broke his leg. Two boxes were lost in the sea. Their weight caused them to sink. No one volunteered to attempt their recovery in twenty feet of water. Workers were drenched by the time they had piled wares onto the pier. They sloshed up a muddy path from the wharf to find shelter in a local tavern.

William avoided the dockside melee while seeking out the harbormaster.

Not far up the main street, he found a two story stone building with green shuttered windows displaying colors of the Union Jack. Inside, he was shown to a damp, musty room occupied by a uniformed officer seated behind a weathered desk. The British Colonel rose and informed William that he had replaced the East India Company clerk when Napoleon arrived. William repeated his cover story which did not seem to create any particular interest. Once names, registration, destinations were provided, fees were paid and William left the building to direct his subjects for the inland trek. The deluge made it impossible to proceed until the torrent passed, so he looked for the men at the tavern.

When William entered, Hibou waved him over to his table amidst a boisterous crowd.

"William, I must speak with you. We're now a man short. The trail from here to Longwood isn't difficult, but there's no telling what surprises may lay ahead. If you help us complete our portage to the Lemoins farm, we'll have a better chance of making up this weather delay."

Unease swept over William. "But, it was agreed I would take the Alouette around to the other side of the island and wait with Charles for your escape."

"I've already sent our ship away," the Frenchman said unequivocally.

William swallowed hard. "What? I will not fight my countrymen for this despot."

"That won't be necessary," Hibou reassured. "From the rendezvous, you can proceed directly to Ass's Ear and wait for our party. After we've completed the mission, we'll meet you there and return to the boats together."

William suddenly found his legs weak with a rush of panic welling up. Hibou had left him stranded. His only way home now lay at the North end of the island. In the back of his mind, he had considered getting a message to the harbormaster to tip off the red-coats an assault was underway. That would be suicidal now since the militia would know he was the culprit who brought Le Nid here. He had to go along with the plan. What else could he do?

"Well, I guess you have me then. I just hope we can pull it off."

The operation did not go well on the North side of the island.

Charles watched French repellers climb a two hundred meter cliff in driving rain. Paying no attention to the wet, he monitored the effort through a telescope. Through drifting moisture, progress appeared imperceptible. Two of the climbers finally made it to a ridge, but a third slipped and plummeted twenty meters to rocks below. Charles could only shake his head in dismay.

Anxiety further increased when the Alouette arrived without William. From a boat separation of twenty feet, the captain related the accident and explained his friend would return with the rest of the soldiers once Napoleon was rescued.

After an hour, rain finally lessened, but the pace did not improve. Despite the climber's excellent physical condition, Charles sensed tentativeness in maneuvering over the slippery formations. By darkness, he could make out a hastily assembled camp near the top of the cliff. He sighed. Those poor men endured the most harrowing ascent of their lives and within twenty-four hours, they would face a still greater test of courage. He could not imagine how the return descent would be accomplished with William and the aging leader in their custody.

Already, William had enough of the tropics.

Rain left everything dripping, steamy, and muddy. His clothes wrapped about the skin like a wet towel. Ten men slogged their way up the trail, pushing through glistening leaves above soggy ground and steamy puddles. Insects buzzed at William face while his hands were pined under a seventy-pound crate carried with another member stepping behind him. He saw no other residents along the path. Occasionally small huts could be seen among lush tropical plants, but they showed no signs of life within the misty jungle.

Eventually, the path widened and ground became level. Vegetation thinned and a mixture of rocks made footing easier. They had reached the plains.

Gloomy twilight greeted the company's arrival at the Lemoins plantation.

Once they entered the main house and unpacked their burdens, many sagged to the floor, too tired to move and fell asleep in their tracks. Hibou looked at the array, his face lined with weariness, and managed only a thin smile of satisfaction, this phase was behind them.

William slumped into a corner of the room and struggled to remove his boots. Air hung thick with oppressive humidity. Strange echoes of nocturnal wildlife grew with intensity, but he no longer cared about his surroundings. His only ambition was a restful sleep to relieve aching in arms and legs. The cadre slept soundly until dawn.

Early morning, a plantation foreman named Jean du Lac came into the room.

After a brief discussion with Hibou, Jean du Lac directed the crew to begin unpacking crates.

They unfolded uniforms ready to don at the rendezvous site at midnight. Despite a predicted full moon, the exchange might be troublesome. Members tied swords and muskets together and sheathed them in cloth covers. The foreman seemed to understand the mission while overseeing the work. Jean du Lac informed the associates that slaves would have nothing to do with the activity, fearing British reprisals. Their lot had improved over the past twenty years and they weren't about to risk losing hard-won freedoms.

Once packages were ready for transport, the men were given time to themselves until sunset when they would set out to cover the remaining five miles to the meeting at Lot's Wife. William noticed a small library within one of the farmhouse's well-appointed rooms. While the others meandered outside, he perused the shelves looking for something interesting to pass the time. A thin calf bound volume caught his eye. The title stamped in gold letters looked vaguely familiar: Old English Baron. He pulled the book and opened it to the title page.

It said: The Old English Baron: a gothic novel by Clara Reeve, fifth edition, London, 1794.

William frowned.

In the upper right corner of the page, he spied a handwritten inscription. His jaw dropped. There was no mistaking the scrawled words.

*Louisa:*
*Thank you for your service at Rosewell Park.*
*Lady Carlisle*

For a long moment, he stared at the letters feeling confused. Had Louisa come to this remote island thousands of miles from England? The inscription obviously referred to actions during the war, but how did her copy get here prior to Bonaparte's exile? It was an unlikely destination unless one was on his way to the Orient. Surely the Hursts would have mentioned such a large undertaking. Perhaps, she actually came here to scout a possible rescue of the Emperor, but it could only have happened during the year prior to her death while Napoleon was present on the island. But that did not make sense either because William recalled her presence at a number of social gatherings during the time, precluding any protracted absence from the British Isles. No, the book must have been carried here by someone else. Of course, the Lemoins farm could be a logical place to find such evidence, a known hideout for French conspirators. Perhaps Louisa gave it to a friend such as Count de Las Cases who subsequently left it here for others to enjoy during their visits.

William settled into a soft chair by a window and began thumbing through the text. The distraction soothed his discomfort and a quiet house soon had him dozing once more.

Sounds of tramping boots at the front entrance brought him back to consciousness. Late afternoon's golden light indicated time was drawing near for their departure. He rose and joined others who had assembled in the living room with the Jean du Lac to partake their final meal.

As he munched a breadfruit, William suddenly felt alone. The enormity of an assault on a garrison staffed with hundreds of armed, experienced regulars overwhelmed him. He would never see Elizabeth again. He could not even remember the last words they exchanged many months ago. If by some miracle, he survived, there would be no leaving Kent ever again, and the Louisa's killer, whoever he was, could go to blazes.

Hibou stood up.

"My fellow freedom fighters, it is time to take up arms and rescue our leader. We shall persevere on this quest, regardless of risk, so France will again see its benefactor free, unfettered by English military. The sun has set, it's time to begin our path to victory."

The squadron climbed to its feet and retrieved their packages. They lined up at the front door, waiting to step outside when a knock burst forth. A deep voice bellowed from the other side with an order to come out in the name of His Majesty. The men froze, looking at each other for advice.

Jean du Lac motioned for silence. He parted the door slightly, then slipped outside to confront the visitors.

A few minutes later, he came back in.

“They're soldiers from the garrison looking for the daughter of one of the governor’s aides. Apparently, she wandered off while the women were returning from town. There's nearly a full regiment out there, so I suggest you all stay inside for a while.”

An hour passed.

William could see torches blinking in the distance, moving through the trees, illuminating their carriers. The members waited quietly without conversation. Time passed slowly at first, until it became clear time was running out. William dared hope the plan might be abandoned.

Hibou motioned for the men to gather around him.

“It’s nearly 2300 hours. The only way for us to make the rendezvous is to put on these uniforms and pretend to join the search. I want each man to carry an extra uniform, two swords, and a musket. The rest of the equipment will be left behind. When we slip outside, do not stay together. You all know the rendezvous location; so each of you is on your own to reach the site in an inconspicuous fashion. Let’s go.”

William had no trouble leaving the plantation in darkness. This development was a Godsend. He could walk slowly to their post-abduction meeting place and avoid all threat from garrison troops.

He made his way across fields and glens nearly three miles in the direction of Ass's Ears. It was nearly midnight. He presumed by now the others had met up at Lots Wife and the assault force was proceeding towards the Longwood farm.

As he trudged on, wooded areas between clearings appeared spooky under ghostly moonlight. Were there animals on the island? He might step on a snake or stumble into the web of the infamous tarantula without warning in the blackness. Even within clearings, rock formations were nearly impossible to make out. He could wander out here until dawn and still not find the correct location. By then Le Nid would be long gone, either off the island or dead. William tried to remember Hibou's map.

At 1:00 AM, he was certain he had finally found the designated spot, but no one was present. He had no idea how long the assault would take, eventually he would make for the cliffs whether or not the rest of the men showed up.

A distant shot rang out. Seconds later another, then two more.

William gulped.

The plot was unraveling. Sounds of commotion were becoming louder. In terror, he heard shouts beyond the trees. Dark foliage rustled and crackled behind him. Were they Le Nid or garrison troops?

He decided not to wait and find out.

He started running toward the cliffs. Tripping, bouncing off tree trunks, fumbling through undergrowth, he fought against slapping branches until emerging onto an open field of tall grasses. Gasping for breath, he removed his heavy backpack, including the uniform no longer needed. As he discarded the last piece, British regulars appeared on the opposite side of his clearing. Twenty men with muskets drawn stepped stealthily into the open area fifty paces in front of him.

William hesitated. Did they see him? Would they ask what he was doing here or just shoot to kill?

In the distance, more reports resonated.

Most of the approaching formation halted. They turned and charged off to his right disappearing into the brush.

He stood still, exposed and bound to be noticed within an instant. All at once, he turned and lunged toward the shelter of the trees. A much louder shot rang out. William cried out at a searing sensation in his right leg. He grimaced, hobbling towards undergrowth ten feet away. He threw himself into the foliage and ran headlong into a tree.

***

William awoke heavy headed, unsure how he had got to the foot of a large tree. His thigh burned and his head throbbed. He sensed the silence. No sounds of gunfire nor approaching troops, only gentle rustling sounds of leaves overhead. All perfectly quiet!

He struggled to his feet.

A bright moon had moved much further to the west. He must have been unconscious for hours. A dread rose. Was it too late to catch the ships? He started to limp towards the cliffs. His footfalls made loud crunching sounds as he threaded his way through ferns and low broadleaf bushes. Ahead, another clearing stood out brightly lit beyond tree trunks' eerie shadows. He set his teeth. There was no choice but to keep going toward the cove. Taking a deep breath, he stepped forcefully into the clearing, but stayed close to the edge where light permitted a safe passage.

Two hours later, he arrived at a low mountain ridge. To his right, the sky brightened in anticipation of an approaching sunrise.

On the opposite face, a hillside sloped downward fifty feet before abruptly ending at the top of a cliff towering above a dark, distant sea. Half dragging the wounded leg, he stumbled down the incline to the edge of the precipice. He squinted in the half-light, searching for boats. The time of escape had passed and those who survived were on the ships by now. He had been left behind.

He started walking parallel to the precipice. He would have to explain his presence in Jamestown. How long before guards tracked the assault to him? If they took any prisoners, it would not be for long.

He rounded a pile of stones. Three hundred yards further along a dimly lit shore far below, he spotted two tiny dots. His heart raced. He ran to the edge.

William clenched his fists and started down, pressing his body against the rock face, gingerly probing for footholds.

Sun peered above the horizon by the time bleeding fingers clutched the edge of a rock formation a hundred yards above the water immediately opposite the Canari. Behind it, the Alouette floated peacefully. There was no sign of French or English troops. He frowned. Where is everyone? Squinting, he could just make out a figure onboard the nearest ship. Was Charles still waiting for our return?

He wasted no time.

Soon, gunboats would arrive from the harbor. A general search was bound to begin with daybreak. The problem was how to scale down the last three-hundred foot crag.

He found a rope left by earlier climbers. It appeared to be securely tied to a large outcrop. William wrapped a segment around his wrist and began lowering himself down the stony overhang. Waves crashed below. Rope slid over his hands burning the back of his wrists, while his boots scraped against the rocks trying to find footholds to slow his descent.

When he descended to fifty feet above shore, he heard a shout from Charles. He looked over his shoulder and saw him pointing overhead. On the cliff above, a cluster of British infantrymen stood. They were not Frenchmen in disguise, their rifles aimed directly at him.

A musket ball shattered rocks ten-feet overhead. Fine particles tore his face.

The last fifty-foot climb became a blur. He let go of the rope and plunged into water below. He swam for the Canari, hearing Charles rouse the crewmen. They helped him onboard after a record-breaking swim in cold morning water.

"The plan's blown! We must leave at once!" William sputtered unnecessarily.

The ship was already coming about.

Charles hugged his companion. "What happened? Where are the others?"

William held his sides, panting. "We were delayed. We got separated. I waited at the rendezvous until gunfire broke out. The whole garrison must have been awakened. I couldn't get to any of the other sites. A squadron of Regulars found me. I ran, but hit a tree and was knocked unconscious. When I recovered, there was no one left. The island seemed deserted."

"Well, it's not empty anymore!"

A British warship came into view around the western peninsula.

With a loud thump, it began firing at the Alouette between them. They had a moment to escape before they were detected.

The little ship passed behind a sheltering outcropping and sped towards open waters to the east. With good wind, the island shrank quickly. No other frigate appeared on their southeastern course.

Days passed without sign of pursuit. Land was again sighted when the Canari neared Cape Town.

"We should scuttle the ship and try to find passage in port," William announced staring at the settlement.

No one on board wanted to encounter another warship. After approaching to five hundred yards off shore, five miles north of the port city, the crew cut holes in the hull and they crowded onto a small dingy to carry them ashore.

"It's a shame to see such a fine vessel go under," Charles remarked as they neared the coast.

"That may be true," said William. "But I'd rather not be reminded of how close we came to losing everything. We should set our sights on an inconspicuous vessel to get back home."

William sighed. Home! A wonderful thought. No Frenchmen. No Americans. Just a peaceful life in Kent. He had almost forgotten why they were thrust into peril as they began a long walk toward Cape Town.

# CHAPTER THIRTEEN

Elizabeth tapped her foot..

"Mr. Gravis, why weren't we informed of the existence of the society of The Nest?"

The agent smiled thinly. "Madam, we were uncertain of your connection with their organization. Members resided within your house who mught well have been responsible for Madam Hurst's death. For all we knew, you did the killing yourself. Once you informed us of the takeover and Lady Carlisle's role in the kidnapping, it became clear you were not part of the operation."

"Is there an explanation for the articles left at her house," Emily asked. "Why were there so many pendants?"

Gravis settled back at his desk. "We believe the Society prepared a refuge for Bonaparte when he surrendered three years ago. Once the Emperor was escorted to Plymouth, Count Las Cases sent word to Lady Carlisle to set up living quarters. Rosewell Park was already under surveillance by British agents, so he must have thought it would be safer at Mayfair Hall. They enlisted Manservant Thomas Reynolds to attend to the leader.

"Within a week, however, nothing came of it. Napoleon's request for asylum was denied, and Admiral Cockburn shipped him out on the *Northumberland*, headed for Saint Helena. The Society was devastated. Determined to force his release, they hatched the kidnapping scheme. According to the Americans, they took the Vice President hostage in order to demand exile for Napoleon in America, but President Monroe refused. Instead, public turmoil nearly caused another confrontation with our former colonies. Fortunately, Hayes sabotaged their operation at your residence. I'm sorry for the damage that resulted."

Elizabeth frowned. "What became of the rest of them, and where are my servants?”

“Most of the Le Nid have returned to France. This letter from William implies another attempt is underway to gain Bonaparte’s release. I contacted Fouche, but he had little to add. Three agents infiltrated the organization counting your husbands. Unfortunately, the body of the other spy turned up floating in the Seine. We shall have to wait to see where Le Nid surfaces next.

“As to your servants, my man Peter tracked them to a Hotel at the address on this card. They were given rooms paid up for a month. I suggest you tell them their holiday is over, and begin the process of restoring your manor.”

“But what of Lady Carlisle?” Emily inquired. “Is she a part of this new mission? William seemed to think she is still in country.”

He shook his head. “As near as we can tell, the Lady has gone into hiding once again. The strain of past events, together with the destruction of Mayfair Hall may have convinced her membership in the Society isn't worth the price. All Montclair ships are accounted for and have been pressed into His Majesty’s service.”

“And what of my sister-in-law’s death?” Emily inquired. “Have you any further speculation?”

“We do have a theory. One of the Society’s rivals is a French faction called the Ultraroyalists. It’s an organization bent upon keeping the French monarchy in place. Many of its members are powerful and ruthless, having succeeded under their deceitful king.”

Elizabeth scowled. “Why would they bother with poor Louisa?”

Gravis shrugged. “Maybe they thought it would prevent Le Nid’s schemes for a favorable Bonaparte exile.”

“And send a killer to my house in Kent? It doesn’t seem very likely,” she countered.

The agent closed his eyes in thought. After a moment, he began pacing the floor. “Some of their strongest constituents live over here. Most Ultraroyalists are wealthy merchants who think revolutionary liberals are bad for business.”

Emily rubbed her chin. “But surely we would have known if one of their kind attended the Darmon’s ball.”

He looked at her curiously. “Recently, we've learned William Crullage is providing money for their cause.”

“William Crullage? Jack’s father?” Elizabeth exclaimed. “Jack did accompany Victoria to our anniversary party. I don't know if they're still friends, but maybe she knows whether he shares his father’s views.”

Gravis nodded. “It might be worth your time. The War Ministry usually doesn't investigate murders unless they're tied to a national threat. If you learn anything further, it could be helpful to Palace Yard.”

The two women thanked Gravis and departed.

In their carriage, Emily turned to Elizabeth. “I thought Victoria and stopped seeing Jack months ago.”

Elizabeth sighed. “She told me he went abroad to tend to his father’s business in India.”

“I guess that leaves us with William Crullage, himself.” Emily offered looking out the carriage window.

Elizabeth watched her sister closely. “It might be worth an interview to see if he’s even heard of the Hursts.”

Emily turned back with glimmer of enthusiasm. “I've heard the old gentleman lives in a castle by coastal cliffs in Northumberland.”

“They say he's quite the recluse, despite his tremendous wealth,” Elizabeth answered with a grin. “Time to pay him a visit.”

They squeezed each other’s hands, welcoming an opportunity to continue the investigation, now, nearly a year in progress.

A cold, gray morning with blustery air greeted the sisters as they set out for a day’s journey to Crullage Castle. The road to the northeast coast of the British Isle wound among fields and low hills in an unpopulated countryside as they crossed from Bagwell Manor in Surrey. Their transport made good speed until noon when it started to rain. Outside dripping, rattling windows, gloomy weather pushed curtains of downpour across long grasses and farmhouses. Their horse steadfastly pulled over muddy lanes which often slowed passage to the pace of a slow walk.

At four o'clock, the carriage finally passed through a large iron gate and started a long approach to an ancient castle under fading skylight. The private road meandered its way toward shore and soon they found themselves on a narrow path bordering spectacular cliffs several hundred feet above a rocky shore.

The stronghold's irregular silhouette enlarged with each turn of the vehicle's traverse up the passageway. Emily shuddered at its ominous appearance in front of the darkening sky. She felt herself being drawn to a sleeping monster waiting to devour unsuspecting visitors. Howling wind battered their compartment making concentration difficult while she tried to remember the history of this decaying eight hundred year old limestone structure, once a symbol of strength, now a relic of antiquity.

The Crullage family had lived in the castle continuously from the year 1653 when Oliver Cromwell granted the property for settlement of debts incurred on the government's behalf. Because of its isolated location, occupants were able to live for generations without threat of confrontation with other landlords. Grounds had been declared forfeit years earlier by an act of Parliament for a reason she could not recall. Now last of the line, Jack would probably abandon the estate he stood to inherit. Only his father and a few servants currently remained within the forty-room mansion.

At last, the carriage swung onto an avenue of lime trees in a final approach to a large Gothic archway. Ahead, the castle stood completely dark, no light appeared in any of its many windows.

A moment later, their conveyance halted.

The ladies pulled their coats tight about the neck before stepping out into a sharp wind. Cold drops immediately began soaking their garments as the driver helped them out of the transport.

They walked towards the entrance. Behind them the driver urged his horse to the shelter of a blowing willow tree. Elizabeth glanced up at turrets barely visible until a flash of lightning shattered darkness.

Feeling vulnerable, she bade the footman to join their position at the front entrance.

Repeated bangs on the massive door brought no response. Even the driver could not get an answer. The trio stood for a moment in cold, dark wet, wondering what to do. They needed shelter or face a precarious journey back down the dangerously narrow road without light.

Elizabeth sent the servant to search the perimeter.

A short time later, he emerged from drenching blackness and reported he had forced open a delivery entrance. Soon, soggy visitors found themselves in a spacious kitchen, dripping puddles of water on a stone floor while the servant fumbled to get a lamp lit.

"Look, I've found two more lights," Emily announced in front of an open cupboard. With three lamps shining, the room seemed less foreboding.

"Let's take a look around," Elizabeth said, picking up a lamp. "Wait here driver. We'll call if we need you."

Elizabeth pushed a door open into a dark hallway.

They called for Mr. Crullage, but heard only eerie silence broken by claps of distant thunder outside. Above the passageway, a series of undersized windows flashed brightly, providing glimpses of a second door fifty feet down the hallway. Buffeting panes strained at the tempest outside, echoing rapid sounds of splattering droplets.

"Maybe we should spend the night in the kitchen with the driver," Emily suggested with a quiver in her voice.

Elizabeth glanced at her sister's worried face. "It might be wise, but not helpful."

She slowly opened the door to a long room furnished with gaming tables, stuffed chairs, ornately carved end tables and statuary. Holding up her lamp, Emily pointed to a painting of Louis XVIII. "Look, Lizzy, isn't it unusual to find such a picture in the home of an English gentleman?"

Elizabeth shrugged. "Maybe, c'mon let's keep going. There's another chamber at the other end."

A small table in the next room held a stack of newspaper

clippings, some dating back to the French revolution. Still, it wasn't evidence of a conspiracy, so they quietly stepped out into another hallway with a stairway at the end, leading upwards.

At the top of the stairs, they paused, hearing puffs of their own heavy breathing.

Fading thunder booms echoed through the castle.

From the landing, an upstairs passageway led past a number of closed doors back in the direction of the kitchen. Elizabeth noticed a dim flickering light under the third doorway. They looked at each other wide-eyed.

A faint, crackling sound grew in the darkness ahead as they cautiously crept forward toward the shaft of light. Popping noises came from behind the portal.

Emily knocked softly. "Mr. Crullage."

She slowly turned the handle and pressed the door open. A fireplace came into view holding a dying fire with sputtering light dancing through the room.

"Someone had to have been here to start it," Emily whispered.

They tip-toed inside.

"Emily, the bed!"

Elizabeth's hoarsely spoken words made Emily jump. She nearly dropped her lamp and swung it around towards an outsized canopy.

On the mattress, a buldge lay perfectly still under a blanket.

Their lamps approached, revealing the face of an elderly man. A dark stain soiled blankets at the man's mid section.

Emily touched the withered face, cold as ice.

"William Crullage," Elizabeth observed, trying to remain steady as she drew back the sheet to expose a ten-inch bloodstain. "Looks like he's peacefully asleep, probably never saw his attacker."

"How long do you suppose he's been dead?" Emily asked.

Elizabeth felt the wound. "The stain is cold. Could be hours, but the fire suggests less than two. We must report this to the police at first light."

Emily swallowed shakily. "It gives me the creeps being in a house where a murder's been committed."

"Thank you," Elizabeth remarked sarcastically, recalling events at Mayfair Hall.

"But, what if the killer is still in the castle?" Emily asked.

Her sister covered the body, and they returned to the passageway.

Once outside the bedroom, Elizabeth took her sister's arm. "We can sleep downstairs with the driver."

Tensely alert to every sound, they quietly hurried down the steps and back through the hallway. Emily pushed open the kitchen door and discovered the driver slumped over a table.

Elizabeth raised his head. "He's unconscious. The large bruise on his forehead suggests he turned to face his attacker just as the blow was struck."

Emily anxiously glanced around the room for a clue to the culprit. Everything seemed in order. "Lizzy, we have to get out of here before he catches us."

Elizabeth shook the servant's shoulders, but he remained lifeless. "Do you think we'd be any safer outside in the carriage?"

"My God, I'm not staying here," Emily blurted on the verge of hysteria.

"Blow out your lamp. We'll hide in the corner of another room. Maybe he's already gone," Elizabeth reassured.

Lightning flashes sent brief images of the hallway they retraced to the gaming room. Nervously, they felt their way inside. Elizabeth locked the door behind her and pulled Emily's arm towards a corner. "Let's sit over there."

Crouched against the wall, they stared out at darkness.

Elizabeth could feel Emily's body tremble, holding each other, waiting. Her sister felt like a wounded bird. Every creak inside the castle made them jump. Where was the stalker now?

The room was not completely dark. High above the floor, five narrow windows provided bursts of light whenever distant lightning struck. Beneath dark wooden beams, the glow created menacing shadows which instantly disappeared until the next flash.

Time slowly passed.

"Maybe we should lock ourselves in a closet somewhere," Emily whispered.

Elizabeth paused. “We'd be just as vulnerable with no means of getting away from a madman.”

“If only we had a weapon," Emily lamented.

Elizabeth shook her head. “Our best hope is not to be discovered. I doubt we possess enough strength to overcome a determined attacker.”

“But he must know the driver wasn’t alone with all the shouting we did.”

“All the more reason not to make any sound,” Elizabeth cautioned.

They paused in silence.

A half hour elapsed. Emily no longer shook.

Did she fall asleep exhausted from fright? Elizabeth wondered.

The wait was excruciating for Elizabeth.

A large stone fireplace under the antlered head of a stag stood majestically at the far side of the room. She decided to edge over to the hearth and look for a tool or piece of wood that could be used against the blackguard. She willed her muscles to move without success. Emily lay against her, making movement difficult. Elizabeth heaved the burden off and propped her sister against the other corner wall.

On hands and knees, she slowly advanced along the room’s perimeter trying not to make noise. Fifteen feet, ten feet, five.., she felt bricks. She reached out for a poker, but had to settle for a two-foot log, three inches in diameter. Clutching her prize, she turned to start back. A new creak punctured the air from the middle of the room.

She froze.

Several tall English chairs and Queen Anne upholstered seats rested between game tables, turned at various angles to her sight. The sound came from there.

She stared at their outlines.

Lightning flashed again. To her terror, a dark form had risen above the middle seat.

Light disappeared before she could see anything more.

Elizabeth's mind raced, wondering if she had been seen.

Another flash. The figure had moved closer to Emily's corner.

"Emily! Emily!" she screamed. "Wake up. Someone's coming at you!"

She could hear Emily stirring, muttering sounds made it clear she did not understanding her plight. Should she run to help? Her legs felt weak and a rush of panic welled up inside her. Maybe, it was best if they remained separated. An attack on one could lead to help from the other.

A glint came again. The visage had stopped.

"W..W..Who are you?" Elizabeth managed to speak, trying to control a shaking voice.

There was no answer.

Light came from the other corner. Emily had struck a flint. Glow from her lamp filled the corner space. Elizabeth quickly looked at the figure.

Lady Carlisle stood holding a pistol.

"Aunt Catherine! What are doing you here?" Elizabeth shouted as if by the force of her voice she could subdue the woman. Her entire body shook uncontrollably.

"You meddlers," came a gruff reply. "This has nothing to do with you."

"Why have you done this? Why did you kill William Crullage?" Elizabeth demanded, managing to find growing strength now the threat was identified.

"You wouldn't understand you ignorant children," the woman answered with disdain. "Perhaps my actions tonight will balance the scales."

"But the American kidnapping, and Louisa Hurst?" Elizabeth protested.

Lady Carlisle met her eyes squarely. "All you care about is that petty murder. She wasn't my doing."

"But you've broken the law. Why are you acting against Britain?

"Only a person born into poverty would understand."

Out of the corner of her eye, Elizabeth saw Emily climb to her feet. With Lady Carlisle's attention on Elizabeth, she edged forward.

The old lady continued. "There's only one possible leader for France. Would that England were so enlightened."

Suddenly, light in the room changed as Emily threw the lamp. It crashed onto the floor in front of Lady Carlisle. Oil spattered and flame burst upward. Her dress caught fire. She thrashed at it, but the flames only increased. She ran to the door, and rushed out. Instinctively, Elizabeth and Emily followed.

The Aunt staggered through the kitchen and lunged outside into the rain. She rolled on wet grass. In the excitement, she dropped the gun. Emily retrieved it and fired into the air after reaching the doorway. Lady Carlisle jerked up. She stumbled toward the carriage and scrambled onto the driver's seat and reining the horse into motion.

The startled animal leaped forward, galloping off at a reckless speed over the narrow road. The carriage veered left, then right, then left again, as the receding horses tried to follow its path. The distant vehicle disappeared over a hillside at the edge of the cliff.

Elizabeth's fainted from exhaustion.

She regained consciousness in front of a warming fire tended by the driver. Wrapped in a blanket, she observed Emily calmly sipping tea. Elizabeth talked for a while. Before drifting once more into a troubled sleep, a thought nagged her. Did Lady Carlisle kill Crullage to 'balance the scales' for Jack's murder of Louisa?

The police found carriage wreckage at the bottom of a two-hundred foot drop, three miles from Crullage Castle. Lady Carlisle's body was not found. Presumably, she fell from the vehicle as it plunged to the rocks along the rugged coastline. Pounding waves then carried her body out to sea.

After a day's search, the matter was officially closed.

# CHAPTER FOURTEEN

William and Charles made port at London Dock on May 20, 1819. Unwashed, tired and hungry, they were very happy to have come back to their homeland. The voyage from Cape Town required four ships, the last of which proved to be a garbage scow hailed in Margate. They did all sorts of abject tasks in exchange for passage and an education in seamanship.

William purchased a *Times* with his last shilling and Charles secured a table at a waterfront tavern, intending to spend his money on a hot meal before the final leg of their journey to Surrey. News was not particularly noteworthy until William's eye spotted a small article on the bottom corner of the second page. It read,

> AUCTION! AUCTION! AUCTION! AUCTION!
> ITEMS FROM THE ESTATE OF LADY CARLISLE DU MONTCLAIR TO BE SOLD TOMORROW IN LANGDON, COUNTY OF KENT
> Possessions of Lady Carlisle du Montclair, who died in a carriage accident last month in Northumberland will be auctioned tomorrow noon at the Langdon Courthouse. Items include memorabilia from the Napoleonic Wars as well as furniture from Rosewell Park and Mayfair Hall Estates.

William slumped in his seat opposite Charles. "My God, Aunt Catherine's dead. Elizabeth is already selling off her things. Why couldn't she wait for our return? I suppose she was anxious to be rid of any reminders of Aunty's imposition. I never appreciated how much of a burden she must have been."

"I'm sorry," his friend consoled. "It does seem a bit coarse. After all, she is a blood relative."

"Knowing Elizabeth, there is a good explanation. Perhaps, she's trying to raise cash for the restoration of Mayfair."

Charles nodded. "Well, we should know the answer by the end of day. I, for one, do not wish to think about foreign intrigue, murder or sea voyages for some time."

"I wish I could share your resolve," William replied, his face pinched with regret. "Louisa's killing will haunt me until the day it's settled. To think among our friends, a lunatic came to my house and took a life is too much to bury."

"Lady Carlisle probably did it and the matter settled itself," Charles snapped. "Chasing your aunt because her actions reflect on the family is one thing, but unless she died at another killer's hand, I say we put the matter to an end."

William regarded his friend, making an effort to control himself.

"You're comfortable to let your sister's killer escape a hangman's noose?"

"I'm not. But, if after all our efforts, all the subsequent deaths and destruction, the killer remains unknown, I say let's retake our lives. We're sacrificing too much of our time to its resolution. There comes a point where the cost of dwelling on the past becomes destructive. Life must go on."

William remained thoughtful. *Maybe the man was right.* Nevertheless, when they got back, he'd offer Elizabeth a chance to visit William Crullage.

The two men ate in silence. They left for Surrey and four hours later, their arrival at the Bagwell manor was greeted with great celebration. Elizabeth's parents and Victoria were present at the house to help with the auction.

Throughout the evening, William heard family members express relief, repeating the phrase: 'It's over now'. Most suspected Lady Carlisle was behind the crime at Mayfair. They listened enthusiastically while William and Charles related their adventures abroad. Their attention also turned to events at Crullage castle.

"Do you suppose her comment of 'balancing the scales' meant she blamed the *Ultraroyalists* for *Le Nid's* failures?" William asked.

"I have no doubt," Elizabeth confirmed without hesitation. She looked around the room. Hostile faces seemed absent of sympathy for the aunt.

Charles stared at his glass. "It's a shame the old gentleman couldn't have been questioned before his death. If he had plotted an attack on the Society's radicals, maybe he's the one who hired the blackguard responsible for Louisa's murder."

"It was suggested his son, Jack might have implemented his father's wishes," William agreed, looking sharply at the youngest sister.

Victoria's brow puckered. "Hold on a minute. Jack would never kill anyone. He's as harmless as a kitten."

Elizabeth frowned in disbelief. "Do you know his politics? Is he anti-liberal like his father?"

"I've not seen him for six months, but he never showed interest in either politics or France. All he cared about was money and women. Unless his father threatened to cut off his inheritance, I wouldn't expect him to do anything for the old man. They weren't on good terms. He hardly ever went to the castle, content to live on an allowance until the father passed on."

"I thought you two were good friends." Emily remarked.

"We were once, but I didn't appreciate his wandering eye. He enjoyed moving among pillars of society, but his enthusiasm waned after the Mayfair ball."

"So where does that leave us?" William sighed, his face bleak. "The list of suspects has been narrowed by deaths of the Blacks, Arthur Hurst, my aunt, and old Crullage; although the guilt of any of the deceased has yet to be proven. The living, of course, all deny responsibility."

"There may be other members of French factions here in England," Elizabeth observed, leaning forward a little.

"It's possible the auction may bring out French sympathizers to claim the war articles," Emily commented with a measure of enthusiasm.

William looked at Elizabeth. "Indeed, why did you assemble an auction so fast? Was it to erase bad memories of her life with us?"

"Didn't I tell you? A room full of French furniture and uniforms was discovered under the Great Hall. Eight pendants were found. Those items together with old Rosewell furnishings you disliked, stored in the North building are the inventory up for auction."

He sighed. "And there's no object which could be regarded as evidence for the crimes committed?"

"Gravis reviewed the inventory. Articles belonging to Bonaparte are the only items of real value," she confirmed.

Discussion turned to news from the village of Hunsford Shire where Elizabeth's parents resided. William's thoughts drifted to Mayfair. He was eager to start rebuilding and intended to visit the site on their way to Langdon the next day. Charles seemed completely distracted. At midnight, the prodigals retreated to bed, extremely grateful for the comfort of a soft mattress.

A cold clear morning with bright sunshine gave signs of approaching spring with greening hillsides and a soft breeze on the roads of Surrey. Elizabeth and William rode to Mayfair in a separate carriage while the rest went on to Langdon.

Ruins of the Darmon estate were an ugly black scar on the countryside, out of place in the pastoral shire of Kent.

William's face became grim when they stopped at the front entrance. He shook his head at the destruction. Elizabeth tried to console him with ideas for restoration. New caretakers were already at work clearing loose rubble within the main building. The couple walked around the perimeter.

Elizabeth showed him where the French articles were found.

"It was a room I played in as a child. We used it for storage, but it was a delight to hide there. I remember during one of Aunty's visits with Uncle Lewis, she came down to retrieve me for dinner, but I hid until father put an end to it. It's strange to think the American Vice President was here. I can't imagine what chaos must have occurred the night of the fire, all because a little boy revealed this room to his aunt."

After an hour, they decided to push on to Langdon. Before they left, William spoke to the servants, suggesting tasks to prepare for replacing exterior walls of the main building.

They arrived in Langdon at mid-day.

A boisterous crowd gathered in front of the Courthouse. Across the street within a grassy park, children played and dogs ran loose in a festive atmosphere.

William recognized many in the audience, friends and acquaintances from Langdon, relatives and servants who thought a piece of history was within their grasp. There were speculators, well-kempt gentlemen who closely inspected the artifacts from Napoleon's regime. Finally, he noticed a few elderly faces, ex-soldiers, perhaps, or families who had lost sons during the war. The group numbered over two hundred persons thanks to the article in the *Times.*

Bidding began with items of little note: some vases and chairs from Rosewell Park. Lady Carlisle's major furniture pieces fetched a good sum, as many were drawn into the pace of the auction.

At last, the auctioneer turned to items retrieved from Mayfair's basement.

William edged forward to view this set of bidders, but it was not obvious whether members of the *Le Nid* were present. News had reached London of the failed Bonaparte rescue. Although the news was sketchy, it suggested annihilation of the entire assault force and further steps underway to eradicate the organization in Paris. Members had also been rounded up in London. Thomas Reynolds was among those who were not expected to be released any time soon. Who knew how many Bonaparte supporters still remained? William could not deny the Emperor's ideas appealed to the common man. One did not have to be a member of *Le Nid* to support the philosophy of individual freedom.

Each pendant went up separately.

Bidding became fast and furious when Napoleon's personal items reached the auctioneer's table. Speculators obtained prized articles at high prices. The last object was a sword displaying the former Leader's inscription, and bidding reached one thousand pounds before the contest ended.

William wondered who would pay such a sum. The gentleman who out lasted the bidding was not familiar nor well dressed. Most likely, he represented a wealthy French exile or a former personal aide to the Man himself. There was no reason to suspect him of a crime. Nevertheless, William could not contain his curiosity. He worked his way forward to mingle with buyers as they retrieved purchases and prepared to depart.

Charles stood next to the gentleman who claimed the sword while he climbed astride his mount. By the time William reached his brother-in-law, the horse trotted off.

"Charles, are you acquainted with that gentleman?"

"Name's Harry McGregor. My sister's servant for several years, but since moved to London and taken other employment."

"Was it a souvenir? I mean the reason why he purchased the sword," William questioned awkwardly.

Charles watched him curiously. "He said his employer bought it and wished to remain anonymous.

"Well, I suppose he could have said that just to avoid attention. It might have been a reminder of his former Mistress," William remarked. hearing an edge to his friend's voice. "Maybe he knew her as a French envoy."

"No," Charles corrected tersely. "He wasn't in Louisa's service. He worked for my sister Madeline."

William stopped. *Madeline? Charles' other sister?* Could she have been involved with Louisa's covert activities? Of course the new owner might just be speculating for future value.

"Did Madeline ever discuss her politics?" William inquired casually.

Charles' face flushed, his demeanor rigid. "Not again. No more. I've only one sister now, for God's sake."

William swore under his breath.

Charles straightened his coat and turned to see Emily talking with a pair of women next to their carriage. He took a step and paused. "If you value our friendship, I beg you, do not think her a suspect. I assure you she cherished Louisa. They were inseparable."

William nodded contritely. “I apologize. I must get over this.”

Charles smiled thinly. “I can tell you one thing. She never would have gotten involved in the Society’s schemes. She hated Arthur Hurst.”

William shrugged and bid his friend goodbye.

He scanned the dispersing throng for Elizabeth. Sunlight filtered through trees to the west by the time he spotted his wife among a small cluster of females down the block. Without urgency, he strolled toward their carriage.

A beggar woman caught his eye.

In her sixties, features still neat and composed, she had large brown eyes, but the jaw line appeared soft and skin hung loose on her neck. She regarded William with interest.

“C’m over ‘ere young man. D’yer want your fortune told t’ya?”

William looked at her dubiously. “I’m sorry, Ma’am. I must be on my way, but here’s a shilling for your time.”

He spun on his heel, hearing a word of gratitude and a strange forecast.

“Beware the woman who carries off a lamb of the throne”

With a puzzled look, he twisted back, but the figure disappeared.

On July 23, Jean du Lac arrived at London Dock. Survivor of *Le Nid’s* aborted rescue attempt, he escaped attention as a respected plantation foreman. Nevertheless, his allegence to Le Nid fired an intent to track down the Englishmen who abandoned those escaping from Saint Helena and cost them their lives.

# CHAPTER FIFTEEN

A month elapsed. Mayfair's buildings began to rise from the ashes.

Workers from Langdon and as far away as London came and went from the reconstruction. Absence of rain permitted steady progress. William spent everyday at the site while Elizabeth and Emily often picnicked on a nearby hill to watch the activity. A refurbished North building permited the Darmons to stay on the grounds, but the main domicile would not be ready for a year.

One morning, an express rider charged into the melee.

Elizabeth accepted the message and found William high upon a cornice, discussing a new roof with an architect. "It's from Michael Gravis at the Ministry of War. He wants to speak with you at your earliest convenience."

"I'll try to make time available," came his terse reply.

She knew he resented interruptions and did not want to be pulled back into an investigation.

The next day, Michael Gravis introduced himself to William.

"Allow me to express my gratitude for your heroic efforts. I know both you and Charles are owed a large debt for service to His Majesty. Your wife was also instrumental in recovery of the American Vice President and eradication of the *Societe Le Nid*. My only regret is for the loss of your Manor, and of course for the killings that took place, especially Mrs. Hurst's murder, which remains unsolved today."

"Thank you for your actions as well," William acknowledged. "Were it not for your quick response, who knows how long those villains might have infested our premises."

"Mr. Gravis also provided direction to Crullage's involvement which ended Aunt Catherine's handiwork," Elizabeth added with mixed feelings.

"Yes, well, we all do our best to serve His Majesty. Now, to the matter at hand. The Americans have finally come to a resolution of the kidnapping affair and wish to tie off some loose ends.

"First, Charles Bagwell has been completely exonerated of culpability in the abduction. Here's a paper to that effect, which I trust you'll carry to him. Second, there are a few bills you incurred during your visit to America to help Mr. Bagwell. An unpaid hotel charge, fee for a missing horse, damage to an apartment, and a few miscellaneous charges."

William looked at the sheaf of papers with surprise. "Won't His Majesty's gratitude extend to payment of costs incurred on a mission vital to the government?"

"Ordinarily, but since you were never authorized to make the trip, it's customary to charge persons who create the expenses."

William sighed. It was not a great deal of money.

"Lastly, the Americans wish to deport a Nina du Bois, with whom you're apparently acquainted. They feel her ties to the *Le Nid* make her an undesirable resident. She's requested immigration to the British Isles and asks if you would sponsor her."

Elizabeth expressed surprise. "She's to be deported? Of course, we'll take her in. Isn't it a bit extreme for the small role she played with the *Society*?"

The agent handed the paper to William. "I'd say so, but here's the order."

William scanned through the text, and noticed several signatures at the bottom. A magistrate, an assistant governor, and Terrence Winthrop!

"Winthrop? Is Hayes still using a cover name? Why should he sign a deportation order?"

Gravis took the piece of paper and smiled. "This is the signature of their Senator from Maryland, a descendant of the famous Massachusetts family. Just to be certain, allow me to retrieve records on file and compare the agent's signature."

While Gravis stepped out of the room William turned to Elizabeth. "Are you happy with her coming to the house? I'm sure any involvement with the *Society* has ended."

"I'd enjoy seeing Nina again," she replied. "She's a nice girl and there are plenty of chores to keep her busy. Was Aigle arrested?"

"Fouche had him replaced with a non-fowl embassy representative."

Gravis reappeared. "The signatures are different. Hayes apparently chose the name by coincidence. He has no known ties to the Winthrop family. You can see from this note, there's no real similarity in the handwriting."

*Madeline*
*Meet me at number 24 West Park Road tomorrow night.*
*Terrence*

Elizabeth frowned. "Is Hayes acquainted with Madeline Bagwell? What is this meeting in the message? It must have been important for you to have kept it on file."

"We save everything attributed to agents of foreign countries. This was filed in the month of June 1814. As I recall, we inspected the address, but found nothing unusual," Gravis concluded.

William glanced up at Michael Gravis. "One more thing, may I impose upon you for the address of Harry McGregor in London?"

The agent nodded and returned moments later with piece of paper.

William gave his approval for Nina's immigration, which Gravis expected would take two months to complete.

He rubbed his chin as they left the building. "So Madeline knew Robert Hayes. I thought she wasn't political."

"Slow down, William," Elizabeth cautioned. "We can't even be certain this is the Madeline related to Charles."

He nodded sheepishly. "We could ask her, but if she has anything to hide, she'd probably deny it. In any case, Charles wouldn't approve our badgering his sister. Let's see what's located at 24 West Park

Road."

Their driver found the address within twenty minutes, one of many apartments located on a shaddy lane. They sought the landlord who had a vague recollection of Winthrop and added that someone else had occupied flat number 4 for several years. There appeared no need for entry, so they prepared to leave. Outside the caretaker's office, William noticed a large cleaning woman dusting the hallway.

He motioned to her. "Excuse me. Do you remember a gentleman who used to reside in Room 4, prior to the current occupant?"

The woman wiped her hands on a filthy rag. "Room 4? I daresay, 'oo knows wot comes and goes around 'ere. I usually mind me own business."

"Please, it's very important."

"Dunno, let me think. Oh yes, 'e came and went months at a time. Seemed nice enough, often 'ad a lady friend inside. Yer could 'ear 'em laughing. Spent the night once too."

"A lady friend," Elizabeth smiled patiently. "Can you describe her?"

"Well, I recall she be tall and thin..."

"Did you ever hear her name?"

"No, but found somtin of 'ers, once."

She took them to her cart at the rear of the building and proudly held up a lace handkerchief with the initials 'M. B.'

"It's Madeline's. I've seen it before," Elizabeth said.

They thanked the woman.

William noticed the cart held a long knife. He wondered what purpose the woman could possibly have for its use. More likely, a relic left behind by a tenant. She probably collected remnants to sell before the manager found out. In any case, she seemed big enough to break a man's neck without the need for such weapon.

Elizabeth whistled softly. "So Terrence Winthrop, excuse me, Robert Hayes, and Madeline Bagwell were lovers? Is it a coincidence the sister of a *Le Nid* envoy took up with an American spy or did he use her to maintain some kind of surveillance on Louisa?"

William nodded. "Perhaps, she wasn't involved in the espionage, but they both were at our anniversary ball."

Their next stop lay across the Thames on Farringdon Road. Harry McGregor's address turned out to be a plain brick hotel of little note. They knocked on his door. When it opened, William instantly recognized the manservant, short in stature, fortyish with a pale face, which carried frameless glasses.

"Hello, I'm William Darmon of Mayfair Hall and this is my wife, Elizabeth. May we have a word with you regarding your recent purchase in Langdon?"

McGregor stiffened. "I remember you from the auction. It was yer stuff we bid on. Yours and that old woman, Lady Carlisle."

He permitted their entry into a clean but sparsely furnished room.

Once seated, William continued. "I'm sorry to impose upon you, but the sword you purchased belonged to my uncle, Lewis du Montclair. His sister desires its return. I will, of course, give you back your money."

"I couldn't do that, sir. My employer gave me strict orders not ta tell anyone 'e'd purchased it. 'E values 'is privacy, yer know."

William smiled sympathetically. "I understand. All I ask is for you to give me his address, so I could tender an offer he might find attractive. The family is willing to pay fifteen hundred pounds, and I'm certain we can provide a consideration for your assistance in this matter."

The man whistled. "Fifteen 'undred is indeed a fortune. What do you mean by 'a consideration'?"

William reached inside the his waistcoat. "Shall we say, twenty pounds?"

Considering the sum involved, Harry smiled, thinking it fair to ask twice whatever William offered. "Make it forty."

An exorbitant fee, but William retrieved his pocketbook.

"The gentleman's name is Colonel Suchet. 'E lives at Rosewell

Park."

William handed the man his bank notes.

He and Elizabeth departed, barely able to conceal their surprise at his aunt's former residence. Once in the carriage, they gave directions to Rosewell and settled back to speculate.

Elizabeth shook her head. "Are we to conclude this Colonel was connected to Lady Carlisle's operation, yet another *Le Nid* member to be apprehended?"

William squinted at the passing buildings. "I think not. It's been two years since she abandoned her estate. Hibou hinted she was forced to leave the place for misuse of the pendants or something."

"Of course," Elizabeth replied with a smile. "You read in the *Times* papers were found at the manor linking her to Terrence Winthrop and the plot to accommodate Americans at Rosewell during the war."

He nodded. "Charles told me Aigle said after Clay changed his mind about the invasion, he asked Hayes to deliver a pendant to Rosewell Park."

"Hayes told me that, too," Elizabeth said.

"Suppose Hayes gave his pendant to Madeline. If the Hursts were using Rosewell Park, maybe Madeline was there too. Since Madeline had no allegiance to France nor the Americans, she may have realized the message needed to reach British hands. Blame for the trap would then fall on Lady Carlisle for *careless use of the pendants*."

"Brilliant!" Elizabeth exclaimed. "But who is Colonel Suchet?"

"I remember a Suchet from the war. He fell from favor with Bonaparte and didn't play a role at Waterloo. If this is the same man, maybe he became a *Ultraroyalist*."

The Bagwells began to put their lives in order. Each day, Charles' struggled to overcome the loss of his sister. Emily filled their days with social calls when they were not with the Darmons at Mayfair's reconstruction. Restoration gave Emily ideas that she would offer to Charles to improve their own manor. They hardly noticed that

Madeline had been in their company only once since Charles' return from Saint Helena.

On this day, the visit to Mayfair was put off. Charles and Emily set about making other plans, when a servant appeared. "Sir, an express just arrived. The rider waits for a reply."

*Dear Charles:*

*Please come to Kensington Palace at your earliest convenience. Your presence is desired for a personal matter. I would be grateful if you kept the visit confidential.*

*Edward, Duke of Kent*

"Another missive from the Duke? Maybe he intends to bestow a reward for your efforts in bringing down the *Le Nid* consipracy." Emily said, looking over Charles shoulder.

Charles scratched his head. "Sounds urgent. I must pen a response. I can be there by 2:00 PM tomorrow."

"Thank you for coming, Charles," Edward greeted his visitor in the Privy room, a chamber designed to impress guests with lavish decor. "I'm indebted to you for your service. I understand the hardships you must have endured from my days at Halifax when I was Commander in Chief of British Forces in North America. I'm of the opinion you may be one of a few trustworthy gentleman in my acquaintance, however so slight it may be."

Charles gawked at the furnishings despite his familiarity with expensive possessions garnered by friends of considerable wealth. The two-story red brick mansion standing behind a wrought-iron gate had been used by royal families dating back to 1689, following purchase by the Earl of Nottingham

He could not help admiring precious artifacts. Hanging on separate walls, three Mortlake tapestries represented seasons of the year, reputedly woven for Charles I in 1623. Below them stood six eighteenth century busts of scientists and philosophers - Samuel Clarke, Sir Isaac Newton, John Locke, Robert Boyle and William Wollaston. The statue of a Moor rose in the center of the room since 1710 according to the Duke. Overhead, a magnificent ceiling painted after ceilings discovered in ancient Rome showed Mars and Minerva surrounded by the arts and sciences. Allusion to the King and Queen was readily apparent to any visitor.

Charles smiled. “Sir, you flatter me. I stand with others of my family, ready to serve England.”

The Duke sighed. “Be that as it may, there is a matter of some delicacy. I hope you can assist in its resolution. A fortnight ago, I experienced a vision so unsettling, I've not slept since. Its’ subject was our four-month old daughter, Alexandrina Victoria.”

“Surely, you don’t believe dreams carry any fact of life,” Charles interrupted.

“I do believe they may serve as warnings,” he replied shortly. “Prudence should never be avoided. In this case, consequences are so monumental I must take action. First, let me give you the background to this development.

“You may know that none of my three bothers have produced legitimate heirs to the throne, and my father, King George III has not been well for many years, requiring my eldest brother, the Prince of Wales to rule in his stead. My brothers and I stand ready to take the throne, however, we are all getting on in years. I am the youngest at fifty-three. The future of England might, therefore, severely change within a decade. This situation was becoming dire for the Hanover line until the birth of our child, Drina. If my father and I were to die, she would be next in line to the throne.”

Charles rubbed his chin. “Surely, you or one of your brothers will reign until she’s a proper age to become Queen.”

“Do you think so?” Edward responded raising an eyebrow. “George, the Prince of Wales, Frederick, the Duke of York, William, the Duke of Clarence and myself may all be dead within the next ten years and Drina will not be of sufficient age to take the throne. But this is the lesser of my concerns.”

Charles looked puzzled. “There’s more?”

“Unfortunately, I’m not a wealthy man. My wife, Victoire is a German Princess. However, her tiny principality has become impoverished by the war. She has two small children from a previous marriage in the village of Amorbach. Last year, I introduced her to London society. Alas, she became homesick after a few months and returned to her village. I was determined our daughter should be born on British soil, so at great expense, I brought her back in time for the blessed event.

“I must confess to you, Charles, I’m so burdened with debt, I cannot afford to keep up appearances as a royal personage in English society. I‘ve borrowed from friends and family to the point where my future can only hold a quiet life in some obscure county residence, perhaps Devon. It’s here my vision struck.

“I dreamt that within a few months, I leave this life. My widow, dearest Victoire is left penniless to care for the future Queen of England. She has only her lady-in-waiting, Baroness Spath and her brother Leopold who remains in Germany. What does she do? She chooses not to reside in England where she's still a comparative stranger and the future Queen is taken from our soil to be raised abroad. Within a short time, rivals take the throne and we Hanovers are turned out forever.”

Charles’ eyes widened. “It's a sad portrayal, indeed. What would you have me do?”

Edward rose from his chair and walked to the window.

“I’ve written to Leopold. He offers to look after his sister in the event of my death. He has an allowance and could supervise her affairs here, if it were not for reluctance by his wife, Charlotte. However, Leopold found a charming house at Claremont in Surrey not far from your home. They might be tempted to move here, if the place were provided. Unfortunately, I am unable to provide financial assistance.”

“Are you asking me to purchase this house on the off chance your dream comes true?” Charles asked incredulously. “What is the price of the establishment?”

"I've been told the building and grounds can be had for fifty thousand pounds."

"Fifty thousand pounds!" Charles repeated squeakly. "That is a fortune well beyond my means. You can't expect me to mortgage my family's future to insure your brother-in-law's welfare."

"Perhaps the sum might be raised among your friends," the Duke plead. "The Darmons, for example..."

Charles stared. "Give me a little time to consider your suggestion."

The two men rose. The Duke called for Charles' coat. Pleasantries were exchanged and Charles left with a promise to return in one week.

"You must be joking," Emily replied.

"How could we assume such debt? Borrowing from Elizabeth and William would be unthinkable on the basis of a nightmare for this, this...possible future queen, Victoria. It's unthinkable.Why should we care what family occupies the throne?

Charles wrung his hands. "Such a request from royaliy should not be lightly dismissed. It's an opportunity to change history and help ensure safe transition for the royal family."

Emily scowled. "Why should we suffer just to please these aristocrats?"

Charles face tightened. "It may pay dividends some day. At least, let's visit the property. We can see if the owner might reduce the price. Then, I'll be able to report back to the Duke its true worth."

Emily nodded. "Fair enough. It will have to be the day following. Tomorrow, I'm to meet your sister for lunch in Chelsea."

# CHAPTER SIXTEEN

An architectural jewel of Kent, Rosewell Park lay isolated behind high foliage encompassing nine hundred acres of gardens, small lakes, and woods. The imposing country house derived its name from the traditional meaning of 'park', a term referring to areas maintained as open space where industry and farming were not allowed so nobility could have a place to hunt. Many such country houses were carefully landscaped to create a mixture of open grassland with scattered trees and sections of rough woodland, often enclosed by a high wall.

Rosewell stood at the center of an agricultural estate large enough for the landowner to be accepted as a member of the nobility. The term nobility often encompassed all members of landowning classes such as aristocracy or gentry and included a landowner's family and owners who had lost their land. Aristocracy, the richest and longest established untitled landowning families, was seen as distinct from the gentry. Aristocrats often lived part of the year in London, played a role in national politics or served as courtiers. By contrast, the vast majority of gentry lived in the country year round. Unlike yeomen, the gentry did not work the land themselves; but hired tenant farmers. Unlike higher nobility, they lacked hereditary titles or privileges and comprised smaller landowners.

Country houses were often used to enhance the owners' ability to influence local and national politics. Country houses served as meeting places for the ruling class to discuss election campaigns. It provided employment for hundreds of people in the vicinity. Those working on estates were most fortunate, receiving secured employment and rent-free accommodation. Of these, the indoor staff slept in proper beds, wore well-made clothes, received three proper meals and a small wage.

The Rosewell mansion was built between 1789 and 1799 by

Phillip Carr for Lewis du Carlisle who made his fortune in shipping. The architect mixed Palladian and Baroque styles in its construction. Palladian architecture came to England many years earlier, popularized by the efforts of Giacomo Leoni who adapted Italian designs. His transformations suited landed classes without abandoning principles of the great masters.

Palladian villas were modeled on Roman temple facades, usually on three floors: a rusticated ground floor, containing service and minor rooms; above this, a piano nobile containing the principal reception and bedrooms; and above this, a mezzanine floor with secondary bedrooms. The piano nobile contained all rooms necessary for a family inhabiting the house. It held a central salon or Saloon, the grandest room beneath the central pediment, and on either side, wings maintained a withdrawing room, principal bedroom and a smaller more intimate room called a "cabinet". Such structures were characterized by a massive Ionic portico with wings sitting atop a rusticated basement and an internal courtyard.

To this style, Baroque architecture was added to impress visitors. Baroque designs embellished an entrance sequence of courts, anterooms, grand staircases, and reception rooms of increasing magnificence.

Lewis du Montclair spent his life as a seaman, a ship owner, and finally, proprietor of the Montclair Shipping Line. His rise to preeminence came through a series of fortunate events and hard work. In the early days, he signed on with a ship of the East India Line and served a term of seven years on vessels sailing around the tip of Africa bound for markets in India and China.

One stormy night off the coast of Madagascar, he happened to be topside when the Captain was stricken by a heart attack. Lewis single-handedly piloted the ship away from rocky shores, and saved a lucrative cargo. The Company awarded him with his own command, and, with steadily improving delivery times, he eventually made enough money to purchase his own ship. Competition with the major lines was difficlt and for a while, his enterprise seemed destined for failure.

The American Revolution changed his fortune. A need for gunpowder combined with the shortage of wood for potash, sent his ship to kelp beds in Scotland. There, he discovered supply for a demand, as John Black put it, which could never be satisfied.

Frequent passage between the west coast of Scotland and an explosive factory at Hastings was augmented by additional ships, and Lewis' reputation grew with the militaries of more than one country. It became common knowledge Montclair ships could be hired for any cargo at the right price.

Following American independence, France became the foremost customer, stockpiling weaponry for the French revolution. An immense fortune befell Lewis, enabling construction of Rosewell Park. Ten years in the making, the huge three-story structure was completed as the nineteenth century dawned, three years before his death.

Upon the passing of her husband, estate responsibilities and many holdings of the du Montclairs came to Lady Carlisle. An acute business sense and a heritage of nobility on her father's side soon made her a powerful figure in the industry and led to the ruin of more than one competitor who could not see past her gender.

Despite the lineage of William's grandfather, his aunt had never truly been accepted into society. Her reputation as an independent woman who championed liberal causes did not sit well in many family circles. Such eccentricities had to be excused when a host prepared invitations to premier gatherings for the presence of such a formidable lady could be considered a crowning achievement.

Widow Carlisle faced overwhelming daily demands with the expansive shipping operation. She found it difficult to enlist the help of English noblemen during the War of 1812 while the country's sense of patriotism ran high and much of the company's income came from France. Only her brother's child, William might have been considered a qualified candidate to restore the company's propriety, but he, too, was forced to cope with maintaining his family's business at Mayfair following the premature death of his father. Without able assistants or heirs to pick up the mantle, she often neglected the company's oversight.

Consequently, Lady Carlisle was receptive to proposals of the Societe de Le Nid as the monarchy of France deteriorated. Prior lucrative French dealings combined with the just cause of individual freedom made her sympathetic to their needs. During the War of 1812, when England once again became a major customer of du Montclair, established relationships on the Continent did not disappear and Rosewell Park continued to be a favorite meeting place for adherents to the politics of Bonaparte.

William and Elizabeth approached the imposing central building along a meandering path, mindful that only a select few ever received invitation to admire Rosewell's the sprawling grounds.

In the distance, across an emerald colored undulating meadow, one could see canals and geometric ponds flowing into a serpentine lake. A lodge sat at the upper edge of the lake together with a boathouse. William also counted a pheasant house with its shooting platform and a summerhouse located behind an orangery planted with flowering shrubs and ornamental trees along a curving walkway. Occasionally, gardeners were spotted, but no sign of other visitors.

Under gathering afternoon clouds, the carriage turned to give view of the enormous residence. An exterior built of gray limestone dressed with stone pilasters presented a ground floor with blocks of ashlar while the upper floors were smoothly dressed stone. A central section exhibited a four-columned arch surrounding a large oak door reached from by a curved double staircase. Above the door, at second floor height, stone garlands flanked two identical wings with tall windows.

Elizabeth cringed at the somber reflection of Lady Carlisle's checkered history.

Their carriage pulled up in front and a servant came out to take the driver to a waiting area while the Darmons ascending two flights of steps to the double door, ten-feet high. A loud clang of the huge doorknocker echoed beyond the entry.

The door slowly opened, and William offered his card.

Moments later the two were permitted inside.

Upon entering, William and Elizabeth were confronted by a marble hall leading to the open courtyard of a Roman villa. Twenty fluted alabaster columns with Corinthian capitals supported a heavily decorated, high-coved cornice. Niches in the walls displayed classical statuary and grisaille panels showed scenes of the estate above the recesses.

They were escorted into an adjoining saloon through a triumphal arch which rose to the full height of the house, sixty feet to the top. Designed as a sculpture gallery, this circular room's theme was based on the temples of Rome with four massive pedestals supporting classical urns.

From the saloon, they passed into a withdrawing room enclosing fine furniture and paintings with a huge Venetian window. Everywhere, the great country house displayed magnificent collections of art, furniture, statuary, and Far Eastern artifacts. The latter left behind by Lady Carlisle who garnered them from Lewis' many travels.

As the servant's receding footsteps resounded off marble surfaces, Elizabeth whispered to her husband. "Does all this belong to the Colonel now?"

She could not stop gawking at the surroundings. Lady Carlisle had never permitted her a visit to the estate. Elizabeth met the woman once before the dowager took up lodging with them at Mayfair. She supposed the aunt had boycotted their nuptials because the woman disapproved their union, and a month after their wedding, her single visit to Mayfair had been a cold formality.

William gazed at the ceiling. "It may still belong to patrons of the Le Nid through business connections. The actual owners could be a collection of noblemen living either here or in France."

The servant returned. "The Colonel will see you now."

He took them down a hallway further into the east wing to a spacious room with ceilings twenty-feet overhead. Paintings and tapestries covered walls and every piece of furniture carried a vase or statuary. Elizabeth could not suppress the impression of an artist's museum. Two peach colored marble fireplaces stood under pictures of Louis XVIII and Louis XIV at opposite ends of the room. Crystal chandeliers provided the room's illumination because heavy maroon velvet curtains were tightly closed.

At the far end of the room, a white wigged gentleman sat at a small desk, writing with quill and ink. Upon their announcement, he rose, smiling thinly while the visitors tentatively stepped forward.

"I'm Colonel Suchet. May I ask what is the purpose of your visit?"

He spoke each word precisely. A tall, angular figure, appeared to be in his fifties, dressed formally in a gray silk waistcoat with French cuffs.

William bowed stiffly. "Colonel Suchet, I am William Darmon and this is my wife, Elizabeth. My Aunt was the former owner of Rosewell Park."

"That means nothing to me, sir," he replied unequivocally. "I now have responsibility of the estate and no interest in former tenants."

William stiffened at the man's coldness. Memories of the manor were a part of his childhood. He was beginning to lose his customary politeness. "Sir, in my youth, I visited these premises many times....,"

"I see. Then you have no need for a tour. If you have no other business, I would appreciate a return to mine."

William gritted his teeth and took a step forward menacingly.

Elizabeth clutched his arm. "Excuse me sir, have no acquaintance with Louisa and Arthur Hurst?"

Suchet did not move a muscle. "No, none at all. Now I must bid you a good day."

He turned to reclaim his seat.

Elizabeth glanced at William, gesturing toward the doorway. "Apparently, the Society's activities are no longer a part of Rosewell. I fear the trail has gone cold since your aunt visited the Crullage estate."

Suchet stopped writing. He looked up with knitted brows. "Did you say Crullage? William Crullage?"

The couple exchanged puzzled glances. William was not about to let an opening slip away. "Why, yes. Elizabeth visited the castle the night he died. His son, Jack, is a good friend of the family."

The gentleman rose. "I beg your pardon. Please sit down. Allow me to offer some refreshment."

He called for a servant.

They sipped tea while Suchet praised the virtues of William Crullage.

"Monsieur Crullage is a distant cousin of Elie Decazes, minister of the French police. He owned Rosewell Park until his unfortunate death two months ago. Alas, I fear his son will not be so kind to us. Perhaps you can put in a good word on our behalf."

"Us?" William inquired trying to put some warmth into his voice.

"We are supporters of the French monarchy. Bonaparte left our country weak and in disorder. He has done more to ruin France than all its enemies accomplished over a thousand years. France cannot afford the luxury of liberals who create chaos to bring down political structure and abolish industry. There are factions in our country that would live in the Dark Ages to avoid allegiance to a king who provides them with a stable economy. It's despicable."

"Are you an Ultraroyalist?" Elizabeth asked.

"All men of noble birth are royalists. I support the policies of Louis XVIII and any ruler who promotes a society of enlightened citizens. It's time to restore order in our country," Colonel Suchet proclaimed.

Elizabeth interjected, "Did Lady Carlisle sell Rosewell Park to William Crullage?"

A flicker of surprise crossed his eyes. "During the war there was a good deal of undercover work here. Unfortunately, it all came to naught. The former tenants were embarrassed by their failure, and Rosewell was closed down. After the war, William Crullage agreed to purchase it for our use."

William turned with surprise. "Did you know the plan for an American invasion?"

He eyed William challengingly. "Of course, we all swore allegiance to Bonaparte in those days."

Elizabeth leaned forward. "Do you know what went wrong?"

Suchet fidgetted with his cup, aware of her scrutiny. "An informant sent word to your Admiral Cockburn of the Essex. With her help, a trap was laid."

William raised an eyebrow. "Her help?"

"Madeline Bagwell."

"She was a spy as well?" Elizabeth exclaimed.

"Not at first. Lady Carlisle invited her to Rosewell when the other sister, Louisa was absent. The Lady gave her errands to run until a fateful day when she was to relay a missive to her brother-in-law at Hastings. Madeline took it to Dover instead. The plot was foiled. Lady Carlisle took the blame."

William rubbed his chin. "You think it was a mistake?"

The Colonel harrumphed. "Madeline hated Arthur Hurst who on more than one occasion tried to seduce her. Although she never admitted it, I suspect she wanted Monsieur Hurst to take the fall."

Elizabeth nodded thoughtfully. "Louisa probably never knew the truth. The sisters remained close after the war. By then, Arthur Hurst became a drunkard and Madeline could ignore his ill-conceived attention."

William frowned. "Lady Carlisle continued to work for Le Nid, and Madeline became an Ultraroyalist."

"As did many of us, disillusioned by Bonaparte's failures." Suchet added, swallowing the last of his tea."

Elizabeth met his eyes squarely. "Colonel Suchet, you seem to know a lot about Madeline. Was it you who shielded her from Fouche's retribution?"

A voice came from the entrance. "Yes, he has been a true friend."

They spun around to see Madeline Bagwell. The tall, pale woman wore a formal white and blue dress of the latest French fashion.

"Madeline!" Elizabeth responded. "Why did you get involved?"

She walked over to the window. "At first, all I cared about was getting rid of that fool Arthur. If it weren't for Robert Hayes, I'd still be fighting for the wrong causes. Robert helped me allay their plans.

"When I passed Louisa's room on the night of your ball, I saw a pendant laying on a table. I was horrified, certain she'd discovered I delivered the wrong message.

“I went downstairs, worrying about her reaction. She seemed pleasant enough, but knowing Louisa, it meant nothing. The more I thought, the more I became afraid she was plotting revenge for my betrayal. I took a serving knife for protection.

“When we went upstairs for the night, I asked her where she'd got the pendant. She laughed, saying it wouldn't be long before it would be on my head. I was certain she knew.

“She seemed puzzled at my anxiety. The more I tried to cover my reaction, the greater became her suspicion. Suddenly, she turned evil. She accused me of being responsible for fifty deaths and destroying her husband.

We went into Lady Carlisle’s room. I pleaded with the old woman to tell Louisa otherwise, but I'd already admitted too much. She grew furious with your aunt, threatening to expose her treason. Lady Carlisle left hastily and Louisa announced she was going to tell Arthur. I knew he'd try to kill me. I reached into in my dress, feeling the knife handle. I thought the threat of it might stop her, but she only sneered. The next thing I knew, she lunged. I thrust the knife to keep her away...”

Tears formed in Madeline’s eyes.

Elizabeth looked at William. “Might it be considered self-defense?”

He too, seemed moved by her confession, but shrugged. “It's for the courts to decide.”

The Colonel scowled. “You see, my dear, this is what's called English justice.”William frowned at the remark. “I'm certain there are extenuating circumstances for a prosecutor to consider…”

“You British are all alike. This heroine does your country a favor, and all you can think of is how she did it. Le Nid commits an unspeakable act to free Bonaparte and Parliament blames the King of France for assaulting their garrison. You people have no concept of justice.”

“Now, wait a minute," William protested. “We have a right to ensure safety from despots who threaten our commerce.”

“Hah! Parliament has no right to impose economic sanctions on the government of France. Your government is deliberately trying to weaken the French monarchy to gain a trading advantage. We won't sit still while England bullies our partners and creates further unrest at home.”

Elizabeth shivered, becoming frightened at the man’s hostility. “What are you suggesting?”

Suchet smiled slyly. “Your attempts to interfere are about to meet with reciprocation. Let's see how well England does without a future monarch.”

William's mouth dropped open. “What? What are you planning?”

Madeline nodded. “By this time tomorrow, there will be no heir to the throne. The daughter of the Duke of Kent will be in our custody.”

Elizabeth gasped. “Madeline, think about what you're doing. Up 'til now you may be accused of an unfortunate accident or an act of self defense, but this is a hanging offense.”

“What have I to live for?” she retorted. “At least I'll die for a worthy cause.”

“You Ultraroyalists are as bad as Le Nid, " William blurted. “Kidnapping, killing and lawlessness are ways you think will restore the status quo. I'm fed up with French subversive practices. I insist you stop this at once.”

Suchet remained calm, reaching into the desk drawer and withdrawing a pistol. “I think not. Madeline, ring for the servants. Let's tie up these misplaced idealists and lock them in the basement.”

Charles and Emily prepared for their trip to inspect the Claremont estate when a servant appeared with the card of visitors. The note announced Sir James and Lady Mary Wellington, sister of Lewis du Montclair, Lady Carlisle’s former husband. The elderly couple was shown into their parlor.

“Mr. and Mrs. Bagwell, please excuse our dropping in like this," Sir James Wellington apologized. “We were in Kent to visit the Darmons and extend our sympathies for loss of the aunt.”

Lady Wellington smiled. “My sister-in-law was never close, but I know William was her favorite nephew. A servant directed us to London, but we found they'd left Palace Yard by the time we arrived. Knowing you lived here in Surrey, I suspected they might be visiting. It was also an opportunity to express our regrets for your sister’s tragic death. Please accept our condolences.”

Emily looked at them curiously. “You're very gracious. Unfortunately, the Darmons aren't here. But please, come sit down. May we offer you refreshment?”

The gray-haired gentleman gripped his cane, and tipped his head toward a basket sitting next to the door prepared by the cook for their outing. “We don't want to impose, especially if you're about to step out..."

Charles shook his head. “Nonsense, we've no pressing engagements. We’re about to view a nearby property up for sale. It's more of a errand for fresh air.”

Lady Mary reacted. “Surrey is such a lovely shire. I'm surprised anyone would want to leave its surroundings.”

Emily glanced quizzically at her husband. “I think Charles is interested in the residence for investment purposes, but it may be well out of our price range. Would you like to join us?”

Sir James nodded. “That would be fine. We love to travel and enjoy visiting our holdings throughout the British Isle.”

Two days later, Charles rode on horseback to Kensington Palace. He was in a good frame of mind for his visit with the Duke. The Wellington's had come to the rescue. Despite vague reasons for the purchase and future donation to the Royal family, the couple agreed to provide thirty-five thousand pounds for the country's rulers. Charles grinned, satisfied he did something important for his homeland.

An hour’s journey from the Palace, he decided to stop at the Inn at Dell Crossing near Notting Hill. Upon dismounting, he heard drumming sounds of galloping horses hooves thundering down the road. In the distance, a carriage approached at great speed, spewing clouds of dust high into the air. Its' driver struggled with reins to keep the pair of racing horses from veering off the path.

Charles froze next to his horse, grateful to be off the road and safely within the tavern circle.

As the speeding vehicle drew closer, Charles caught a glimpse of the passengers within the open vehicle. His eyes widened at the sight of his sister, Madeline and another gentleman exhorting the driver onward. Once they passed, he stood dumbfounded while the receding transport quickly became lost to view.

"Charles, good of you to return," Edward exclaimed, cheerfully shaking Charles hand. "We've been expecting you. I trust the news is not entirely bad?"

Charles took a chair within the familiar Privy room of Kensington Palace. He smiled broadly and withdrew a paper from inside his coat. "Sir, I do believe the Claremont property will soon be at your disposal."

"Wonderful, my good man. You have performed a valuable service for our family. I won't forget this," replied the portly Royal. "Your sister said the news might be favorable."

Charles blinked. "My sister? You've spoken to Madeline?"

"Why yes, she was just here. She came to the door, saying you requested she be present during our meeting. I presumed you invited her because she was one of your investors."

Charles frowned. How could she have known of the meeting? Then it came to him. Emily! She met with Madeline in Chelsea and must have divulged the details.

"And where is she now?" Charles asked, still uncertain why she came.

"Well, when I introduced her to Victoire, she was so taken with Drina, she and Nurse Spath took the baby out for a walk."

Charles scratched his head. "If you don't mind, I'll leave you with these papers while I track her down to see if she has any comments regarding our agreement."

"Of course," he responded. "I believe they went out the South entrance. Our grounds are beautiful this time of year, makes one forget London is only four miles away."

Charles walked swiftly to the tall doorway and outside onto a terrace. He scanned the gardens. No one in sight. A guard at the door said the nurse mentioned they were on their way to Sunnybrook Lake. He pointed west beyond the perimeter wall to a road winding toward a distant grove of trees.

Charles thanked the sentry, clamored down the steps and rapidly paced a broad walkway to the gate. He called Madeline's name several times at the South fence, shaking his head, mystified at his sister's behavior.

The Lake was deserted. Charles called again. Distant buildings brought an idea they might have gone to visit a neighbor.

He sighed. Whatever the reason for her being here, it had nothing to do with the transaction, so he might as well return to the Duke and conclude his dealings.

He started back along the road when his eye caught sight of a black object within a cluster of trees. He went over to it. A cold shiver gripped his spine. The pram lay on its side, empty. His knees felt weak. Were the women waylaid and the princess taken?

Charles picked up the baby carriage and pushed it wildly along the road toward Kensington. A disturbing thought came to mind. Why had they been in such a hurry at the Dell? He slowed. Were they bent upon coming here to harm the Duke and his family? Why?

He swallowed hard, remembering William's suspicions. A sinking sensation wrenched at his stomach. French conspirators had struck again!

# CHAPTER SEVENTEEN

Michael Gravis paced a polished floor in Kensington's Cupola Room.

Having heard Charles' story, the family quickly notified Palace Yard. George, the Prince of Wales, arrived to comfort his brother, and Victoire fainted upon learning the news. She rested upstairs in the Queen Mary bedchamber. The Palace's large stateroom now filled with red-coated guards and policemen, including Inspector Matthews who barked orders at those reporting for duty.

A search of the grounds resulted in the discovery of nurse Spath, bound and gagged inside a building they called the 'Greenhouse'. Originally designated the Orangery, the enclosure housed many orange trees situated on Palace terraces during cold winter months. The shaken baroness confirmed Madeline's role in the abduction and noted the presence of a man hiding behind the Greenhouse who had waited to overpower her.

George, or Prinny as commonly known, and his brother sat on overstuffed chairs in stunned silence.

Strain showed in the tightly drawn face of Edward Guelph, the Duke of Kent. At fifty-four, he was a tall, vigorous man with bushy eyebrows, balding with remaining hair dyed glossy black.

He picked a hair from the shoulder of his impeccably tailored coat with an air of stiffness. "Long ago a gypsy in Gibraltar prophesized I was to have many losses, but I was to die in happiness, and my only child would be a great queen. Now I wonder if it can be true."

"We will do everything humanly possible, sire," Agent Gravis reassured. "A crime of this magnitude never succeeds."

Devastated, Charles sat glassy-eyed, watching chaos build inside the Palace. Gravis dodged a fast walking courier weaving his way through the throng of officers waiting for assignment. The agent made his way over to him.

"Charles, you have my sympathy for your sister's betrayal and the shame this brings to your family. I want you to know neither the Duke nor I hold you in any way responsible for this unthinkable act. Your service in bringing the Le Nid organization to justice earned our gratitude. I only wish you were given a better fate."

"Thank you," Charles mumbled. "I still can't believe it."

The agent pulled a folded sheet of paper from his coat pocket. "We must get to the bottom of this. Did you know, during the war, Madeline worked with the American agent Robert Hayes or Terrence Winthrop as you know him?"

Charles raised his head unsteadily. "I'll believe anything at this point. If Louisa was involved in espionage, I guess it's not much of a stretch to think Madeline, too, was part of the operation."

"The Darmons mentioned a 'Harry McGregor'. Does that name mean anything to you?" asked the official, perusing the note.

Charles bit his lip. William had been right afterall. "He was her servant for a time. I saw him in Langdon two weeks ago after purchasing a sword belonging to Napoleon at the Carlisle auction. William asked me who he represented."

Michael Gravis nodded. "I've just received word from my men that the Darmon's also visited him. He sent them to Rosewell Park to see a gentleman named Colonel Suchet."

"Rosewell Park?" Charles groaned.

He always disliked the idea William's aunt lured his sister away from his family. Apparently, Madeline also denounced her upbringing.

He looked at him with a twisted smile. "Lady Carlisle's former residence. I'm sure you know its notorious history."

Constable Matthews stepped forward. "Aye, we're aware once she left the place, a group called the Ultraroyalists took over."

Edward put a hand on Charles' shoulder. "Do you think they're behind the attempt to snatch little Drina?"

Matthews nodded. "I'll send some men around to Rosewell Park, but I expect if they're involved, the culprits are already on their way to France. We may need Fouche's help on this one."

Charles looked dubious. "You think they'll seek asylum there? It could start a war if that government helps them in any way."

“Where else would you expect Madeline to find a safe hiding place?” Gravis challenged. .

“Well, don’t forget about our cottage in Edinburgh,” Charles answered, his face turning red at the thought of how his family had become invoved in espionage.

Gravis whispered something to Matthews, who nodded and charged off.

Charles looked up wretchedly. “Can't Parliament enact a law to rid the country of foreign conspirators?”

The agent sighed. “We don't know if Suchet is involved. As an Ultraroyalist, he hasn’t broken any law although His Majesty’s government doesn't condone activities subversive to neighboring countries. We've tried to make life unsuitable for these French fraternities by surveillance and restrictions. We could evict them from Rosewell, but I fear they'd simply move to a more hidden location. The more these people are exposed, the more difficult it becomes for them to blend in with our communities.”

Police moved in on Rosewell Park to find an empty house. The two had fled, but left behind two prisoners locked in the basement. William and Elizabeth burst forth, happy to be rescued after spending three days without food or water. They were horrified, hearing the exploits of their jailers.

Two days passed. Seaports from London to Plymouth were searched without success. Fouche’s men reported no detection of their arrival in France. Authorities in five countries were unable to determine where on the Continent they might have taken refuge. The cottage on the Forth of Firth was searched without success, and Northern borders secured.

Upon their return to Mayfair, William and Elizabeth quickly packed their belongings to spend whatever time necessary to comfort the Bagwell's in Surrey until the travesty passed. They could not imagine the pain their brother-in-law endured, waiting for his sister's apprehension.

“William, isn't there anything we can do to help bring this situation to an end?” Elizabeth said, thinking aloud.

He shrugged, feeling a strange emptiness. “I suspect the Ministry and Palace Yard are doing everything possible. I'm amazed Parliament hasn’t gotten involved. There's no reason to declare war over the crime, but, our citizens should be on the alert to find out where they're hiding. I guess Gravis must be waiting for a break.”

“Do you think they’ll harm the baby? Madeline seemed bent on revenge the last time she spoke to us,” she said, face pinched with remorse.

He put his hand to touch her. “Not if they intend to extract allowances for France. They’ll look after her while Parliament debates concessions.”

“It's so frustrating not knowing…" She trailed off.

A servant appeared. “Your bags have been loaded, Madam. The carriage is ready.”

Outside, a footman waited patiently as the couple bid last minute instructions to their staff. William escorted his wife down steps to the vehicle.

After Elizabeth was helped aboard, the head gardener approached, wiping his hands.

“Sir, I know we’ve been told not to enter the shed at the west end because of fire damage, but the stablehand, Roberts reports hearing noises coming from inside.”

William frowned. “When were you told not to enter the structure?”

“We found a note pinned to the shed's door after you'd left for London," he replied.

“Let's go see," Elizabeth admonished.

Caterwauling grew louder as they walked up to the building.

“Sounds like an animal’s trapped inside," William observed, trying the door.

Gardener nodded. “It's locked from the inside. Boy, get me an axe.”

A splintered door opened moments later. Their mouths fell open at the sight.

"McGregor, what are you doing with that baby?" demanded William.

"Blasted thing wouldn't shut up," he blurted.

"William, it's the baby!" Elizabeth shouted. She took the infant wrapped in a small blanket. "Why on earth did you bring her here?"

McGregor shrugged. "We thought it would be the perfect hiding place. Once the sword got you to Rosewell, Suchet was certain your grounds would be clear for sometime."

Elizabeth held the baby close and directed a servant to fetch some milk. "How awful. She might have starved to death if we'd remained locked in the Rosewell basement much longer."

They returned Little Drina to grateful parents. For the time being, the future Queen was safely ensconced at Kensington, and the Royals heaved a sigh of relief. The perpetrators were still at large, but fewer agents were assigned to the task. Palace Yard received no further reports of sightings.

Two months passed.

The Darmons were happy to have resolved Louisa's murder and devoted their time to restoration of their manor. Eventually, William and Elizabeth were able to move out of the North building and back into the main building. Charles' despondency at the loss of his missing sister was evident whenever they visited. His mood eventually improved, but the strain of events took a lasting toll.

# CHAPTER EIGHTEEN

Rain danced in waves across the pond located east of the new Mayfair Manor. For weeks, servants and family worked diligently to restore priceless furniture and valuable livestock to Mayfair's grounds. Although some scars remained, the Darmons were satisfied the premises resembled its condition prior to evacuation.

From the easternmost window of the Great Hall, Elizabeth gazed upon the scene, but her thoughts were directed to their long anticipated Fifth Anniversary Ball. She looked forward to another reunion of relatives and friends not possible during the past three years.

At last, the celebration day arrived.

Her parents insisted they come with Victoria a week early to fully appreciate Mayfair's restoration and help with the party's preparation. Their assistance soon took the form of frequent advice regarding the proper way to entertain society's elite.

The Bagwells came next, mid-morning before the event. They were warmly greeted by the Darmons. Charles announced he had received a letter from an old friend soliciting interest in a recently vacated Chair of the Commons.

A while later, members of the London police department appeared on their doorstep, including Michael Gravis and a few familiar faces from the night of the Mayfair fire. Among other invitees to arrive throughout the day were Sir James and Lady Mary Wellington. Of special note was the presence of Nina du Bois, their charge from America who, at age twenty-three, came to live at Mayfair Hall and learn the ways of English society.

Crowds formed around host and hostess during the evening, many curious about their recent adventures, but the Darmons quickly changed the subject to Mayfair. They took pleasure in describing changes to the Manor and expressing relief at moving back inside their home.

The Wellingtons spent a good deal of time with Charles and Emily. Once more Lady Mary expressed sympathy to Charles for the loss of another sister. They seemed to enjoy each other's company.

William proposed a toast to Charles' success at a chance to become a member of Parliament. Charles joined in without objecting to the news made public. He was not, however, looking forward to a three-month's stay in London without his wife for Emily chose to remain at home, having no desire to leave Surrey for such a length of time.

During the evening Emily caught up to Elizabeth. "Lizzy, can we have a moment with you and William in the drawing room? Mr. Wellington told us something I think you both will want to hear."

Elizabeth retrieved her husband, and soon they were sitting on a rosewood settee facing the marble hearth of a massive fireplace. Crackling flames masked party sounds and distant storm rumblings rattling windowpanes. Emily and James Wellington sat on two beige upholstered fauteuils. The brocaded armchairs were positioned on opposite sides of a sofa facing the Darmons. William adjusted his charcoal velvet jacket while waiting for their address. Elizabeth frowned at her sister dressed in a yellow glown.

"What's bothering you, Emily?" she asked.

Emily opened her hand toward the elder gentleman. "Mr. Wellington, please."

James straightened. "Emily thought you might be interested in hearing about out trip to France last summer. In particular, we spent some time in the Alsace region at Obernai, a town located in the foothills of the Vosges, an hour's ride from Strasbourg."

William shifted slightly. "We know the area. Elizabeth and I visited there a few years ago. An agreeable district."

He nodded. "While staying at a local hotel, we happened to speak with a gentleman who spent many years there. He was not in good health, but we talked for a while before he retired to his room."

"He lived in the village?" Elizabeth asked, mystified.

"At one time, he owned a large villa, a medieval castle or some such, which had been restored atop a hill in the vicinity," Wellington continued.

William's attention drifted to the ball. He should return to the guests. "And what did you conclude from this?"

"Much to my surprise, he turned out to be a distant relation of yours."

"Who do you mean?" William's focus returned.

Wellington smiled thinly. "He said his name was Henry Hurst, brother of Arthur Hurst, Louisa's husband."

Elizabeth's eyes widened. "Really? You mean to say he was landlord of the Castle du Philippe?"

Wellington grinned. "Precisely, my dear. Not only that, he professed an acquaintance with Charles' other sibling, the now infamous Madeline Bagwell."

William's eyes riveted on the man. "How did this happen?"

The elder gentleman glanced furtively at the back of the room. "I'm afraid circumstances were not proper. Apparently, she once had an affair with Arthur, and they used the Castle for rendezvous. The brother supported Arthur until the liaison ended tragically."

Elizabeth could not contain herself. "I can't believe it. Madeline hated Arthur!"

Wellington's hands trembled slightly. He gripped the arms of his chair. "There was a child. Madeline remained at the villa until it was born. Arthur insisted it be put away, lest Louisa learn the truth. Madeline would not have it. She and Arthur eventually returned to England, leaving the baby in Henry's care."

William scowled. "You mean to tell me Henry raised the infant as his own? Next you'll tell us the child grew up to be Francois Hurst, the lad who perished at sea during the war."

"No, no," James responded, signaling William to calm down. "It was a girl. However, when Madeline returned to the Castle months later, the child was no longer there."

Elizabeth stopped. "What happened to her?"

James looked squarely into her eyes. "Henry said Arthur sent word to put the infant up for adoption. He never told Madeline who the parents were, but assured me they were a respectable couple living in the town below."

Emily nodded. "Poor Madeline. She must have been devastated. Little wonder she disliked Arthur Hurst."

William sighed. "The child was never heard from again?"

Wellington gazed at each of them. "There's one thing more. Apparently, the new parents were killed when Bonaparte's troops pushed back the Prussians, marching through town on their way to the Russian front. The body of the child, then twelve was never found in the rubble of their home. When Henry learned of this, he sent a servant to the town to search for orphans of that age."

Elizabeth leaped up. "My God, could it be Nina? She might be Madeline's daughter?"

James shrugged. "Anything's possible, I guess. They took in a number of children for kitchen help."

"Francois and Nina might have been first cousins," William concluded.

Emily smiled. "Charles may have a niece unknown to him."

Music played until long after midnight.

Most of the guests departed the next day. Elizabeth bid an emotional farewell to the Hudsons. Her mother thanked Elizabeth several times for allowing Victoria to visit Edinburgh with Nina under tutelege of the Wellingtons. Her father also chuckled with gratitude. The Wellington carriage left with its crew of new acquaintances.

When departures were completed and the household quieted, the staff began cleanup chores. William and Charles settled back in the drawing room to discuss Charles' assignment in London, if he were elected.

"We'd decided to spend the rest of summer up at our cottage before the Commons seat opens up," Charles said. "Emily and I have had little time to ourselves since we returned from Saint Helena. Now, it looks like we can only afford a month until I must begin campaigning in Surrey. At least we'll have a few weeks rest. It's been three years since we've used the place. Nina will join us there. It will be a good opportunity to get to know her."

William agreed. "It will be good for both of you. The chance for both Victoria and Nina to visit with the Wellington's is appreciated."

"By the way," Charles remarked, "I received a letter from Doctor Kinkade. I believe you used his services to repair your leg. He sends his greetings."

William remembered the brief encounter with Estee Black at the cottage. He and Elizabeth almost drowned coming back. Strange, how the pendant's message took them to such far-flung places, all in the cause of justice for Louisa Hurst.

"I wonder if Madeline ever tried to find the child?" he mused. "Perhaps she still seeks her daughter."

William paused.

It made sense Madeline and Colonel Suchet would flee to France. She knew the Castle du Philippe well. It could be an ideal hideout, and Inspector Matthews might not be aware of it's relevance.

The next day, William set out for London's Metropolitan Police headquarters.

By afternoon, his carriage had threaded its way through the country roads of Kent's farmlands.

Suddenly the transport slowed. William stuck his head out just as a gunshot rang out. The vehicle lurched, then halted abruptly, throwing him back against the seat.

The door flung open. Jean du Lac peered inside holding a pistol.

"Good day, Mr. Darmon. I suggest you remain within the carriage until I have you in a secure location."

William gasped. "Jean du Lac, I thought you were dead."

"No thanks to you. We all were stranded when you and Bagwell sailed off. I vowed to seek revenge for my comrades from that day forward."

"We waited hours until a patrol started shooting at the ships. We weren't part of Le Nid. We were there as a favor to Fouche."

"You sabotaged the operation. What if we had captured Bonaparte?"

"Look, we got involved to find Louisa Hurst's killer. She was one of your Le Nid members and also Charles sister."

"And did you learn why she was killed?"

"She died as a consequece of Ultraroyalist actions during the war."

"Ultraroyalists? I despise those bastards."

"Well, I'm on my way to tell the Police where I think one of their leaders is hiding, Colonel Suchet."

"Suchet? That traitor who abandoned Bonaparte during the war? Where is he?"

"In France, at a little known chateau in the Alsace region."

Jean du Lac sneered. "You're not going to inform the Police. This gentleman is mine. Do not try to escape. I advise you to think of your wife."

"Don't worry, my other sister-in-law is there, too. I must bring her back."

Their vehicle lunged forward with the Frenchman holding the reins.

Four days later, they arrived at a hotel in Obernai. The manager directed them to an upstairs room. There, they found Madeline sitting beside Henry Hurst on his deathbed. She told them Colonel Suchet was at a nearby brasserie.

An hour later, Jean du Lac and William approached the ultraroyalist sitting at a table with an acquaintance.

Jean du Lac smiled. "So we have found the coward at last."

"I beg your pardon?" Suchet said, turning from his friend.

"Dishonoring our former leader was not enough to satisfy you," du Lac spouted. "Now you and your whore have taken to kidnapping helpless babies from English noblemen."

The friend bowed slightly and quickly left the premises.

"You watch your tongue, dog or I'll ...."

"Or you'll what? I hereby challenge you to a duel. My second, William here, will see to the details as quickly as possible to rid this planet of your kind."

William jerked his head. "Huh?"

Suchet scowled "Your behavior is unpardonable. I accept your challenge and will be glad to eradicate you, scum."

Jean du Lac and Suchet met at Marcel's Mill on the River Noire in the forest of Saint Germain the following afternoon, May 30, 1821. The men were to stand at eight paces, turn and fire. Suchet was a well-known sharpshooter and Jean du Lac felt his only chance to kill him would be to allow enough time to take an accurate shot. Thus he allowed Suchet to fire into his body. The bullet struck his stomach, but Jean hardly quivered, calmly leveling his pistol at Suchet. The trigger was pulled, but the hammer of his gun fell to the half-cocked position and did not fire. According to dueling etiquette, this could have been the end of the duel. Jean, however, was not finished. Re-cocking his pistol, he aimed and fired, striking Suchet dead. Unfortunately, Jean du Lac also bled to death before he could be taken to a hospital.

William returned to London with Madeline two days later. Given recovery of Drina and the possiblility Nina could be her daughter, he was able to convince the Bagwell sister to turn herself into the police.

The ensuing trial was a long affair, with emotional testimony and international attention. Newspapers had a field day with the intrigue conducted by the aristocracy.

DOUBLE AGENT ARRESTED. MADELINE BAGWELL RESPONSIBLE FOR FRENCH AGENT'S DEATH.

AMERICAN DEATHS DURING 1814 RAID ATTRIBUTED TO FEMALE AGENTS.

LIBERALISTS AND ULTRAROYALISTS DRAG HIS

MAJESTY INTO FRENCH POLITICS.

TRIAL EXPECTED TO LAST SIX MONTHS WHILE MAGISTRATE SORTS IT ALL OUT.

Madeline's extenuating circumstances resulted in a small leniency for her crime. Michael Gravis testified that her wartime actions benefited His Majesty's position. Even an American envoy argued she helped defeat Bonaparte and America would not look favorably on severe punishment. Louisa's death was ruled an unfortunate accident. Madeline was sentenced to fifteen years in prison for the sole crime of abduction. Charles was relieved to have his sister alive, free from a hangman's noose. It meant he could still visit her and introduce her to the daughter she never knew.

The explosives factory at Hastings was taken over by the British government. Given possible future challenges to England's authority on the high seas, it was decided to bring such manufacture under direct control of His Majesty.

Activities of the Ultraroyalist coalition continued to have considerable influence inside the French government. Fouche was unable to gain more than a disapproving nod from the King.

With the passing of Edward, Duke of Kent, all ties to these events ended and the case of the Mayfair Hall murder was officially closed.

# CHAPTER NINETEEN

Elizabeth sat on grass near the manor's east pond. Morning mist had lifted to an afternoon warmth, linguring in the last days of summer. Ducks languidly floated on the water, not yet concerned about the season, a peaceful scene much appreciated by Elizabeth after the trial's ordeal.

She reread the morning's post from Emily. Despite the efforts of Lady Mary, the experiment to teach Victoria and Nina proper etiquette met with limited success. During their visit, the two girls walked to the center of Edinburgh without escort on several occasions. They were also seen in the company of young men prior to Emily's intervention. Emily forcefully expressed her concern to Charles that Lady Wellington's knowledge of propriety was insufficient to guide girls of Nina's age. It was clear she and Charles would have their hands full for a number of years.

Some distance away, in front of the main building, William sat reading a book with his leg propped on a cushion. Elizabeth leaned back thinking of the turmoil over the past three years. They survived voyages abroad, which she might have declined under different circumstances, and Mayfair had been restored with a completely new, trustworthy staff.

The cost in lives was a sad outcome. Of all the casualties, Lady Carlisle would be missed the most. Perhaps, because Elizabeth respected the woman's resilient maneuvering and keen insight into foreign politics. William's aunt was a lady of action, and Elizabeth could not believe she was gone. The aunt had her faults, impatience, occasional flashes of temper, adherence to a strict code of decorum, yet she went up against the law of the land, even risking a charge of treason for a cause she believed in, the cause of Bonaparte, permitting those without station to be respected and have a say in their choice of leaders. She sympathized with individuals no matter their class or style of life. She had been a formidable lady indeed.

Elizabeth smiled, reflecting on the sphere of Montclair influence and drifted to sleep.

A sound came from the front doorway. Elizabeth opened one eye. Maid Claudia emerged, walking steadily toward her, despite interrupting her mistress' reverie.

She controled her voice with difficulty.

"Mrs. Darmon I think …, I thought you'd like to know. When I cleaned the withdrawing room this morning, I noticed one of the cushions of the settee had a little tear. I tried to push the fabric back in place, but there was something hard inside. I dug my finger into the stuffing and found this."

The maid held out her fist and opened the hand. Sitting in her palm was another pendant, complete with *fleur-de-lis* engraving.

Elizabeth frowned. "Another one? I thought we'd auctioned them all except Louisa's, which Gravis kept as evidence."

Curiosity building, she took the item to twist it open. Another note fell out. She scooped it up and anxiously unrolled the missive.

A coldness touched her.

*Madame Carlisle*
*Your efforts to secure Emperor Bonaparte's freedom have been commendable. I wish we could have done more to help you recover Rosewell. You will have to confront old Crullage on the matter. If things go badly, your protection can be arranged.*
*Sage Hibou*
*14th day of March 1819*

Elizabeth read each word carefully. The aunt must have hidden the message hurriedly. Perhaps, its delivery came just before fire broke out. She knew what happened next. The woman went to Crullage castle and killed the old gentleman in a futile effort to remove *Ultraroyalists* from her former premises.

She glanced at William, but he had taken no particular notice of the maid's approach.

A flock of birds suddenly lifted from nearby trees. Sounds of a horse trot grew. Elizabeth squinted for a better view. In the distance, a carriage moved up the road.

In a seconds, the vehicle pulled to a stop at the entrance. William struggled to his feet and stepped to the carriage. She saw him halt suddenly. He glanced in her direction, mouth open.

Lady Carlisle emerged!

Elizabeth ran to the driveway. She arrived in time to hear heard the woman speak.

"Well, I am here again. Please show me to my room!"

THE END

BLACK ROSE
writing™

CPSIA information can be obtained at www.ICGtesting.com
Printed in the USA
LVOW10s0146110114

368901LV00004B/115/P